Roberta Rich divides her time between Vancouver and Colima, Mexico. She is a former family law lawyer. *The Midwife of Venice* is her debut novel.

Visit Roberta at http://robertarich.com

THE MIDWIFE OF VENICE

Hannah Levi is famed throughout Venice for her skills as a midwife, but as a Jew, the law forbids her from attending a Christian woman. However, when the Conte di Padovani appears at her door in the dead of night to demand her services, Hannah's compassion is sorely tested. And with a handsome reward for her services, she could ransom back her imprisoned husband. But if she fails in her endeavours to save mother and child, will she be able to save herself, let alone her husband?

ROBERTA RICH

THE
MIDWIFE
OF VENICE

Complete and Unabridged

CHARNWOOD
Leicester

First published in Great Britain in 2011 by
Ebury Press
an imprint of
Ebury Publishing
London

First Charnwood Edition
published 2012
by arrangement with
Ebury Publishing
The Random House Group Limited
London

British Library CIP Data

Rich, Roberta.
The midwife of Venice.
1. Large type books.
I. Title
813.6–dc23

ISBN 978–1–4448–1233–6

Published by
F. A. Thorpe (Publishing)
Anstey, Leicestershire
Set by Words & Graphics Ltd.
Anstey, Leicestershire
Printed and bound in Great Britain by
T. J. International Ltd., Padstow, Cornwall

This book is printed on acid-free paper

To Mimi Meehan
1920 – 2007

1

Ghetto Nuovo, Venice
1575

At midnight, the dogs, cats, and rats rule Venice. The Ponte di Ghetto Nuovo, the bridge that leads to the ghetto, trembles under the weight of sacks of rotting vegetables, rancid fat, and vermin. Shapeless matter, perhaps animal, floats to the surface of Rio di San Girolamo and hovers on its greasy waters. Through the mist rising from the canal the cries and grunts of foraging pigs echo. Seeping refuse on the streets renders the pavement slick and the walking treacherous.

It was on such a night that the men came for Hannah. She heard their voices, parted the curtains, and tried to peer down into the *campo* below. Without the charcoal brazier heating her room, thick ice had encrusted the inside of the window and obscured her view. Warming two coins on her tongue, grimacing from the bitter metallic taste, she pressed them to the glass with her thumbs until they melted a pair of eyeholes through which she could stare. Two figures, three storeys below, argued with Vicente, whose job it was to lock the gates of the Ghetto Nuovo at sunset and unlock them at sunrise. For a *scudo*, he guided men to Hannah's dwelling. This time, Vicente seemed to be arguing with the two men, shaking his head, emphasizing his words by

1

waving about a pine torch, which cast flickering light on their faces.

Men often called for her late at night — it was the nature of her profession — but these men were out of place in the ghetto in a way she could not immediately put into words. Stealing a look through the protection of the eyeholes, she saw that one was tall, barrel-chested, and wore a cloak trimmed with fur. The other was shorter, stouter, and dressed in breeches of a silk far too thin for the chill of the night air. The lace on the tall man's cuff fluttered like a preening dove as he gestured toward her building.

Even through the window, she could hear him say her name in the back of his throat, the *h* in Hannah like *ch*, sounding like an Ashkenazi Jew. His voice ricocheted off the narrow, knife-shaped ghetto buildings that surrounded the *campo*. But something was wrong. It took her a moment to realize what was odd about the two strangers.

They wore black hats. All Jews, by order of the Council of Ten, were obliged to wear the scarlet *berete*, to symbolize Christ's blood shed by the Jews. These Christians had no right to be in the ghetto at midnight, no reason to seek her services.

But maybe she was too quick to judge. Perhaps they sought her for a different purpose altogether. Possibly they brought news of her husband. Perhaps, may God be listening, they had come to tell her that Isaac lived and was on his way home to her.

Months ago, when the Rabbi informed her of Isaac's capture, she was standing in the same spot where these men stood now, near the wellhead, drawing water for washing laundry. She had fainted then, the oak bucket dropping from her arms onto her shoe. Water soaked the front of her dress and cascaded onto the paving stones. Her friend Rebekkah, standing next to her under the shade of the pomegranate tree, had caught Hannah by the arm before she struck her head on the wellhead. Such had been her grief that not until several days later did she realize her foot was broken.

The men moved closer. They stood beneath her window, shivering in the winter cold. In Hannah's *loghetto*, dampness stained the walls and ceiling grey-brown. The coverlet that she had snatched from the bed and wrapped around her shoulders to keep out the chill of the night clung to her, holding her in a soggy embrace. She hiked it higher around her, the material heavy with her nightmares, traces of Isaac's scent, and oil from the skins of oranges. He had been fond of eating oranges in bed, feeding her sections as they chatted. She had not washed the blanket since Isaac had departed for the Levant to trade spices. One night he would return, steal into their bed, wrap his arms around her, and again call her his little bird. Until then, she would keep to her side of the bed, waiting.

She slipped on her loose-fitting *cioppà* with the economical movements of a woman accustomed to getting ready in haste, replaced the coverlet over her bed, and smoothed it as though Isaac still slumbered beneath.

While she waited for the thud of footsteps and

3

the blows on the door, she lit the charcoal brazier, her fingers so awkward with cold and nervousness that she had difficulty striking the flint against the tinder box. The fire smouldered, then flared and burned, warming the room until she could no longer see clouds of her breath in the still air. From the other side of the wall, she heard the gentle snoring of her neighbours and their four children.

Peering through the eyeholes, now melting from the heat of her body, she stared. The tall man, his voice strident, pivoted on his heel and strode toward her building; the stout man trotted behind, managing two steps for each one of the tall man's. She held her breath and willed Vicente to tell them what they wanted of her was impossible.

To soothe herself, she stroked her stomach, hating the flatness of it, feeling the delicate jab of her pelvic bones through her nightdress. She felt slightly nauseated and for a joyful moment experienced a flicker of hope, almost like the quickening of a child. But it was the smell of the chamber pot and the mildew of the walls playing havoc with her stomach, not pregnancy. She was experiencing her courses now, and would purify herself next week in the *mikvah*, the ritual bath that would remove all traces of blood.

Soon she felt vibrations on the rickety stairs and heard mumbled voices approaching her door. Hannah wrapped her arms around herself, straining to hear. They called her name as they pounded on the door, which made her want to dive into bed, pull the covers over her head, and

4

lie rigid. From the other side of the wall, her neighbour, who had delivered twins last year and needed her rest, rapped for quiet.

Hannah twisted her black hair into a knot at the back of her head, secured it with a hairpin. Before they could burst through the entrance, she flung open the door, about to shout to Vicente for assistance. But her hand flew to her mouth, stifling a cry of surprise. Between the two Christian men, pale as a scrap of parchment, stood the Rabbi. Hannah backed into her room.

Rabbi Ibraiham kissed his fingers and reached up to touch the *mezuzah*, the tiny box containing Scripture fastened to the right-hand side of her door jamb. '*Shalom Aleichem* and forgive us, Hannah, for disturbing you.' The Rabbi had dressed in haste; the fringe of his prayer shawl dangled unevenly around his knees, his yarmulke askew.

'*Aleichem shalom*,' she replied. She started to put a hand on the Rabbi's arm but stopped herself just in time. A woman was not to touch a man outside of her family, even when not having her monthly flow.

'These men need to talk with you. May we come in?'

Hannah averted her eyes as she always did in the presence of a man other than Isaac. They should not enter. She was not properly dressed; her room could not contain all four of them.

In a voice pitched higher than normal, she asked the Rabbi, 'Your wife is better? I heard she was suffering from the gout and has been in bed since last Shabbat.'

The Rabbi was stooped, his clothes redolent with the fusty odour of a man lacking a healthy wife to air them and ensure he did not sit hunched all night reading over beeswax candles. Perhaps, Hannah thought, Rivkah had finally gone to the Jewish quarter in Rome to live with their eldest son, as she had often threatened.

The Rabbi shrugged. 'Rivkah's hands and feet remain immobile, but, alas, not her tongue. Her words remain as cutting as a sword.'

'I'm sorry to hear that.'

The Rabbi's marital troubles were not a secret from anyone in the ghetto within earshot of their apartment. He and Rivkah had not enjoyed a peaceful moment in their forty years together.

'Gentlemen, this is our midwife, Hannah. May she be blessed above all women.' The Rabbi bowed. 'Hannah, this is Conte Paolo di Padovani and his brother Jacopo. May God his rock protect them and grant them long life. The Conte insisted that I bring him to you. He asks for our help.'

Our help? Hannah thought. Did *she* deliver sermons? Did the Rabbi deliver babies?

'But as I have explained to the Conte,' said the Rabbi, 'what he asks is not possible. You are not permitted to assist Christian women in child-birth.'

Only last Sunday in the Piazza San Marco, Fra Bartolome, the Dominican priest, had railed against Christians receiving medical treatment from Jews, or as he phrased it, 'from enemies of the Cross.'

The Conte tried to interrupt, but the Rabbi

held up a finger. 'Papal dispensation, you are going to tell me? Not for a humble midwife like Hannah.'

This time it seemed the Rabbi was on Hannah's side. They had common cause in refusing the Conte's request.

The Conte looked to be in his fifties, at least twice Hannah's age. Fatigue showed in his hollowed cheeks, making him appear as old as the Rabbi. His brother, perhaps ten years younger, was soft and not as well made, with sloping shoulders and narrow chest. The Conte nodded at her and pushed past the Rabbi into the room, ducking his head to avoid scraping it on the slanted ceiling. He was large, in the fashion of Christians, and florid from eating roasted meats. Hannah tried to slow her breathing. There seemed to be not enough air in the room for all of them.

'I am honoured to meet you,' he said, removing his black hat. His voice was deep and pleasant, and he spoke the sibilant Veneziano dialect of the city.

Jacopo, his brother, was immaculate, his chubby cheeks well powdered, not a spot of mud disgracing his breeches. He entered warily, placing one foot ahead of the other as though he expected the creaky floor to give way under him. He made a half bow to Hannah.

The Conte unfastened his cloak and glanced around her *loghetto*, taking in the trestle bed, the stained walls, the pine table, and the menorah. The stub of a beeswax candle in the corner guttered, casting shadows around the small room. Clearly, he had never been inside such a modest dwelling, and judging by his stiff posture and the way he held himself away from the walls, he was not comfortable being in one now.

'What brings you here tonight?' Hannah asked, although she knew full well. The Rabbi should not have led the men to her home. He should have persuaded them to leave. There was nothing she could do for them.

'My wife is in travail,' said the Conte. He stood shifting his weight from one leg to the other. His mouth was drawn, his lips compressed into a thin white line.

The brother, Jacopo, hooked a foot around a stool and scraped it over the floor toward him. He flicked his handkerchief over the surface and then sat, balancing one buttock in the air.

The Conte continued to stand. 'You must help her.'

Hannah had always found it difficult to refuse aid to anyone, from a wounded bird to a woman in childbirth. 'I feel it is a great wrong to decline, sir.' Hannah glanced at the Rabbi. 'If the law permitted, I would gladly assist, but as the Rabbi explained, I cannot.'

The Conte's eyes were blue, cross-hatched with a network of fine lines, but his shoulders were square and his back erect. How different he appeared from the familiar men of the ghetto, pale and stooped from bending over their second-hand clothing, their gemstones, and their Torah.

'My wife has been labouring for two days and two nights. The sheets are soaked with her blood,

8

yet the child will not be born.' He gave a helpless wave of his hand. 'I do not know where else to turn.'

His was the face of a man suffering for his wife's pain; Hannah felt a stab of compassion. Difficult confinements were familiar to her. The hours of pain. The child that presented shoulder first. The child born dead. The mother dying of milk fever.

'I am so sorry, sir. You must love your wife very much to venture into the ghetto to search me out.'

'Her screams have driven me from my home. I cannot bear to be there any longer. She pleads for God to end her misery.'

'Many labours end well, even after two days,' Hannah said. 'God willing, she will be fine and deliver you a healthy son.'

'It is the natural course of events,' the Rabbi said. 'Does not the Book of Genesis say, 'In pain are we brought forth'?' He turned to Hannah. 'I already told him you would refuse, but he insisted on hearing it from your own lips.' He opened his mouth to say more, but the Conte motioned for him to be silent. To Hannah's surprise, the Rabbi obeyed.

The Conte said, 'Women speak of many things among themselves. My wife, Lucia, tells me that although you are young, you are the best midwife in Venice — Christian or Jew. They say you have a way of coaxing stubborn babies out of their mothers' bellies.'

'Do not believe everything you hear,' Hannah said. 'Even a blind chicken finds a few grains of corn now and again.' She looked at his large hands, nervously clasping each other to keep from trembling. 'There are Christian midwives just as skilled.'

But he was right. There was no *levatrice* in Venice who was as gifted as she. The babies emerged quickly and the mothers recovered more speedily when Hannah attended their *accouchements*. Only the Rabbi understood the reason, and he could be trusted to keep silent, knowing that if anyone discovered her secret she would be branded as a witch and subjected to torture.

'Now from her own lips you have heard,' said the Rabbi. 'Let us depart. She cannot help you.' He gave a brief nod to Hannah and turned to leave. 'I am sorry to have disturbed you. Go back to sleep.'

Jacopo clapped his hands together as though they were covered with dirt, rose from the stool, and started toward the door. 'Let us go, *mio fratello*.'

But the Conte remained. 'I would bear Lucia's pain myself if it were possible. I would give my blood to replace hers, which as we waste time talking is pooling on the floor of her bedchamber.'

Hannah's eyes were level with the buttons of his cloak. As he spoke, he swayed from fatigue. She took a step back, afraid he would topple on her.

She lowered her voice and said to the Rabbi in Yiddish, 'Is it unthinkable that I go? Although Jewish physicians are forbidden to attend

10

Christian patients, they often do. Christians needing to be purged or bled turn a blind eye to the Pope's edict. Many Jewish doctors are summoned under the darkness of night and slip past sleeping porters. They say even the Doge himself has a Jewish physician . . . '

'Such tolerance would never extend to a woman,' the Rabbi replied. 'If a Christian baby was, God forbid, to die at birth, and a Jewish midwife was attending, she would be blamed. And along with her, the entire ghetto.' The Rabbi turned to the Conte and said, speaking again in Veneziano, 'There are many Christian midwives in Venice. Any one of them would be honoured to help.'

Paolo di Padovani looked pale in the dim light of the room. 'You are my last hope,' he said in a soft voice. 'They say you have magic in your hands.' He picked up Hannah's hands and clasped them. His own hands felt cold, the palms soft as kid leather. Hers were rough from lye soap and hard well water. 'Is that true?'

Embarrassed and shocked, she pulled her hands away.

The Rabbi leaned toward her and said in Yiddish, 'Is this what you want, Hannahlah?' He used her childhood nickname. 'Your body tipped from a barge some night into that part of the lagoon where no fishing is allowed and where no one may draw drinking water?'

A prudent woman would not reply. But Hannah could not hold her tongue. 'Is the suffering of a Christian woman different from the suffering of a Jewish one?'

11

'Tell this illustrious Conte that you cannot help him. Let his wife's death be laid at the door of someone other than a Jew.'

The Rabbi was ignorant of what it meant to be female: to bear stillbirths, to suffer puerperal fever, to hear the rustle of the wings of the Angel of Death over cradles and birthing stools. Hannah took a deep breath and said, 'I have a talent, Rabbi. Surely God wants me to use it.'

'I curse the day you brought your, your . . .' — he floundered in search of the right word — 'your device to me and asked me to make a *brokhe*, a blessing, over it.'

Hannah regretted it too. If only she had kept her creation a secret.

'He is rich,' the Rabbi continued. 'A merchant and a Christian. Every man, woman, and child in the ghetto will pay the price if this child dies under your care.'

The Conte said to the Rabbi, 'I can protect her if, God forbid, there is trouble. I am a member of the Council of Ten and I have friends in the Courts of Inquisition.' He made an effort to encourage her. 'Ready yourself, Hannah, and come with me under cover of darkness, in my gondola. No one outside my household will know of your attendance.'

The Rabbi muttered in Yiddish, 'Hannah, you do not know the world as I do. This will not turn out well. Yes, he wants you now. Yes, he will protect you now. He and his lofty Council of Ten. But do you think for one moment that he will give a fig about you if his wife dies?'

Hannah tried to swallow, but her throat was

too dry. The Conte had ventured into the canals at night, courted disaster from roving bands of ruffians, bribed Vicente to unlock the gates, and roused the Rabbi from his bed. Few husbands would take such trouble. She glanced at the Rabbi, whose black eyes, below wiry eyebrows winging up toward his bald head, fixed her with a scowl. He was blocking the door, standing in front of her with the air of a man who would not step aside for God Himself.

When Hannah's sister, Jessica, converted to Christianity in order to marry a gentile, who later abandoned her, the Rabbi had, in accordance with Jewish law, ordered the family to sit *shiva*, the traditional mourning ritual for the dead, and to never utter her name again. 'Jessica, may her name be obliterated and the teeth rot in her head,' he had said as Hannah wept and her father covered the family's only looking-glass. The Rabbi had forbidden anyone in the ghetto to have contact with Jessica from that moment on.

Her sister lived only a few canals away. Hurrying to the Rialto market at dawn, Hannah had often crossed paths with Jessica as she made her way home from a party or fancy dress ball, attired in a gown of rich silk, sequins, and a mask. Each time, obedient to the Rabbi's injunction, Hannah would duck her head and take another route.

A year later, a midwife's apprentice arrived at the gates of the ghetto, out of breath from running, to summon Hannah to Jessica's confinement. The Rabbi barred Hannah from accompanying the apprentice and chased her away.

The Rabbi addressed the Conte now. 'With all due respect, the authorities cannot always protect the Jews when the priests foment trouble. You and I would not have to ponder the matter long to think of examples — during outbreaks of the plague, when the infidel pirates seize Venetian ships . . . '

If he heard the Rabbi, the Conte gave no sign, shrugging off his cloak and laying it on the only space available, the bed. A look crossed his face, and for a moment Hannah thought he would wrap her up in his cloak, sling her over his shoulder, and carry her out into the night.

'Conte,' said Hannah, 'I do not perform miracles, nor is there magic in my hands.'

'You must try,' he replied.

Jacopo tugged at the Conte's arm. 'Come. Let us go. We were fools to think a Jew would help. Holy Mother of God, Paolo, I will leave without you if I have to.' He held his handkerchief to his nose. 'The smell of this room is making me quite nauseous. Paolo, conclude this matter. Offer her money. This is the only thing Jews understand.'

Hannah should have been accustomed to such remarks — she heard them often enough. But she whirled on him, ready to say the first thing that came into her head, to curse him as the whore son of a pig. Instead, she cleared her throat and addressed his brother.

'Conte, pay me two hundred ducats and I will go to your wife.'

Jacopo let out a snort of laughter.

14

Hannah kept her eyes fixed on the Conte, who was not laughing. His eyebrows knit together as he pondered the demand. It was a shocking sum. Two hundred ducats was sufficient to buy a hundred bolts of printed silk, a cargo of timber, or Isaac's life. No one, not even a nobleman, would pay such an amount for her services. A few silver coins was her usual fee.

This would end the discussion and send the Conte back to his palazzo. The Rabbi was right. If Hannah failed to save the Contessa, the Inquisition would force her to submit to the *strappado*. Her hands would be bound behind her back and she would be dropped from a great height.

Hannah said, 'My husband is being held as a slave in Malta by the Knights of Jerusalem. They demand this sum for his ransom. I will try to save your wife's life if you will save my husband's.'

The Rabbi was angry now, his voice slow and deliberate. 'Hannah, as I have told you, the Society for the Release of Captives will fund Isaac's release. It is only a matter of time.'

'Time is running out,' Hannah said.

The Rabbi shook a stiff, blue-veined fist in her face. 'Your first obligation is to do nothing to endanger the ghetto. Isaac is only one Jew; the ghetto is three thousand.' He was so close Hannah could feel the heat of his breath on her face. 'I am your Rabbi and I forbid you. That is the end of the matter.'

These were the hands that had blessed her many times, had circumcised her brothers, and had held the silver *kiddush* cup to her lips at Seder dinners.

'Rabbi, I did not stand under the wedding canopy with three thousand Jews. I stood under the *huppah* with one man — Isaac.' Her husband, she wanted to add, who had married her without a dowry, and had continued to love her in spite of her barrenness. In the synagogue, she had overheard the Rabbi assuring Isaac that the law would release him from a childless marriage. The Rabbi had urged him to divorce her and find a wife who would bear him a son. Isaac had pulled his prayer shawl more tightly around his shoulders and shaken his head. Most husbands would not have shown such patience — for is not a child the *takhlit*, the purpose of all women?

And how had she repaid this husband who, when she was aching from bending for hours over the trestle bed of a labouring woman, would take the *bahnaches* glasses from the cupboard, heat them over a candle, and apply them to her back? In the week before Isaac sailed, she had hurled at him an arsenal of wounding words — said that if he loved her he would not sail to the Levant in search of wealth and prosperity, that he thought only of himself and was deserting her. The words he flung back were like knives. He told her that she was a timid little ghetto mouse, afraid of taking a chance, that he was risking his life for her, for a better life for both of them. Then there was silence between them. They did not look at each other, and slept far apart in bed. She had refused to see him off

16

in his ship, *La Dogaressa*. Now the thought of him alone in Malta, believing she no longer loved him, was more than she could bear. If the Conte would pay, she would go with him. The Rabbi could be as angry as he wanted.

'Will you pay what I ask?' she said to the Conte.

'I will pay this outlandish sum,' he replied. 'You can sail to Malta and ransom your husband before they work him to death in the stone quarries.' He picked up his cloak.

Hannah had no time to be astonished by his agreement. She draped a scarf over her hair and slipped on her thin leather sandals as Jacopo and the Rabbi watched. The Rabbi was silent but his frail old body was rigid with fury.

'Take me to your wife,' Hannah said to the Conte.

She hurriedly gathered her equipment — an apron, an iron knife, clean gauze, vials, swaddling cloths, packets of medicinal herbs, and a silver amulet, a *shadai*, inscribed with the Star of David, meant to be hung over the cradles of newborns. *May it not be too late; may it be needed tonight.* She placed her supplies in a bag made of unbleached linen. But before she pulled the drawstring closed, she raised the lid of her *cassone*, patterned in bright marquetry, reached in, and quickly took out a long and narrow object wrapped in cloth. A corner of the material fell away and the light of the candle caught the sheen of her birthing spoons, two silver ladles hinged together. Her face, drawn and white, reflected in the bowl of one of the spoons. Before

17

the men noticed, she tucked them into the bottom of her bag under the swaddling cloths.

Her birthing spoons could save babies, but they could also maim. At a recent confinement, she had exerted too much pressure and had crushed the skull of the baby instead of easing it out. The mother was left with a tiny blue corpse to cradle in her arms. If Hannah made the same blunder tonight, she would be denounced as a slayer of newborns.

'Brother,' said Jacopo, 'you are a fool and I will not be a witness to it a moment longer. I will take leave of you.' He bowed from the waist as well as a man so stout was able. 'I have need of some fresh air. I will make my own way home.'

The stairs creaked as he descended and then the door at the entranceway slammed. Hannah wondered at Jacopo's risking his life on the streets alone at night. Roving gangs of ruffians were commonplace — a well-dressed man might be robbed of his clothes and then shoved off a bridge into the fetid waters of the canal. But she said nothing.

'Come, we can be at ca' di Padovani in a few minutes. My gondola is moored on Rio di San Girolamo,' the Conte said.

The Rabbi pulled his prayer shawl higher around his shoulders. Hannah waited for him to move from the doorway, but he did not. He glared at her. When he slowly raised both his bony hands to her face, she thought for an instant he meant to strike her. Instead, he made slow circles above Hannah's head, as he davened from the waist and said in Yiddish, 'May God in

His Greatness guide you. Be a credit to the Jews and to all women, Hannah. Do not bring destruction upon us.'

The Rabbi then stepped aside to allow her and the Conte to pass through the door.

Once outside, the Conte draped his cloak, smelling of tallow smoke and sweat, over her shoulders. 'It is damp on the canals tonight.'

She sagged under the weight of the fur-trimmed wool.

Clutching to her breast the linen bag containing her birthing spoons, she marched in the wake of the Conte toward the gondola. The Rabbi followed closely behind. She could not help remembering the incident that had occurred last Purim at a house on the Calle del Forno. The midwife attending the birth had been unable to turn the fetus into proper position. To save the mother's life, the midwife had used a *crochet* to pierce the baby's skull, and then had used a silken cord to rip the arms and legs from the child's body in order to extract it. Tiny limbs had been strewn about the woman's bedchamber, tossed there by the midwife in her panic. Hannah prayed the same spectacle would not greet her tonight.

2

During the full moon, unseen currents ran in the canals, washing over the crumbling walls and wetting the slimy steps of the ghetto. At high tide, *acqua alta*, the entire *campo* disappeared under a layer of mud. Tonight was such a night. Hannah held up her skirts as she, the Conte, and the Rabbi made their way across the *campo* toward the gates, the Conte grasping her elbow to prevent her from slipping in the silt. Overhead in her building, shutters opened. A tiny flicker of a candle showed through the window and then the shutters banged closed. Hannah shivered as a rat leapt into the canal, leaving greasy ripples in the water.

The Rabbi bid them good night, and headed in the direction of his *loghetto*. Then, except for their footsteps on the cobblestones, the silence was complete.

When they reached the heavy wooden gates, the guard Vicente, his hat upturned in case the Conte wanted to drop a few *scudi* in it, unlocked the gate leading to the Ponte degli Agudi. The Conte and Hannah hurried toward the boat on the Rio di San Girolamo. The gondolier was snoring so loudly he had scared away the pigs rooting in the garbage along the Fondamenta. He woke up when he heard them approach and sprang to attention, offering his forearm to Hannah to help her over the gunwales. Then he held to one side the heavy brocade curtains of the *felze*, the cabin of the gondola, until she settled in a chair. The boat dipped and swayed when the Conte climbed on board. Inside the *felze*, it was dark as a cave, concealing her from anyone who might be watching on land. The seclusion should have made her feel safe, but it did not.

When the gondolier cast off, she wanted to hurl herself out of the boat and onto solid ground again. On the prow the six iron teeth of the *ferro*, each tooth symbolizing a *sestiere*, a district of the city, sliced through the water. They did not speak. The only sound was the drip of the oar as they glided over the black waters. No light reflected from the houses of the Cannaregio.

When they reached the Grand Canal, hardly a pine-pitch torch hissed or flickered from the docks of the splendid palazzi. The Conte's cloak was heavy around her shoulders, pressing her down. It did not warm her any more than a hunter's snare gives heat to a trapped quail. She struggled to sit upright. It would avail her nothing if the Conte realized how frightened she was. Confidence must radiate from her. Isaac had taught her that.

Was not the flesh of a Christian noblewoman fashioned the same as a Jewess's? she thought. Did they not bleed and moan and labour in the same manner? Did they not also have tight wombs that refused to expel their contents, and babies who presented buttocks first? She had enticed unwilling infants from half-dead Jewish mothers; she would do the same for a Christian. It was for Isaac that she risked a watery cell below the Doge's palace and a midnight visit from the strangler. His handsome face appeared before her, his aquiline nose and sensual mouth.

In the cabin of the gondola, listing to one side with the weight of its load, the Conte spoke to her in a voice so low she had to ask him to repeat it. 'My wife, Lucia, is frail. For years, she has coughed blood. In spite of this, she has had many confinements. None have resulted in a living child.' He studied her in the shaft of moonlight penetrating the half-closed curtains. 'You are young, but I am sure you have seen such cases.'

With each intake of breath, the Conte seemed to suck all the air from the small enclosure, leaving none for her.

'I will do my best.'

'I believe you will, my dear. Like most men, I know nothing of the ways in which children enter the world. But heed my words: if you must make a choice between my wife's life or my child's, save my child.'

Before she could stop herself, Hannah said, 'But Jewish midwives are schooled to favour the mother's life.' Seeing his troubled face, she added, 'With God's help, I will not have to make such a choice.'

'I love Lucia, but under the terms of my father's will, I must produce an heir before I turn fifty. Otherwise, the family estate will pass from my hands into the hands of my brother Jacopo. I will celebrate my fiftieth birthday next month.'

It was not the first time Hannah had heard such confidences. Fathers-to-be were often consumed with *maninconia*, a combination of anxiety and distress that made them disclose things they had no business telling strangers.

'Jacopo and my younger brother, Niccolò, are feckless and will ruin the family businesses. If the estate falls into their hands, it will mean the devastation of the family. Niccoló has already gambled away a small fortune. Jacopo is a worry to me for reasons I cannot discuss with a woman.'

What did this talk of his father's will and family business have to do with her? Rolling out dough for matzo she understood. Delivering babies she understood. But the inheritance laws of rich Christians?

It would not be a kindness to tell him what every midwife knew: that for every five babies born, one died; that for every ten labouring mothers, one would not live to give suck to her child. Nor would she tell him she had bettered those dismal odds with the device hidden in the linen bag resting at her feet.

One Shabbat she was ladling beet soup, so hot and steaming it made her hair spring into tiny curls. The silver soup ladle in her hand, with a concave belly and a curved handle, plunged deep into the tureen. She dropped the handle when it grew too hot and it slid along the side of the bowl, coming to rest against the curve of the bottom. An idea took shape in her mind. She took an identical spoon down from the cupboard, and with her hands still stained red from the beets, she crossed one spoon over the other to form the letter X. Such an instrument, she thought, could bring a child's head farther down the birth passage and hasten deliveries.

She made a rough sketch, which the silversmith then used to fashion the instrument, sculpting the bowl of the birthing spoon more deeply than that of an ordinary spoon and making the handles longer. A hinge held the two spoons together in the middle, so that they could be opened and closed like a pair of scissors. At first, she had practised in private, extracting onions from the cavities of raw chickens. When her dexterity improved, she used them at confinements, draping a bedsheet over the mother's bent knees so she could not see, and shooing all the other women from the room. Midwives were burned as witches for less cause than this, so Hannah knew she must be circumspect.

'I want you to know I am not a man without sentiment,' said the Conte, 'one who thinks only of his estates and horses and how many ducats he can make on every business transaction.'

'I know you care for your wife or you would not have taken the risk of summoning me,' Hannah replied.

The Conte patted her hand. 'My brother spoke harshly to you because he is indebted to the moneylenders. Jacopo is as profligate with his money as a dyer.'

Several moments later, with a creak and a muted thump, the gondola slid alongside the dock of a palazzo with a stone façade and arched windows. On the last curve of the Grand Canal, this palazzo overlooked the *campo* of St. Samuele. A liveried servant on the dock caught the bowline from the gondolier and lashed it around a mooring pole painted in the colours of the family, gold and green. The Conte helped Hannah out and escorted her inside. A manservant held open the door for them and bid them good evening. She followed the Conte through the *piano terra*, where the commercial business of the family took place. This ground floor — used as a warehouse, judging by the wooden crates — was heavy with the fragrance of cardamom, cinnamon, and raw wool. It seemed as large as the entire Campo Ghetto Nuovo.

She tried to keep pace with the Conte, noting how large his head was. If his wife was small, this did not bode well. A delicate wife and a substantial husband often caused the mother to carry a baby with a head too big to make good the passage through the sharing bones.

Before they reached the main entrance hall, Hannah returned the Conte's cloak to him, feeling lighter with it off her shoulders. A servant woman greeted them, her dark hair clinging to her face with perspiration and her apron stained with blood.

'Hannah, this is our midwife, Giovanna.'

Hannah smiled and nodded, but the woman did not acknowledge her greeting.

'Giovanna, this is Hannah. Take her to the Contessa. Not a word to anyone. She has come to assist,' said the Conte. 'Any change during my absence?'

'I think you must summon a priest, sir,' Giovanna said, speaking with downcast eyes.

Hannah backed toward the door. A priest would know from her red scarf and modest dress that she was a Jewess. If a priest arrived, she must leave, or her arrest would follow as surely as blood trickled downhill.

To her relief, the Conte replied, 'We will wait to see what Hannah can do for her.' He must have sensed Hannah's nervousness, for he turned to her and said, 'Do not worry. You shall have your chance. Now go quickly.'

Giovanna curtsied to the Conte, and then led Hannah up a wide staircase, the stone walls radiating damp. Accustomed to the enclosed, rickety staircases of the ghetto, Hannah felt dizzy at this expanse of stone. She stopped mid-flight and clutched the cold balustrade. To regain her equilibrium, she looked down, and saw in an alcove below two men drinking at a table, a flask of wine between them, a spaniel lolling at their feet. One was the brother Jacopo, flushed from his walk home in the night air. The other, she surmised, was Niccolò, the youngest brother. He was handsome, with curly dark hair and the rumpled look of a man recently risen from bed.

Jacopo took a pair of ivory dice in his hands, blew on them for luck, and then cast them onto the table. Hannah moved slightly and her leather sandals made a squeak on the marble staircase, and Niccolò glanced up, giving her a mocking salute with his glass.

Nothing in this palazzo seemed familiar or safe. She felt the way a small animal must feel in a field surrounded by predators. Too much space and nowhere to hide. The Conte must have experienced the same sense of discomfort in her humble *loghetto* with its damp walls and smoky brazier as she did now amongst the silk-tasselled curtains, gleaming silver, and coffered ceilings of his palazzo.

Up the stairs she continued, feeling the chill of the stone radiate through the soles of her sandals, putting her thoughts of the two men out of her mind. Of one thing she was certain — the Contessa would be like any other woman, with sharing bones, a belly, and a matrix.

Hannah had heard that Christians filled their grand palaces as well as their churches with images of the human figure. And sure enough, at the landing at the top of the stairs appeared a fresco in brilliant colours depicting two women washing the feet of Christ. Hannah gathered her skirts and walked with her head down. The Torah forbade the worshipping of graven images. She thought of her beautiful *shul* in the ghetto, with a carved wooden pulpit for the Rabbi to deliver his sermons, a gilded Holy Ark to hold the Torah, and a filigreed screen to separate the main floor of the men's section from the women's gallery above. It seemed austere by contrast to this palace.

She followed Giovanna's ample behind down a hallway covered with a carpet patterned in ruby and emerald and topaz. The moon shining through the high clerestory windows cast rhomboid shadows on the jewel colours.

As she walked down the hallway, Hannah did

not need Giovanna to direct her to the Contessa's bedchamber. The woman's screams drew her to a room so large that at first she could locate the bed only by the screams issuing from it. She paused in the doorway, dazzled. There seemed more gold in the room than could be found in King Solomon's mines. Moonlight shining through the front and back windows, and light from lamps and candles, filled the bedchamber. Light was everywhere, dancing in gilded looking-glasses, mirrors, and bronzes. Even the terrazzo floor, glass smooth and fashioned of coloured stone embedded with semi-precious gems, glowed. Adorning the windows were curtains of silk taffeta woven with a gold brocade weft forming loops to catch the moonlight.

Above the bed hung a small devotional painting of Madonna and child. The Madonna, wearing a gown of lapis lazuli blue, offered him a breast with a look of rapture on her smooth face. For Christians, it was a tender scene, but Hannah felt her stomach contract in revulsion. Only God could make another human being. It was wickedness to attempt to emulate Him by creating graven images. If only she could ask Giovanna to remove it and in its place substitute her *shadai* of hammered silver. Hannah looked away and placed her bag on a chair.

In the corner was an elaborate child's crib identical to the Contessa's bed but on a smaller scale. May it be filled soon, Hannah thought. The screams drew her to the woman on a bed supporting a canopy on four pillars.

There lay the Contessa, so pale she was almost translucent. Around the bed was a ring of salt to protect mother and child from the Evil Eye. No doubt this was Giovanna's contribution, and a useful one against Lilith, the slayer of newborns. Hannah wished her amulet, the *shadai*, was in her hands and not in her bag on the chair. When the contractions started, Lilith heard the screams and hovered close to savour the scent of blood. The more protracted the delivery, the bolder she grew. Humble *loghetto* or palazzo, it made no difference. Lilith was no respecter of social class.

Hannah took Contessa Lucia's hand, her fingers as cool and waxy as candles. Her blue eyes were swollen and her hair matted with sweat. Her cheeks were too flushed, her eyes too bright. Had it not been for her coughing and a thin blue vein throbbing on her forehead, Hannah would have thought her dead.

She said, 'Contessa, I am Hannah. I've come to help you give birth to your baby. Can you hear me?' Hannah felt the rustle of the wings as she bent over the bed and thought she saw the rosary dangling from the headboard shift in response. She murmured a swift prayer.

Putting her arms around the Contessa, Hannah pulled her up into a sitting position to make it easier for her to cough. Her shoulder blades cut into Hannah's arms. Blood dotted the handkerchief Lucia held to her mouth.

'You must listen to me. I know it is difficult. You have laboured long and hard without result. I must examine you.' Hannah studied her patient's face. It was as Hannah had feared: the

Conte had waited too long to summon her. If only he had fetched her at dawn, before Lucia had lost so much strength, there might have been some hope. Now, it was well after midnight and the Contessa looked too weak to push out a mewling kitten, much less a baby.

Lucia peered at her through half-closed lids, as though trying through her pain to work out who Hannah was. 'Do I know you?'

'Your husband fetched me. I am a midwife. I have come to help you.'

A few moments passed, and Lucia blinked, seeing what must have looked like an apparition in a blue *cioppà*, shawl and head scarf. 'Hannah, yes. All the women speak of you.' She tried to smile. 'They say you work miracles. That is what I require.'

And what I require as well, thought Hannah, but she said, 'One must not rely on miracles.'

Now that the coughing fit had passed, Hannah lowered the Contessa into a supine position and pulled back the covers sodden with sweat and blood.

'I will be gentle, but I must feel your belly and see if the child is in the correct position.'

'Hand me my rosary.'

Hannah was about to reply that it was forbidden for Jews to touch the religious objects of Christians, but she stopped herself. God would make an exception. To give comfort, to hand a rosary to a dying woman, would be a *mitzvah*, not a violation of either the *Mishrat* or the Papal Edict. Hannah took the rosary from the headboard and handed it to Lucia. The

30

beads felt warmer and more lifelike than Lucia's fingers. Lucia held them to her lips and kissed them.

'You are a Jewess?'

'From the Ghetto Nuovo.'

'Thank you, Hannah, for having the courage to come. Whatever becomes of me or my baby, I am grateful to you.' Then she lay still and her eyelids drifted closed. 'You touched my beads as though handing me a serpent.'

'So you noticed? Good for you. There is life in you yet.' Hannah smoothed the damp hair off Lucia's forehead. She turned to Giovanna, who was wiping her hands on her apron. 'How far apart are her pains?'

'Only a few *pater nostrums* apart for the past three hours. She started two days ago, but she has made no progress. Now she is exhausted and has lost a lot of blood, as you can see, I have told her she must push. But she is too feeble.' Giovanna studied Hannah for a moment, taking in the red scarf and dark hair, and then said, 'You know as well as I do that it is forbidden for Jews to deliver Christian babies. What if, God forbid, the child requires immediate baptism?'

'Then you can provide that service.'

'As I have for all the other babies born to her,' Giovanna said, her broad face set in a frown.

For a Jew to have Christian foes was dangerous. She would have to handle this midwife with care. Hannah went to the washbasin beside the bed, wrung out a wet cloth, and placed it on the Contessa's forehead.

'To give birth is hard work, is it not?'

31

Lucia nodded as Hannah palpated the Contessa's stomach. Hannah did not like what her hands told her. Not sure how much Lucia was capable of understanding, Hannah said, 'The head is twisted and is stuck in the womb. I must try to move it.' Lucia opened her eyes and gave Hannah a look of incomprehension.

'Imagine this, if you will: I am trying to push you out of that window.' She gestured with her chin to the narrow casement window adjacent to the bed, through which could be seen a silver beam of moonlight. 'I could come up behind you, give you a firm shove, and you would splash into the canal below quick as a wink. That is the way it is if the infant's head is well positioned. But imagine this: You are at the window, standing crookedly to one side, or hanging on to the window ledge with your hand. Even a great shove would be of no use. If the babe lies wrongly, strong pains and pushing will be of no avail.'

Lucia's eyes drooped shut again; it was unlikely she had heard a word.

Hannah continued, as much to visualize the difficulty for herself as to explain it to the Contessa. 'But suppose I clasped you by the shoulders and moved you to the middle of the window and then stood outside on the window ledge and with an instrument drew you out.'

'Such a thing is possible?' Lucia's voice was barely audible.

So she had been listening. 'Before I can answer that question, I must place my two fingers inside your sheath. I will do it now, while

32

you are between your pangs.'

Hannah drew the candles on the side table closer. She groped in her linen bag, pushing to one side the silver birthing spoons, extracting a vial of almond oil. Holding her hands over the flame of the candle, she poured a spoonful of the oil on her palms and rubbed them together to warm them.

Too exhausted to plead modesty, Lucia remained still as Hannah reached down, hugged one of Lucia's legs against her, and braced the other against a large pillow. She pushed Lucia's nightdress up to her waist, trying not to wince at the sight of apple red blood pooling on the sheets between her legs. Giovanna could not render any assistance, but at least she should have changed the bed linen. The Contessa's belly was high and full, but otherwise she appeared emaciated. Her limbs were thin, as though the baby had greedily seized all nourishment, sparing none for Lucia. Hannah ran her hands over the taut mound, trying to ascertain whether the head had descended into the birth canal. The infant's buttocks were high above Lucia's umbilicus. Hannah put her hand between Lucia's legs.

'I need to feel your womb to see if it is locked shut or opened.' She hoped to feel the soft and flexible opening of the mouth of the womb and the top of the infant's head, but knew this was unlikely given what she had felt from the belly. If she managed to touch the baby's head, she would move her two fingers like a compass over it to see if it was descending straight. It was always a wonderful sensation to touch the head and feel the flutter of a tiny pulse in the skull.

'Don't push. It is not time for that.' Unnecessary words. Lucia's faint panting indicated there was little chance she would have the strength to bear down.

It was as she had feared. The head was not in position. It remained above the pelvic bones, deep within the womb, difficult to feel, impossible to manipulate. Her birthing spoons could be of no help unless the head progressed farther into the birth passage.

Dear God, she must fight her growing sense of panic, her urge to flee before the woman died in her arms. Never had she attended a weaker mother. Never had she seen a case where a tragic outcome was so certain. Hannah felt her own breath quicken and her heartbeat increase. She withdrew her fingers from between the Contessa's thighs and wiped them on a clean cloth.

She considered the Conte's admonition to save the child above all. Since Lucia was so near death, would it not be better to slice through her belly now and extract the baby before it smothered? To save the child would ensure the Conte's gratitude. But could Hannah cut open a woman who had tried through her pain to smile at her, a woman who had even made a feeble jest?

'I want you to breathe as deeply as you can. Deeply and slowly. Then we'll see what can be done to get this obstinate baby out of your belly.'

The Contessa's head lolled back, her face as white as the damp rectangle of pillow framing it.

Hannah pressed her fingers to the Contessa's wrist and, after searching, felt a pulse faint as a thrush's heartbeat. 'God come to my aid and guide my hands,' she murmured in Yiddish.

'Save my poor mistress,' Giovanna said. 'You'll never get this baby out alive. Use the *crochet*.'

Hannah motioned for Giovanna to be quiet, hoping that Lucia was too dazed for the words to penetrate. The *crochet* was a sharp hook used to gouge a hole in the anterior fontanel of the infant's head so that a midwife could insert her fingers through the fractured skull and pull, thus extracting the dead fetus. No. If she was to use any instrument, it would be her iron knife. Kill the mother, save the child. If she went against the Conte's orders and saved the Contessa by using the *crochet*, she could expect neither protection from the law nor her fee. Better to have Giovanna out of the room.

'Please, go and fetch fresh linen. Let us see what can be done to make her more comfortable.' Giovanna's only skill would be to dismember the fetus. Was it any wonder Lucia had suffered so many unsuccessful confinements?

After Giovanna left, Hannah realized she had not asked if the waters had broken. She lifted up the covers and patted the bed linen. There was blood, but no water from the matrix. She grabbed her bag on the chair, took out the iron knife, and concealed it under Lucia's pillow. It would be at the ready if she had to slice open the belly.

Lucia's eyes opened and she whispered, 'Am I

35

going to die? It would be just punishment for my sins. What is the purpose of my life if I cannot give my husband an heir?' With those words her head drooped to one side and she appeared lifeless.

What possible sins could this coughing, feverish woman be guilty of? Hannah kissed her on the forehead. The smell of burning tallow mingled with blood and flux.

'You are tired and discouraged, but it is too soon to surrender hope.' If by some miracle the Contessa survived, this would be her last confinement. At her age the sinews and ligaments of the womb were tough and did not willingly give way.

'Is the child alive? I have not felt movement for some time,' Lucia said, but before Hannah could answer, her eyes closed and she grimaced as her belly hardened and she twisted with pain. The spasm lasted for several moments, and then, spent, she collapsed back against the pillows.

'Whether the child is alive, I cannot say until I put my ear to your belly.'

If she did not hear a heartbeat, she would reach for the *crochet*, dismember the child, and extract it limb by limb from the Contessa's body. Then perhaps the Contessa would have a chance. On the other hand, if the baby was alive, she must slice Lucia open,' grope about amid the flooding blood, and scoop out the child before it died.

She picked up the Contessa's hand and held it to her cheek while Lucia endured another spasm. When the belly relaxed, Hannah pressed her ear against it, listening for the flutter of the baby's heartbeat. She held still and waited. Moving her head lower, below the umbilicus, she listened again. Nothing. Next she tried a location higher up, just below one breast. She listened again. Yes, perhaps there was a faint beat. She did not trust her ears. Was it her imagination? No, there it was again, the muted heartbeat of a small being. But it was so slow and so faint. The child was dying. The Contessa was dying. Hannah had no time to vacillate.

She must open Lucia's belly, reach in, and fish out the slippery child. But could she bring herself to gut the Contessa like the *shochet* slaughters the spring lamb before Pesach? If she could perform this horrific deed, the two hundred ducats would be hers, and Isaac returned to her side. Of what importance was the life of a Christian woman to her? The Conte would approve; the Contessa had given her permission. God would forgive.

But could Hannah forgive herself?

She slid the knife out from under Lucia's pillow. Tipping a drop of almond oil from her vial onto the blade, Hannah rotated the knife from side to side to distribute a coating over the surface. Then from her bag, she removed a whetstone, poured a drop of oil on it, and in quick, circular motions honed the blade. The knife made a rasping noise on the stone. Hannah checked Lucia's face to see if she had heard, but Lucia remained motionless, unresponsive.

Hannah placed two fingers against Lucia's neck but could not locate a pulse. She reached over to a small table next to the bed and took up a silver-backed looking-glass. She held it to the Contessa's lips. No reassuring moisture clouded the glass. Lucia was dead. There was no reason to delay. Taking up the bottle again she oiled the mound of belly. With the tip of the knife she drew an imaginary line in the oil from above the umbilicus to the sharing bones of the pelvis. Then she raised the knife.

Giovanna entered the room and stood staring, fresh bed linen stacked high her arms. 'Hail Mary, full of grace, blessed are thee and the fruit of thy . . . '

'May you forgive me for what I am about to do, *cara*,' Hannah whispered.

Giovanna took a sharp breath and looked toward the windows.

'Dear God, steady my hand. Let me not slice so deeply that the child is harmed, nor so shallowly that the womb remains shut fast and I cannot reach the child before it drowns in its mother's blood. Help me to split open this woman's belly as neatly as one halves a white peach to free the pit.' Her heart was racing.

Hannah said to Giovanna, 'When the blood spurts from her belly, use a linen cloth to wipe it from my face so that I may see clearly and seize the baby's head and shoulders.'

Suddenly Hannah heard ringing in her ears, and it seemed as though all light had left the room. Waves of dizziness passed over her. Her legs refused to support her.

'God forgive me,' she said, 'I cannot do it.' She tossed the knife to the terrazzo floor, where it clanged and skidded under the bed. Sinking to her knees, Hannah buried her face in the silk coverlet. Her entire body trembled, her shoulders shook with sobs.

Then she felt something as light as a moth settling on her hair. It was Lilith come to thrust her aside and claim Lucia for her own. The hand stroked her hair, but it was Lucia's thin, hot hand pushing Hannah's curls behind her ears. The tension drained from Hannah. She would have continued that way, head buried in the silk coverlet, drifting, if Giovanna had not grabbed her by the arm and hauled her to her feet.

'Holy Mother of God, the Contessa is alive. Do something!'

Relief flooded her and Hannah straightened her *cioppà* and took a deep breath. After dipping her hands in the almond oil, she inserted two fingers into the birth passage, hoping the baby had righted itself. The waters still had not broken; the womb remained wet, a small mercy. With the baby in such a poor position, lack of water would have made repositioning impossible. Hannah reached farther between Lucia's thighs, her index and middle fingers slippery with almond oil. She felt the route leading to the matrix, but before she could touch the mouth of the womb, her hand collided with what she had most feared.

A tiny, limp hand.

3

Valletta, Malta
1575

Isaac Levi had gambled with fate and lost. Trade between Venice and the Levant was so lucrative that huge profits, sometimes upwards of three thousand percent, could be gained from buying and selling spices, timber, and printed silk. And so he had borrowed heavily and bought a warehouse full of silk to resell in Constantinople, planning to buy spices with the profits and sell them in Venice. He had not calculated on his ship being fired upon and mercenaries in the pay of the Knights of Malta, reeking of drink and sweat and religion, clambering over the rail, screaming and brandishing swords and muskets.

There had been twenty of the brutes, savage, hairy men with swinging crucifixes and hearts bursting with hatred for the infidels and greed for their rich Venetian cargo. The smell of gunpowder from their blunderbusses filled the air. Most of his fellow passengers were murdered before they had a chance to gather their wits about them and ask God's forgiveness for their sins. Isaac thought he would soon be watching his own blood congealing on the foredeck. But God had other plans for him. In the months that followed, he learned the power of His punishment.

Now he was in Valletta, capital city of Malta,

40

stronghold of the Knights. During their long nights and endless days in jail, Simón, another Ashkenazi Jew and a fellow prisoner, had explained to Isaac that in 1530, Charles V of Spain had bestowed this island of rock and wind on the Knights of St. John in exchange for their protecting the archipelago against the infidel Turk. The Knights succeeded in defending the land from the rapaciousness of the Ottomans, but over the years they had grown greedy. Bewitched by their victories, they used the pretext of defending their island to prey not only upon the infidel ships of the Ottomans but on Christian ships as well, seizing cargo and enslaving all on board, rich or poor, merchant or servant, woman or child. They called themselves Knights but they were little more than pirates, grown rich through crimes sanctified in the name of the Holy Crusade.

The Knights had spared the lives of Isaac, Simón and some others in anticipation of large ransoms. They had been trussed up and thrown into the hold of the ship, so slippery with rat excrement that they had difficulty remaining upright. For many days and nights the steady protest of the ropes and the thrum of the heavy sails made sleep impossible. Isaac's stomach grew queasy from the stink of pine pitch and rotting timbers, and he vomited from the motion of the ship, the rolling most severe in the hold.

After they landed in Malta, he had languished in a stone cell no bigger than the bed he and Hannah used to share, with a dirt floor and a grated window that allowed little light to penetrate, even at midday.

Worse than the food had been the waiting — weeks of being held in this stinking garrison, expecting death from starvation, hoping for it. Now, at last, the wait was over. He was to be sold to the highest bidder at the slave auction in the main square. Then he must try to stay alive until word of his capture arrived in Venice and the Parnassim dos Cautivos negotiated his ransom.

Isaac peered through the barred window into the corridor, empty except for dust motes settling onto the floor. He was thinking about what he always thought about — his plan of escape. There had been little else to occupy his mind while he was shackled to the wall of his prison cell.

He heard footsteps and the clanking of keys. The door to his cell swung open and two guards strode in. One grabbed him, yanking him to his feet. The other one checked his leg iron, dragged him from the cell, and half-thrust, half-carried him outside. Isaac squeezed his eyes shut against the barbs of sunlight. They frogmarched him and other prisoners, including his friend Simón, from the Grand Master's palace, across to the town square, where a platform had been erected. The guard shoved him up the steps.

Once his eyes adjusted, Isaac noticed that the platform, raised a few feet from the ground, was surrounded by a crowd of men and a few women, all shoving and pushing, craning their necks to examine him and Simón and the other prisoners from *La Dogaressa*. In the distance, over the ramparts of St. Elmo, ships bobbed at their lines.

A rough hand pushed him forward and a voice behind him shouted in Maltese — a primitive stew of Italian, Sicilian, and Arabic, which, after weeks of listening to the guards converse, Isaac was beginning to comprehend.

'What am I bid for this Jew? Thirty-five years old or close enough, from Venice, fit to work, free of cholera and rickets.' The auctioneer took a baton and tapped the backs of his limbs. Isaac's feet, swollen where he had been *bastinado*'d fifty blows, gave way at the touch of the baton. He stumbled. One of the guards caught him and held him upright. The auctioneer tossed the stick to his assistant and said to Isaac, 'Open your mouth. Let us have a look at your teeth.' Grabbing him by the jaw, he poked a dirty finger around in Isaac's mouth, and then turned to the crowd and said, 'An impressive set of grinders. White and strong. How many of us can say that?' He grinned, revealing two missing canines. The crowd roared with laughter. 'Those who have teeth can eat, and those who can eat can work.' The auctioneer felt Isaac's limbs. 'No fractures, no dislocations, no spavin, or ring-bone.' Motioning Isaac to show his hands, the auctioneer examined the palms. 'Delicate and tender hands. Neither callused nor brawny. He is a merchant or a gentleman and will fetch a good ransom for the Knights. In the meantime, some fortunate purchaser will have the benefit of his labour.'

The sun heated the iron ring around Isaac's ankle into a circle of fire. He heard a stocky man in the crowd call out, 'Tell him to remove his shirt! I want to see if he is strong enough for me.' The man's face was dotted with smallpox scars. His gold tooth caught the sun.

Isaac had heard tales from his fellow prisoners about farmers who harnessed men to plows like draft animals and worked them to death. *Please, God, by all that is holy and great, not a farm*, he prayed. The auctioneer nodded at him to comply with the man's request. It was not necessary to remove his shirt — it was little more than a rag, and Isaac's arms and muscular chest shone white through the tatters — but he pulled what little remained over his head.

The man nodded in appreciation. Then he said, 'But if he is a Jew, where is his beard?'

Isaac reached up to rub his chin. He had had a beard ever since he was old enough to grow one. Every Jew did, for the Torah says, 'The adornment of a man's face is his beard.' Now his face felt as vulnerable as a newborn's. When he had arrived in Malta, one of the jailers had insisted his beard be shaved. 'To keep down the lice,' explained the barber who had shaved both his head and his face with a dull razor, leaving ribbons of bloody gashes on his chin and cheeks. When his beard started to grow back, they shaved him again.

The jailer had also stripped him of all his possessions, his extra clothing, his prayer shawl, his thousand ducats destined for the purchase of cardamom and cloves in Constantinople, everything except for a tiny cloth sack no bigger than a walnut shell, filled with the eggs of *Bombyx mori*, the prized silkworm. Another prisoner on

44

the ship, an old Turk who knew he would not survive to see dry land, had pressed the cloth sack into Isaac's hand and, in exchange, asked Isaac to pen a letter to his wife in Constantinople. Isaac hid the sack inside the shirt of a dead prisoner who had been left to putrefy. A few days later he snatched the bag back just before the Knights skidded the poor man's body off the aft deck and into the sea. He tucked the bag past the waistband of his breeches, snug up against his *shmekele*. Now the sack was his sole possession. Although he knew nothing of the cultivation of the worms, he knew the value of printed silk fabric and the lure it held for well-born women of Venice. Someday perhaps his worms would serve him well on this island of rock and soldier monks.

The auctioneer turned back to Isaac, scrutinizing him to determine his other marketable virtues. Next to him, Simón stood swaying in the heat of the afternoon sun. As the silence lengthened, the crowd started to drift away. Isaac could imagine what confounded the auctioneer — his broad chest was now so devoid of fat that his muscles showed as though in a painting of Christ in the final stages of exsanguination. His legs, once straight and hard, were no thicker than a table's.

Isaac whispered a few words in the auctioneer's ear. The man nodded and called out, 'Not only is this slave a Jew, but he is a learned one. One who can read and write and compute.'

The stocky man heckled. 'How do I know he is learned if he has no beard? Does not the Jew obtain wisdom from his hairy chin?'

Isaac raised his head and managed to say to his tormentor in a voice hoarse from disuse, 'If men be judged wise by their beards, then that billy goat over there' — he motioned with his chin in the direction of the livestock pen across the square — 'would be the wisest among us.'

He felt the sting of the baton on the back of his legs. He staggered and nearly toppled off the platform. Laughter rose from the crowd.

'What use is a clever tongue to me?' said the man. 'I need slaves for galley ships making their way to and from the Levant.'

And of what use has my clever tongue ever been to me, Isaac thought, except to get me into trouble? Flies collected around his eyes. He could not summon the will to brush them away.

Simón said under his breath, 'Do not antagonize that one. His name is Joseph. He is a *Judenfresser*, a Jew-eater. By the time the galleys arrive here, the slaves are more dead than alive from starvation and beatings. This bastard replaces the poor creatures with fresh slaves and leaves the old ones to die. The petty officers are so desperate for crew, they buy anyone.'

God would understand if I killed myself, thought Isaac. In such circumstances, it would not be a violation of the law. Had not the Jews at Masada killed themselves to rob the Roman soldiers of the pleasure? But then the memory of Hannah came to him. Hannah with her narrow waist and black eyes, waiting for him in Venice. He forced himself to stand straighter. God might understand and forgive if he hanged himself in

46

his cell by the ragged sleeves of his shirt, but Hannah would not. Isaac put the thought of suicide out of his mind, just as he had put aside the memory of their quarrel and their last miserable day together. When their love was strong, they could have slept together on a bed the width of a sheaf of wheat. That last night, a bed measuring sixty cubits would not have been sufficient.

The sound of a rough voice brought him back to the present. Joseph yelled to the auctioneer, 'I would not bid ten *scudi* for this hairless Jew, but satisfy my curiosity, Auctioneer. Did you shave his private parts too? Is that hair missing along with his foreskin?' A collective guffaw rose from the crowd. Encouraged, the man continued, 'Maybe he is not a real Jew at all, but a Marrano from Spain: Christian on the outside, Jew on the inside, eh? Ask him to drop those shit-caked breeches.'

He who tolerates insults invites injury, Isaac reminded himself, the blood rushing to his face. If he did not reply, the crowd would join in and soon he would find himself at the receiving end of a hail of rotten oranges, or worse. What an abomination to be mocked by an illiterate lout who no doubt signed his name with a greasy thumbprint and slept in a hay rick with his pigs. He grinned at Joseph and called out, 'I cannot oblige you, sir. The sight of my member would excite envy in the heart of every man present and desire in the heart of every woman.'

The crowd pressed closer, jostling one another to approach the platform. One of the guards took a step toward Isaac and raised his baton. Isaac mentally cursed his ill-advised retort and stiffened, preparing for the sting of the beating.

To his relief, the auctioneer said, with a shake of his head, 'The Knights will want him alive until they receive the price on his head.' He motioned the guard to hold back his blows, but he shot Isaac a warning glance.

Joseph laughed and shouted up to the auctioneer, 'He amuses me. Perhaps I can find a use for him: to bait my rat traps!' He jiggled the coins in his pockets. 'Come to think of it, what better function for any Jew?' More and more men had ambled over to join the throng, drawn by the jeers and hoots of approval. Joseph faced the crowd and took a deep bow before turning to Isaac to ask, 'Shall I buy you, Jew?'

'No,' Isaac replied.

'And why not?'

'Sir, how can you take me for a slave after you have taken me for an adviser?'

The crowd jeered.

'All of Christendom knows your people killed Christ and must be forever punished,' called Joseph.

'Enough!' The auctioneer held up a hand. 'What about fifty *scudi*, sir? You will get your money's worth out of him.' Meaning before he died of overwork. The auctioneer raised his gavel. 'What do you say? Shall I knock him down to you?'

'Here is ten *scudi*, Auctioneer. I will buy him for the pleasure of seeing him starve.'

'Any other bids?' The auctioneer scanned the

crowd. 'No? Very well, then. Sold to Joseph.' He thumped his gavel on the plank in front of him and then motioned to the guard. 'Take him down.'

As Isaac stumbled in front of Simón, his friend whispered, 'May God protect you.'

The guard kicked Isaac down the stairs to where Joseph waited, stomping his boots in the dust. He tossed a ten-*scudi* coin to the auctioneer, who caught it and said, 'Thank you, sir.'

The auctioneer now turned his attention to Simón. 'And next is a Jew from Leghorn, a trader in gemstones.'

As Joseph grabbed Isaac by the shoulder and started to lead him toward a dusty cart in the middle of the square, a female voice from the back of the crowd called loudly, 'Auctioneer, wait!'

The men parted to make way for a woman built like one of the battlements of St. Elmo. Over her robes was an apron covered with a dusting of flour. She pressed a small dog to her bosom, white against the brown of her scapular. Whether the animal was white by nature's hand or white from flour was difficult to say. She grabbed Isaac by his arm. In Maltese, she said, 'This man will never last a fortnight on the galleys. Release him. This is nothing less than murder.' She shook a finger at Joseph. 'You are an abomination.'

'The bidding is closed,' the auctioneer called down to her.

'Joseph will have him strapped to an oar,

sitting in freezing water up to his waist. Surely you can see that, Auctioneer.'

'I only sell slaves, Sister Assunta, I do not predict their futures.'

The auctioneer turned his attention back to Simón, but before he could continue, the nun said, 'Once he is scrubbed and deloused, he will do well enough for me, cleaning and working in the garden of the convent.'

Joseph made a grab for Isaac's other arm and, turning to the nun, said, 'With respect, Sister, this man has been bought and paid for. Now let us pass.'

The auctioneer looked down at the nun, his expression apologetic. 'Sorry, Sister Assunta. You are too late.'

Isaac studied the woman's face, her rough serge habit, her red hands, and her wide hips. An *unsoggolo*, a wimple, concealed her jaw and part of her cheek. She reached into her pocket and withdrew ten *scudi* and waved it in Joseph's face.

'Here, Joseph, be gone. Go murder someone else.'

'Let me pass.' Joseph began to haul Isaac in the direction of the horse cart at the edge of the throng.

Isaac could not help imagining the peace of a convent, perhaps a garden of olive trees and hives for bees. He halted.

'If you refuse to walk,' Joseph said, 'I will pick you up and sling you across my shoulders like the carcass of a goat.'

The sister tried to thrust the coins in Joseph's pocket, but he ducked out of her reach.

Isaac felt as a snapper must feel being fought over by two housewives in the Rialto fish market.

'This Jew is mine. Report me to the Grand Master if you do not like the way I treat my slaves,' Joseph said. He gave Isaac a shove into the cart and climbed in after him as the nun finally released her hold.

'It is God's will that I have him, Joseph. Sell him to me and buy that brute over there.' She gestured to a large Nubian standing at the back of the platform. 'He will last longer than this one. Leave the Jew to me.'

Joseph picked up the reins of his cart horse. 'Let me pass, Sister.'

A man in the crowd called out, 'Save your soul, Joseph. Let the convent have him. The nuns need the services of a man with a large member more than you do.' The man doubled over with laughter.

Joseph flushed red and made a clucking noise to his horse but did not slap the reins. 'Since it is you, Sister Assunta, give me fifteen *scudi* and he is yours.' He gestured to the dog in her arms. 'Then you can pamper him like your lapdog.'

Sweat trickled down Isaac's legs and he felt the cloth sack of worms slip down his breeches. Working his hand down his leg, he managed to tug it up surreptitiously and press it under his waistband. Joseph and Sister Assunta continued their haggling.

'Take my ten *scudi*. This is all the money I have. My convent is poor.' She tried again to put the ten *scudi* coins into Joseph's hand, but jaw set, he shook his head.

51

Sister Assunta grunted in frustration. She grasped the skirt of her habit in her hand, strode up the steps to the auction platform, and elbowed aside the guard. She addressed the crowd. 'Ladies and gentlemen, I am in need of a donation of five *scudi* for the convent. Whoever has pity for this Jew and wishes God's light to shine upon him, open your purse,' her voice rang out.

Isaac sat stiffly in the cart and waited for someone to volunteer, but not a soul stepped forward.

God was not through shitting on him.

4

Moments passed as a pair of seagulls shrieked overhead and Joseph's hand on Isaac's arm grew as tight as the iron circle around his ankle. Would no one in the crowd take pity and rescue him from this loutish gentile? It was a trivial sum, but the throng, their hope of further excitement gone, began to drift away.

Finally, a fair-haired woman with wide, angular cheekbones and dimples stepped forward. 'Here are five *scudi* for your blessings, Sister,' she said.

Assunta accepted them with a barely discernible nod of her head. The nun tossed the coins at Joseph and hauled Isaac out of the cart. Joseph stared at the fair-haired woman and seemed about to follow her, but she disappeared quickly into the multitude.

Sister Assunta thrust her white dog into Isaac's arms. 'Hold him while I fetch my wagon.'

The dog, entranced by the smell of Isaac's unwashed body, wriggled in his arms, licking his face. Assunta returned leading a wagon missing several floor slats, pulled by a spavined roan mare. Isaac, dog under one arm, climbed in.

Sister Assunta's wrists were as big around as Isaac's biceps, her face as harsh and angular as Malta itself. Clean water, fresh air, prayer, and wholesome food evidently made nuns grow massive in Valletta. What manner of female was she? Isaac wondered. With those hands and feet and low voice — was she male, female, or a member of a sort of middle sex with the most unpleasant aspects of each gender? Hannah, with her soft voice and silky hair, was as different from Assunta as one woman could be from another.

After a silent, bumpy journey along the coast road, Assunta finally pulled up the pathway to a graceless and stolid building overlooking the sea. Isaac took a deep breath and gazed around. The air was perfumed with the scent of pines and wild roses and salt air. He congratulated himself on his good fortune. A neat vineyard covered the nearby hillside. An orchard filled with orange trees bloomed in the field behind the chapel. Plump, bossy chickens pecked in the yard. Assunta tossed the horse's reins to a waiting sister and led Isaac into the convent kitchen. Bags full of turnips, carrots, and onions slumped against the walls. A side of beef hung aging from a hook on the ceiling. There were worse places to wait while the Society negotiated his release.

Assunta threw off her shawl, pushed back her wimple, allowing a hank of brown hair to escape, and busied herself mixing bread dough, measuring handfuls of flour into an enormous bowl and then, with a wooden paddle, blending in water and soured milk. After stirring and mixing until she had the right consistency, she shaped the dough into a ball the size of a goat kid, hoisted it over her head, and thwacked it on the table in front of her.

Isaac stood with his arms dangling at his sides,

trying to think of a way to make himself useful. The dough appeared sticky and might require more flour.

'I thank you for rescuing me,' he said, dragging a sack of flour from the cupboard to the centre of the kitchen and shoving it within reach of her arm. 'You have saved my life.' For the first time since his arrival in Malta he felt that was something to be grateful for. 'God will reward you for your charity.'

It had been months since he had tasted bread that was not crawling with weevils. There was a bowl overflowing with grapes on the table in the centre of the room. As for fruit, he had not eaten so much as a wormy apple since he left Venice.

Assunta ignored the sack of flour and paused in her kneading. 'You can also thank that woman in the crowd if you ever come across her. Her name, I believe, is Gertrudis.' In a voice that did not invite questions, she continued, 'A woman of some notoriety.' She tucked a sweaty tendril of hair under her wimple. 'It would have been a sin to allow you to be sold to Joseph.' She executed a stiff pivot of her torso so she could see him in spite of her wimple. A gleam came to her eye. 'Joseph and I have crossed swords before. I have always got the better of him.'

'When your enemy falls, do not rejoice,' Isaac said, quoting from the Torah.

'Well said,' she replied. 'But a difficult injunction to obey.'

He wished she would turn her head to him when she spoke so he could read the expression on her face, but her habit seemed to make all her movements awkward, as though she were encased in a suit of armour. The Maltese dialect was all spongy vowels and harsh fricatives. Some of her words were unfamiliar, but he could guess at their import; others left him perplexed.

Assunta said, 'The Bible does not prohibit slavery. In fact, it says, 'Slaves, obey your earthly masters with fear and trembling, and with a sincere heart, as you would Christ.'' She resumed her kneading, gave another thump to the dough, and continued, 'But the Bible forbids doing nothing when you see a wrong about to be committed. I knew Joseph would kill you.' She slammed both fists into the dough, making a huge crater in the middle of it. 'You should know,' she said, jabbing a floury finger toward the seashore, 'the Knights of St. John have terrorized the seas surrounding Malta for years. They have become no better than brigands.' She rubbed her cheek with the back of her hand, leaving a streak of flour behind. 'Yes, I helped you, as I have helped others.' Assunta pinched off a piece of dough and dropped it into the upturned pink mouth of her white dog. 'I have my reasons.'

Isaac spoke in Veneziano, which, if he enunciated slowly, she seemed to comprehend. 'What work can I perform to show my gratitude?' He glanced out the window. 'I can prune your vines, help with the harvest. No doubt another pair of hands would be welcome?'

'Do not thank me for buying you. I am not compassionate, at least not the way a nun should be. If I cannot get to heaven by being kind I will do so by righting wrongs, thus ensuring that I

56

ascend to heaven at the proper time.' She gathered up the stray bits of dough and then, cupping her hand, skidded them onto a plate.

'A *mitzvah* is a *mitzvah* regardless of motive,' said Isaac.

She rubbed olive oil on the top of the dough and placed it to rise in a crockery bowl. She patted the top. 'Bread for tonight. We have many sisters, all of them hungry from gardening and working in the orchards.' Then she reached into a burlap sack and took out an onion, which she began chopping into small pieces.

Isaac said, 'I am a good worker and learn with ease. I am versed in the Venetian method of double-entry bookkeeping. I can keep your books of account.'

'Our vows are poverty, chastity, and obedience.' She waved the knife in his face. 'We have no books and nothing to account for.' She laughed so hard at her own jest that she began to cough, then wiped her hands on her apron and looked around the kitchen, considering her next chore. 'Reach that bunch of rosemary hanging from the ceiling and chop it for me. Sister Caterina will return soon to help me prepare the rest of the meal.'

Isaac took the rosemary, rolled it between his fingers, and held it to his nose. It evoked memories of Seder dinners and roasted lamb, and he felt a rush of homesickness. He grabbed a knife and began to chop.

'My wife, Hannah, grows rosemary in a pot on the windowsill,' he said.

Assunta watched Isaac wielding the knife,

57

hacking off ragged sections. 'Not like that — small pieces, like so.' She took the knife from him, minced the herb into even pieces.

Why were his hands so clever when it came to writing, turning the pages of a book, and caressing his wife, and so clumsy when doing a task any simpleton could manage? Even the rooster, which had wandered in from the courtyard, seemed to mock his ineptitude. The air was yeasty with the aroma of rising dough. Soon it would be baking in the oven above the hearth. His mouth watered.

'What other skills have you?'

'Buying and selling spices and timber.'

'Somewhat of a problem if you have none,' she observed.

Through the window, he noticed a mulberry tree growing in the courtyard in front of the convent. His cloth sack of silkworm eggs was tucked safely into his waistband. Soon greedy worms would hatch, demanding to be fed.

'There is something I could do . . . with your help. I have some silkworm eggs. Worms are creatures I know nothing of. But silk fetches a high price. Perhaps together we could find a way to make my worms thrive. This island could use some commerce other than the trafficking in Jews.'

'Isaac,' she said, glancing up long enough from her work to ensure she locked eyes with him, 'Malta is a military fortress. Knights and soldiers do not wear silk. You will find no grand ladies here swanning about in silk ball gowns. We are an island of simple people. You should have

58

stuffed your satchel with hides of beef and sheep rather than silk eggs.' She marched to the corner of the kitchen and picked up a sheepskin dotted with lumps of fat. 'This is useful.' She shook it in his face, close enough that he could smell the odour of rancid lanolin and see it glisten on her fingers. 'Silk is for the Grand Master who rules this island. Wool is for the rest of us.'

'I can read and write,' said Isaac.

He was about to elaborate, but she patted the back of his hand, leaving a smudge of flour behind. 'Good. I will give you the loan of a quill and parchment and you can post a NO TRESPASS sign on my kitchen door to keep the chickens out. In the meantime' — she flapped her apron — 'I shall chase them out.'

The rooster scuttled past Isaac.

'Let me explain my true reason for buying you,' she said. 'My family was originally from Toledo in Castile — La Mancha. They were heretics like you. Eighty years ago they converted to Christianity. It was not their choice. King Ferdinand and Queen Isabella forced all the Jews to convert.'

A sinking feeling seized Isaac. If her family were *Conversos*, then she would be more earnest than most Christians about demonstrating her piety. 'Yes, the Alhambra Decree,' Isaac said. 'Convert or be exiled. But not all Jews converted. Many fled to Venice. The Venetian ghetto is filled with Spanish Jews, the Sephardim. Others fled to Constantinople.'

She continued as though she had not heard him. 'To be ignorant of the ways of Christianity

59

is forgivable, but only if no one takes the trouble to educate you.' Assunta took an apple from the bowl on the table, cut off a slice, and handed it to him with the point of the knife. 'Eat. It is from our orchard.'

He bit through the red skin. The juice flooded his mouth with such sweetness that he choked. If she would cease talking, he could enjoy the nectar to its fullest.

Assunta ate the remainder of the apple. 'I have made it my mission to buy Jewish slaves with the small number of coins that come my way and then persuade them from their heretical beliefs. Many of my most devout nuns, for example, Sister Caterina, are New Christians. I will do the same for you.' Assunta polished another apple on the skirt of her habit. 'So,' she said, crunching down on the second apple with her square white teeth, 'let us discuss the salvation of your immortal soul and how we may best accomplish your conversion.'

Convert? To the Christians, he would be no better than a *marrano*, a pig rooting around for scraps. By his own people he would be seen as a traitor and a coward. The Knights had taken everything — his dignity as a free man, all of his property. Being a Jew and the hope of seeing Hannah again were all he had left.

The rooster pecking in the corner of the kitchen squawked and raced out the door. Isaac considered following, but the bowl of apples was in front of him and the rising dough would soon be baking. How long it had been since he tasted fresh bread.

'Ordinarily, it would be improper for a man to live in our convent,' Assunta said. 'But if you accept Jesus as your Saviour and convert, I will talk to the Bishop about making an exception. I will give you shelter, food, and work. You can sweep out the chapel and help with the laundry. You are a handsome man, or will be when you have been fed. A man such as you will be a temptation to the novices, some of whom, I regret to say, are here not because of their spiritual devotion but because their families cannot afford their dowries. So I will watch you like a dog guarding a flock of ewes. You will sleep in the goat shed. So what do you say? You will live in comfort until your ransom is paid.' When he did not reply immediately, she said, 'Or would you prefer to beg in the streets of Valletta?'

Given what he had experienced of the flinty-hearted Maltese, he would starve as a beggar if she threw him out. 'My people were slaves in the land of the Pharaoh. The ancient Israelites prevailed. So shall I.' Even to his own ears, the words sounded quixotic.

'You are being foolish. Convert. You will not regret the decision.'

There was no need to make an enemy of her. He cleared his throat. 'Perhaps someday. In the meantime' — he raised his knife — 'I will finish chopping this rosemary.'

'You do not understand,' she said, taking the knife from him. 'Unless you convert, you cannot remain here. You would be defiling consecrated ground. I could not permit it.' She gave him a severe look. 'I am giving you a chance to enjoy life both here on earth and in heaven. As Christ said, 'Follow me and I shall give you life everlasting.''

'I am grateful to you, Sister, for all you have done, but I cannot convert.' It would not do to answer her candidly. He wanted to shout, *I will convert when my foreskin grows back*, but the word *foreskin* would have embarrassed her. Christians were squeamish about matters of the body, like foreskins and the monthly flow of women, yet they adored their paintings of Christ's crucifixion, his hands and feet dripping with blood, and thorns gouging his scalp. There was no fathoming the gentile mind.

So this was the price of Christian compassion: she would give him shelter and food but only if he converted. He felt his face flush. He was a slave, in no position to be angry. His task was to survive. Perhaps he could distract her as one does a child.

'Shall I read the Bible to you?' Isaac offered. 'Perhaps that is a more useful form of labour than digging turnips or minding goats.'

'Where would I get a Bible? There are no books at the convent.' She looked at him with impatience. 'I am offering you the gift of Eternal Life.'

And along with it, the miracle of the Immaculate Conception, the miracle of loaves and fishes, and Lazarus rising from the dead. The credulity of gentiles was boundless.

When he said nothing, Sister Assunta's face became set and hard. 'Why cling to such a ridiculous religion? That a pig is not suitable for human consumption? That I offend God if I eat a piece of cheese and meat in the same meal? That' — here she blushed in a way he found both touching and grotesque — 'that a woman must be cleansed each month before she can return to her husband's bed?'

At least she knew more of his religion than most Christians.

'I am offering you a chance not only to have food and shelter but to renounce a religion that will always garner scorn and hatred.'

Isaac regarded her determined face and considered his future. He must stay alive long enough to make the journey back to Hannah. Could he *pretend* to convert? Was it within his ability to act with duplicity in a matter of such importance as belief? Sephardic Jews had been forced to convert by King Ferdinand and Queen Isabella, yet many of them had continued to practise Judaism in secret. Could he? A man never knows what is within his capacity until he tries. God would understand and forgive. He would at least make an attempt.

Isaac held on to the edge of the kitchen table and tried to lower himself to his knees. This was the way Christians prayed: on their knees, head bowed, hands clasped, all signifying abasement before God. Man is nothing; God is all-powerful. It was as though his joints had rusted up like the hinges on the gates of the ghetto. The memory came flooding back of the Rabbi davening back and forth with the speed of summer lightning while intoning the morning prayers.

Isaac extended his hand to Sister Assunta. He

opened his mouth to recite the only Christian prayer he knew, the *pater nostrum*. "'Our Father,'" he began, "'who art in heaven . . . '" And then, although his lips continued to move, the words stuck like fish bones in his throat.

Assunta knelt beside him, intoning the next words to encourage him. "'Hallowed be Thy Name . . . '"

He tried once more to repeat the words but his tongue had grown thick and refused to obey. He felt a dark flush of shame creep over him, as debilitating as a fever. The weakest man is the first to submit. Here he was on his knees, holding the hand of a Christian nun. He was the most craven of men.

He said, 'Sister, I am a Jew. I do not know how to be otherwise.' He lurched to his feet and brushed dried chicken excrement off his legs.

She rose from her knees. 'In that case, I pity you your folly and wish you well. You will find life harsh. This climate is not pleasant. The sun is blistering during the day. At night you will freeze with no clothing or blankets. And in the winter months? From the wind off the sea, many die of exposure.' She went to the shelf along one side of the room, took out a simple wooden rosary, and handed it to him. 'Take this. It will remind you of my offer. You reject the notion of conversion now, but mark my words, after a few months you will beseech me to teach you your catechism.'

Not to accept a present, especially from one who has saved your life, was unforgivable. He took it in his hand. 'I am sorry, Sister, but I have no talent for being a Christian.'

64

'There is no way to flee this island. Abandon any thought of that.'

'I have no thoughts of escape,' Isaac lied. 'The Society for the Release of Captives in Venice is funded by a levy that Venetian Jews pay according to the value of their cargos. They will ransom me.'

'Good, because as you stroll around town, you will see the Knights' guards roaming the docks. No captain will risk the displeasure of the Grand Master by giving you passage. If the captain were to be caught, he would be forbidden from docking here to take on water and provisions. And no ship sailing to the Levant can make the voyage without putting in to Valletta. We are a victualling port. Take this — ' She tossed him a sheepskin, catching him in the chest. 'It is beginning to stink up my kitchen.' She rinsed her hands in the bucket in the corner. 'And let us be off.'

He accepted the skin, wondering what use he would have for it. If only she had offered him a chicken instead, even the stringy old rooster. He said, 'Perhaps you would do me the honour of allowing me to write a letter for you one day. You are the only one on this island who has shown me the slightest kindness.'

'Isaac, you will not live long enough to write me fancy letters, nor read to me from the Bible. No man survives the galleys.'

'What do you mean?'

'I am selling you back to Joseph. Being tied to an oar on a galley ship will give you a different view of the world.'

65

He looked at her. 'Please, not to Joseph.'

'I need my fifteen *scudi* back.'

'The Society will repay your fifteen *scudi*. Just let me go and I will somehow forage for food and make my own way.'

'I do not have time to argue.' She marched out to the courtyard, where her wagon stood waiting, the horse munching oats from his feedbag. 'Joseph should be at the docks now. Let us depart.'

From the expression on her face, he knew argument was useless. He clung to the sheepskin and followed her out the door with a backward glance at the bowl of apples and the dough rising on the table.

'I thank you for your help. One favour, if you will. I have no place to store these silkworm eggs. They will not trouble you. When they hatch, send for me.' He tried to hand her the small cloth sack.

'I do not want them befouling my kitchen.'

'Please take them. Just keep them warm and dry.'

Giving a martyr's sigh, she said, 'Very well. I see you are determined to saddle me with their custody.' Her lips compressed into a coy expression. 'Give them here.'

He dug in his waistband and handed the tiny sack to her. She thrust it into the folds of her habit, and then glared at him, her head moving in tandem with her torso in that stiff way of hers. Then she seemed to think better of it. Through the kitchen door, he watched as she walked to the hearth, removed a brick, and placed the

66

bag in the crevice. Then she slid the brick back into place.

Isaac started to climb into the cart, but she shook her head and unbuckled the harness from around the mare.

'My poor little mare is exhausted.' Assunta motioned to Isaac. She placed the yoke of the horse's harness around his neck and let the lines flap at his sides. 'Not a perfect fit but you will get us into town.'

She hitched the breeching straps onto the shafts of the cart, then took up the crupper strap and leaned toward him. For a terrible moment Isaac thought she was going to wind it under his private parts, but she tucked it out of the way under the yoke.

'My horse needs a rest. And you need practice with hard labour if you are to survive.' She climbed into the cart and slapped the reins down on his back with more force than she had shown her mare. He struggled forward, dragging the cart no more than a few paces before the road inclined. He shuddered to a halt, the cart threatening to pull him backwards and toss them into a ditch.

All Isaac had to his name was a sheepskin, which even in the open air made his eyes smart from the stink of it. The harness dug painfully into his neck and shoulders. This bride of Christ was right. He would be dead before the week was out.

5

Venice,
1575

Hannah pinched the hand, praying it would retreat back up into the womb. At first, she compressed it with as slight a pressure as possible so as not to rupture the membranes holding back the waters. When it failed to respond, she squeezed again, this time more firmly, feeling a fingernail as small as a seed pearl. In response, she felt an almost imperceptible quiver. The child was alive but weak. Again, she pinched — and the hand moved.

Then, to Hannah's surprise, the womb hardened in another pang. She withdrew her fingers and waited for the matrix to relax. The pang had been feeble. Yes, Lucia was alive, but for how much longer?

When Hannah reinserted her fingers, she sought the baby's hand again, but it had retreated into the safety of the matrix. She touched the inner mouth of the womb; it was open sufficiently to permit the head to emerge but as long as the head was twisted, there was no hope of delivering the child alive.

Giovanna stood next to her, the stack of bed linen dropped at her feet. Hannah said to her, 'The Contessa is alive and so is the child, but both are weak. Help me lift your mistress. Put these pillows under her bottom. The womb is too constricted. The pains have little force. Hold her thighs in the air so we can straighten her spine.'

Giovanna stacked pillows under the unresisting Contessa, casting Hannah a sideways look. 'You seem to know a great deal. Have you borne children yourself?'

'To my regret, I have not.' She remembered her optimism each time she and Isaac had joined together when her period of *niddah* was complete, and her despair each month when her monthly courses commenced.

'Odd that you should choose to be a midwife, having never experienced birth yourself.'

In other circumstances the words would have stung. She thought, Do not physicians provide medicaments for illnesses they have never suffered? But Hannah held her tongue. Two in her care were suspended between life and death. She had more important matters to worry about.

Giovanna went on, 'Do all midwives from the ghetto poke their fingers into crevices where they do not belong?'

'The child may turn if the spine is straight,' Hannah said. She grasped Lucia's hand and bent low to her ear. 'Listen to me, *cara*. Your baby is alive, but you must help me get it born. When the time comes, you must push with all your might. I know you are tired from this endless travail, but you must think of the child and do your best.' Sometimes a whiff from a pot of cayenne pepper and the strong sneezing would expel a child when the mother was too weak to bear down, but this was not such a case because the child was not well positioned.

Some colour came back into Lucia's face. 'You are certain the child is alive? You heard the heart?'

Hannah nodded.

'The Holy Virgin is merciful.'

'Yes, but we have little time.' Hannah stroked the Contessa's forehead, pushing back a strand of wet hair. Then she grasped both of Lucia's hands in hers. 'I am pouring my own strength into you. I have enough for both of us. Feel it enter your body and make use of it.'

Lucia gave an answering squeeze.

Hannah released her hold and took a step toward the foot of the bed, slipping on a puddle of blood and catching herself clumsily on one of the bed pillars. She thought she saw a dark form fling itself from the top of the canopy and flutter toward the ceiling with a low cry. Perhaps it was a bat from one of the fruit trees outside. Giovanna must have seen it too, for she grew pale and pulled her shawl higher around her shoulders.

In a voice louder than necessary, Hannah said, 'God is on our side. With His help, we cannot fail. We will wait a moment and see whether this baby turns on its own or whether I must manipulate your belly and force the turning. Better that the child does the work on its own.' If the child would only turn, she could then use her birthing spoons to pull it out.

While Lucia lay motionless between pangs, her belly thrust in the air, Hannah darted around the enormous room, opening drawers, cupboards, and all the doors, releasing the sashes holding back the drapes, and lifting the lids off chests. It was well known that this would facilitate the opening of the birth passage.

Giovanna, who should have completed this task earlier, was now in the corridor speaking with the Conte. The murmur of their voices drifted into the bedchamber. Hannah could hear the Conte asking Giovanna about their progress.

'Sir, how can any good come of an infidel attending a birth?'

Hannah could not hear everything the Conte said in reply, but she did hear, 'Do whatever you can for the sake of the baby. Hannah is my last hope for an heir.'

Hannah wiped the Contessa's face with a moist cloth. 'Let me see if the baby has turned.' She ran her hands over Lucia's belly. 'Good, the head has dropped. Not enough, but better. We will try now.' Hannah called Giovanna back into the room. 'Hold her legs for me. Hurry. She will push now.'

Giovanna genuflected and took Hannah's position at Lucia's side. Hannah went to the end of the bed and said, 'Now, Lucia, with all your strength, push. Yes, that is right. Good — your baby wants to be born. Push harder!'

Hannah prayed, *Please, God, do not let this child tarry too long in the birth passage. Do not let the mother's sweat and pain and blood be for the sake of a small blue corpse. Do not force me to take up the iron knife and take Lucia's life for the sake of an heir.*

The Contessa's face flushed as she bore down,

grunting with the exertion.

'Grab her legs, Giovanna, and hold them up and back.' Hannah bent low and looked. 'I see the little one's head, dark and wet. Just a few more pushes and it will be born. You are a strong and brave one, *cara*.'

Lucia dropped back against the bed, exhausted. 'Rest until you feel another pain, and we will try again.'

A few moments later, her belly tightened and Lucia said, 'I am ready to try.'

Her lips pulled back in a grimace; she grunted and pushed, although not as forcefully as before. She slumped back against the pillows, and Hannah feared she was too exhausted to do more. The baby's head disappeared. Blood obscured the passage. Then Hannah felt Lucia's belly harden with a fresh pang.

'Give me another push, *cara*. Please try, for the sake of your infant.'

But it was no good. She could not be roused. Hannah reached for Lucia's wrist. Her pulse was thready. She pressed her ear to Lucia's belly and listened for the baby's heartbeat, but she heard only the faint echo of the Contessa's heart.

It was time to use the birthing spoons. With God's help, she would not splinter the tiny skull into fragments or rip open the birth passage. Hannah reached into her bag and withdrew the spoons from the folds of cloth. She passed them quickly through the glow of the candle so they would not feel cold to Lucia. The silver turned black from the heat of the flame, until Hannah could no longer see her own anxious face reflected in the handles.

Giovanna stared at Hannah as though she had seen a witch. If only Hannah could have banished Giovanna from the room — but she needed her to support Lucia's legs and position her belly. It could not be helped. Besides, Hannah could no more stop the gossiping tongue of such a woman than the *shochet* could staunch the flow of blood from a slaughtered lamb.

As Hannah rubbed the birthing spoons with almond oil, she repeated the prayer she had heard physicians say, 'God, if it pleases you, first let me do no harm.'

She eased the spoons into the narrow passage, slowly and gently, manoeuvring them until she felt them clasp the infant's temples. She was grateful for Lucia's unconsciousness.

Giovanna watched as Hannah worked the spoons up Lucia's passage. 'Is she not dying fast enough for your liking?'

'Please, a woman's mind is unstable during her travail. Do not speak so. Let us work together. Your mistress needs you to give her hope and confidence.' Hannah worked the spoons in farther. 'Hold her limbs higher.'

'God may forgive you, but I will not. Neither will my master,' said Giovanna, but she continued to hold the Contessa's legs open, one knee resting against her side. 'Better to slit open her belly than torture her slowly. Even the Inquisitioners do not have such an instrument.'

Hannah had no time to answer, and instead prayed silently, *Please, God, may I not have the murder of this Christian woman on my conscience.*

73

'Come on, my child, we are waiting to welcome you. I will bathe you in warm water and rub you with fragrant oils. You will have a life of joy. Come out and meet your mama.'

With the next weak contraction, she pulled, but she felt nothing until the next contraction, and then she tugged more forcefully, careful not to compress the spoons. Lucia's flesh ripped and blood splattered onto the bed. Hannah took advantage of this ragged gash to slide the spoons in deeper.

God, place your hand over mine. Give me the wisdom to know how much pressure to apply and when to pull. When she pulled again with slow, steady force, she was rewarded with a glimpse of dark, wet hair. With the next attempt, the head emerged, and then one shoulder. She released the spoons and tossed them on the bed. With her hands, she freed the other shoulder, which was caught under the bridge of the sharing bones.

With a final burst, the slick body fell into her hands.

The sight of the baby soon extinguished whatever relief Hannah felt. It was the mottled colour of autumn plums, deep purple with patches of white where no blood flowed.

'Quick, Giovanna, get two basins — one with hot water, the other with cold.'

'I would do better to fetch the priest,' Giovanna said. 'That babe is soon to be Lilith's.' She hurried from the bedroom.

Hannah scrambled under the bed, retrieved the knife, and cut the navel string, which felt like

74

cutting through a boneless finger. Seizing a candle from the table next to the bed, she cauterized the severed end of the cord, which made a *pfsst-pfsst* sound when she held the flame to it.

Fitting her mouth over the baby's, Hannah sucked mucus from its nose and mouth and spit it on the floor. The infant remained limp.

Giovanna returned with the basins and said, 'Just use a damp cloth. Immersion in water is not good for a child. It will die and all our hard work will be lost.'

Hannah knew of the Christian indifference to bathing. The Rabbi had told her once — in jest, perhaps — that when a Christian baby is baptized, an old priest dressed in smelly black robes pours water from a chalice over his head and declares that forever more the child is relieved from the responsibility of bathing.

'It is not to cleanse but to bring the child back from the edge of death.'

Giovanna said nothing, but watched as Hannah plunged the tiny form into the basin of warm water, then into the basin of cold water, back and forth.

Come. Breathe, child. A life of ease awaits you. Fine clothes, private tutors, loving parents, a palazzo on the Grand Canal. All that is required of you is to suck air into your little body and then exhale it. Try. It is not so difficult.

'The child should be christened,' said Giovanna.

'I will blow smoke into the lungs.' Hannah took the same candle she had used for cauterizing, held it above the baby, careful not to let the tallow drip onto its chest, and through pursed lips blew the smoke in the direction of the baby's face. She did it several times, but the child remained blue and lifeless. Perhaps a dish of singed rosemary under the baby's nose? But there was no time. She grabbed it by the feet and, holding it upside down, slapped its bottom and back, careful to keep the slippery body suspended over the bed.

'I am doing my part, God. Please help me.' Holding the small body, she made a plunging vertical motion as though scrubbing clothes on a washboard. 'By all that is great and good, breathe.'

'Only God can give him life,' said Giovanna.

'Tonight He needs my help.'

'You blaspheme.'

Hannah righted the child, but its colour was no better. Again she submerged the infant into cold water, the waxy coating nearly making the tiny body slither from her grasp. This time, the shock of the freezing water elicited a shrill cry of outrage. Hannah's shoulders sagged with relief, and she placed the baby on the bed.

'May your screams be heard all the way to the Piazza San Marco.'

As the baby wailed, its colour turned from purple to pink. The birthing spoons, lying on the end of the bed in plain view, had left tiny red marks on either side of the babe's forehead. It would do her no good if Giovanna snatched her spoons and presented them as evidence to the Inquisition. She grabbed them and thrust them,

76

sticky with mucus and blood, into her bag.

She heard a faint moan from Lucia, and said, 'Your child lives. I will attend to you in a moment.'

Turning her attention back to the baby, she scrubbed off the layer of waxy cream with a rough cloth. The infant was large, the private parts so swollen it took Hannah a moment to realize he was male. The slate blue eyes in the wrinkled face opened. He would be a beauty — if he continued to breathe. Seeing the tiny abdomen rise and fall like the soft belly of a kitten, Hannah smiled with joy. He was plump, with strong, even features, a high brow, and full cheeks. His hair would be reddish when it dried. How unlike the dark, complaining babies of the ghetto, who entered the world red and protesting, born instinctively sensing that a life of struggle awaited them. She held the child to her breast and rocked him as he appraised her, clenching his tiny fists.

'Bring the candle closer, Giovanna. Let me examine this little man.'

Giovanna obliged and held the light high, illuminating the baby's skin, which now bloomed a healthy pink. She did not want to put him down, he was so beautiful. A Jewish child would now be oiled and covered in a layer of salt for his own protection. On the eighth day, he would be circumcised. None of these things would be done for this child of nobility.

In the corner stood the cradle with four marble posts supporting the canopy of red silk, embroidered with fauns.

She placed the child inside and pulled the coverlet up to his chin. Swaddling would have to wait until she had attended to the Contessa.

The afterbirth, like a veined piece of calf's liver, should have glided out of its own accord and fallen into the basin. In biblical times, a Jewish midwife would have straddled the mother's thighs, ramming her head into the mother's belly until the liver cake dislodged. Hannah's method was kinder. She tugged on the navel string that hung out of the birthing passage, but as she pulled, the cord, engorged with blood, broke. Was it too much to ask of God that one small detail go smoothly? If Lucia had been able, Hannah would have asked her to stand so that the liver cake would drop from between her legs, but Lucia could no more stand upright than could the baby she had just birthed. If the afterbirth did not emerge, putrefaction would result. There was only one thing to be done.

'Giovanna, clasp her by her shoulders. I must feel what is wrong.'

Hannah pushed back the bloody sleeves of her *cioppà*. She plunged her forearm into the warm darkness of the womb, clutched the resistant afterbirth, braced herself, and tugged. Lucia's back arched. There was a tearing sound, and Hannah staggered back, gripping a raw piece of the organ. She dropped it to the floor and reinserted her arm, groping in the womb, seizing more spongy flesh, tugging, holding it fast, and reeling back with another purple fistful. Her arm was shaking and glazed with bright blood. This time, Giovanna held a basin for her to cast the tissue into.

Once the afterbirth was extracted and the matrix cleaned of tissue, the flow of blood slowed to a trickle. Now, according to Jewish custom, the placenta should be wrapped in a clean cloth and buried in the ground. For reasons Hannah could not fathom, Christians preserved it in a jar of fine oil.

A clicking sound brought Hannah to attention. Lucia's teeth were chattering and her whole body trembled. Hannah grabbed a feather quilt from the armoire and buried Lucia under it. She put a hand on Lucia's forehead. The Contessa was burning with fever. Hannah prayed there would not be prodigious bleeding that could not be staunched.

Hannah's vision was blurry with fatigue; her arms ached from the effort of extracting the afterbirth. She had been at Lucia's bedside the entire night and needed to sit down, drink a bowl of strong broth, then sleep — but her work was not yet completed. She pulled up a chair and sat next to Lucia.

'It is over, *cara*. You did well.' She took Lucia's hand. 'You have suffered, but you have a beautiful boy to show for your pains. A boy with a large head, as I do not need to tell you, and your husband's blue eyes. Just wait until you see him.'

Lucia squeezed Hannah's finger. Motioning Hannah to lower her head, she murmured, 'You have been so kind. The Holy Virgin will watch over you all the days of your life.' And then her eyes fluttered closed.

Rest and nourishing food were all the medicaments Lucia needed now. In a few months, God willing, she would be well again.

'We should change the bedding, Giovanna.'

They tackled the task together, rolling Lucia from one side of the bed to the other as they worked, the bed linen so drenched they could have wrung it out and filled a laundry tub with the blood. But there was colour in the Contessa's cheeks and her pulse was growing more regular.

From her bag, Hannah took out packets of fennel and some wild sage and handed the herbs to Giovanna. 'If you combine this with some wine, honey, and hot water, we will feed the infusion to her. It will draw the matrix closed and ensure that all the bleeding ceases.'

Giovanna returned a few minutes later with a cup of the mixture, and Hannah spooned it between Lucia's unresisting lips while Giovanna held her head upright. From the cradle came the sounds of the baby beginning to cry. When Lucia had swallowed as much of the liquid as she seemed able to, Hannah asked Giovanna for a basin of warm water, and when it arrived, she bathed Lucia with a square of cotton. The water turned watery pink. Hannah kneaded her belly with almond oil until the candles by the bed burned out and Giovanna had to replace them. The massaging would close the matrix tight and slow the bleeding.

While they worked, Giovanna often looked at Hannah strangely, opening her mouth as though to speak. Finally, she said, 'The Contessa will live, God be praised, but her child was brought into the world with an implement of the devil.'

'Why should a midwife not have her tools? Does not the farrier have his nails and hammer? The glassblower his *borsella*, his pinchers? My spoons are no more an instrument of the devil than those.'

'Birthing is God's work. We are here only to cut the cord and encourage the mother, not to shove God aside and take over the job ourselves.' Giovanna balled up the bloody linen sheets and tossed them into a rush basket.

'God has given me the spoons and He, in His Wisdom, directs my hand as I use them,' said Hannah.

Giovanna was about to make a retort when from the cradle came the tremulous cry of the baby, growing lustier as he gained strength. In response to the cries, two wet spots appeared on the front of Giovanna's apron.

'You are with milk?' Hannah asked.

Giovanna nodded. 'My baby girl was born six months ago.'

Hannah scooped up the infant and motioned for Giovanna to sit. When Giovanna had arranged herself on the chair and had undone her bodice, Hannah handed the child to her. He tossed his head from side to side, searching out the nipple, and when he found it, he latched on as though he would never let go. Giovanna gave a start from the strength of his suck. Hannah's breasts ached in response. How she wished someday to hold Isaac's child to her breast and feel the quick tug of a baby's lips drawing the milk from her.

The bedchamber had grown quiet, aside from the sucking, rooting noises of the baby. Even Giovanna's face relaxed as she gazed down on the nursing infant, the deep grooves of her forehead softening. Hannah walked to the casement window, where the full moon radiated silvery arrows of light. She threw open the window, looking out at the canal below, seeing nothing but black waters. When she felt the rasp of dark wings on her face and sensed her hair shift in the slight breeze, she knew that, for the moment anyway, death had been defeated. She slammed the window shut.

Isaac would be proud of her. She had saved both the mother and the child. She had succeeded where most would have failed. Soon they would celebrate her triumph together. Because of her skill, and her birthing spoons, she had saved Isaac's life as well. If only he were waiting for her at home, ready to apply the *bahnkes* to her back, which ached from hours of bending over Lucia. The cupping would draw out the pain, leaving her relaxed, ready for sleep.

Giovanna said, 'The master is in the hall. Let him see his healthy brute of a child who is draining me dry. Then you can collect your fee and get out.'

6

The woman was already a foe, but why make it worse?

'I thank you for your help, Giovanna,' Hannah said, and walked out of the room.

In the light from the clerestory window, the Conte was slumped in a chair in the hallway, dozing, his head resting on his chest. Dawn was gilding the city. Long fingers of sunlight illuminated the palazzo. This glowing light was so unlike the darkness of her cramped room in the ghetto, which required candles even at noon.

In her weariness she slumped against the wall, but winced and drew herself upright as marble moulding jabbed her in the back. She shook the Conte's shoulder, waking him up. 'I have wonderful news for you. You have a fine, healthy baby, one with all his limbs and a cap of fine reddish hair.'

He stared at her, seemingly unable to absorb what she was saying.

'A healthy child,' she repeated. 'Shall I show you?' When he made no reply, she asked, 'Have you been here all night?'

'How is Lucia?' He rubbed his eyes. His voice was subdued, as though expecting bad news.

'She is alive but has had an unhappy time.'

'But she will recover?'

'Perhaps, if it is God's will.'

'I swear if Almighty God spares my wife, I will

never bed her again.' He got to his feet and shook himself awake.

Jews had experience in the art of restraint. No marital relations were permitted for twelve days of the month during the woman's unclean period, or for forty days after the birth of a child. But Christians, it was well known, demonstrated little self-control in the marriage bed.

'You are tired,' Hannah said. Risking the impropriety, she rested a hand on his forearm and gave a slight pat. 'In truth, if she lives, I do not think your wife will conceive again. This will be your only child. Come and bid him welcome. He is enjoying his first meal.'

'You did say a boy?'

'Yes, may God be praised, a fine and healthy one.'

The Conte grabbed her in an embrace so strong she felt her ribs compress. He lifted her off the ground and twirled her around the corridor. The folds of her blue *cioppà* flew out around her.

'Please,' she said.

The Conte grinned and set her down. 'God's blessing on you, Hannah. After all these years, I now have an heir. You have made me a very happy man.'

They entered the bedchamber, still scented with the coppery odour of blood. The Contessa lay under her quilt, shivering. He glanced at the baby suckling at Giovanna's breast and then went to his wife's side and sat on the edge of her bed. He picked up her hand and massaged it in his own.

'My darling, thank you for this child. May God restore your strength and make you well enough to dance at his christening party.' He bent and kissed her forehead. 'Now sleep.'

Although Lucia continued to shake with fever, her eyelids fluttered open and she smiled at him.

When the baby appeared to be sated, Hannah took him from Giovanna and walked over to the bed. She held the infant out to the Conte, who bent to peer into the baby's sleeping face.

'Can you see him, my darling?' he said to his wife. 'A boy. A beautiful, red-faced boy.'

Lucia gave no sign that she heard her husband.

The child curled his hand around Hannah's finger and waved with the other at the dawn's light. She continued to offer the child to the Conte, saying the words she had said many times before at confinements. 'God, thank you for sparing this baby's life and may the child just born grow to be . . . ' She halted, at a loss. She had been about to say 'a Torah scholar,' but recovered herself in time and concluded, with only a slight stammer, 'a blessing to his parents.'

The Conte was not the first father she had encountered to show apprehension. She pitied him. He had more reason than most to fear the baby's death.

Still the Conte did not hold out his arms for his son. Instead, he lowered his head and turned away. Hannah heard the catch in his voice when he spoke.

'He is as fragile as porcelain. Swaddle him well.'

Hannah gave the baby back to Giovanna, who began wrapping the infant in long, narrow strips of fabric.

The Conte took a handkerchief from his pocket and blew his nose. 'You will think me unfeeling not to hold my child, but I am too old for another disappointment. Some of our other babies lived, too. A girl for a fortnight, then a baby boy for a few days. I loved them. I could not help myself. Maybe my love for them lured death to their cradles. I will not demonstrate my affection yet, lest I make God jealous. When he is older and I am certain he will survive, it will be different.' He gave Hannah a look. 'Will he live? He is as small as a puppy. Do I have reason to hope?'

'I think love, as much as milk and amulets and prayers, keeps babies alive,' Hannah said. 'It is not natural to withhold love from a child. When death sees him protected by a strong, loving father, she will keep her distance. And if, God forbid, the baby dies, at least he will have known your love.' Hannah wanted to take the Conte in her arms and comfort him. But even if he were a Jew from the ghetto, it would not have been proper for her to do so. Instead, she said, 'He is pink now, but he is too hot, perhaps with fever, perhaps with the exertion of being born. If he lives, he will grow into a man with a great deal of endurance. A child's character is forged by his journey into the world.'

Giovanna finished wrapping the baby and, settling back onto the chair, began to nurse him once more. Jacopo entered the room with a suddenness that caused Hannah to start. When he bent down to peer at the baby, the infant lost his latch on Giovanna's nipple and began to fuss.

Jacopo straightened and said, 'A wrinkled, wizened little wonder he is.' He sat on a chair beside the Conte on the side of Lucia's bed. 'Congratulations, brother. You have a fine son.'

Hannah wished he would leave; his presence made her uncomfortable. Moreover, it was not fitting for this man, who was not the father of the child, to be insinuating his way into the birth room. Giovanna must have been in agreement, for she glowered at him and turned her body, shielding the baby from his view.

'Jacopo,' said the Conte, 'Lucia is exhausted. Perhaps you can come tomorrow when she has composed herself.'

But Jacopo did not move from his chair.

Ignoring his brother, the Conte leaned forward to speak to Hannah. The face of the dignified nobleman was gone. Hannah saw only a man in pain.

'Tell me, Hannah, how should I protect this infant? If I can do anything to ensure the baby's safety, I must know.' He turned to Jacopo again and motioned to him to leave, but Jacopo remained where he was.

'I want to hear how this Jewess will answer you,' Jacopo said.

Hannah said, 'I have a silver amulet in my bag, one that is said to keep away Lilith, the slayer of newborns.' She reached into her bag and held out her *shadai* in the shape of a baby's hand. 'It has been of great assistance at times like these.'

The Conte asked, 'Can I persuade you to give it to me?'

'When I tell you the story of how it came to me, you will understand why I must refuse you.' It was a story that was well known to everyone in the ghetto.

'Many years ago, in the ghetto on a bitterly cold winter evening,' she began, 'a baker's wife found a baby in a rush basket abandoned under the portego near the Banco Rosso. The infant was blue from exposure and screaming with hunger. Since she discovered the baby on a week-night, when the ghetto was filled with gentile visitors either borrowing money or shopping for second-hand clothing or gem-stones, she was not certain whether it was Jewish or Christian.'

The Conte bent toward her, eyebrows drawn together. It was not her custom to speak so frankly in front of a Christian, but under his attentive gaze, her shoulders relaxed and the words tumbled from her mouth.

'Nor could she understand how the baby had survived. She unwrapped the infant and exam-ined the child's linen for clues to its identity. Then this *shadai* fell out of the swaddling cloths.' Hannah passed the *shadai* to the Conte, who took it and held it between the palms of his hands. 'And she understood it was this that had protected the infant from freezing February rains and ravenous canal rats.'

The Conte dangled the *shadai*, suspended on a slender red cord, between his fingers. The amulet caught the light of the candles and shimmered as it moved, no bigger than a newborn's hand.

The Conte glanced up at Hannah, his head inclined, a hand clasped around his bent knee, as though he had nothing more important in the world to do than listen to her. 'And how did you come to have it?'

'That half-frozen bundle left to die was my mother.' To Hannah's surprise the Conte's eyes moistened and, in response, her eyes did as well. 'This *shadai* has safeguarded every baby in my family, including my sister, Jessica, who was born with the birth string wound around her neck. The amulet saved my sister, but not our mother, who died a week later of childbed fever.'

'We have that in common, my dear,' the Conte responded. 'My mother died giving birth to my youngest brother, Niccolò, whom you saw playing cards with Jacopo when you arrived.' He reached over and patted her hand. 'I understand you must keep it. Someday, you will require it for your own baby.'

He must have surmised from her home that she had no children. She replied, 'May your words lodge like wax in God's ear.'

'But may I borrow your amulet?' asked the Conte. 'Giovanna will return it to you when the period of confinement is over.'

'Let me see it, brother.' Jacopo took the *shadai* from the Conte. 'What manner of writing is this?'

She wanted to snatch it out of his smooth, manicured hands, but replied, 'Hebrew. It is inscribed with the names of the three angels who protect newborns. That' — she turned the amulet over and showed him the other side — 'is the Star of David.'

'So you would have us believe a Jewish amulet will protect a Christian baby?' Jacopo said. He turned to the Conte and said, 'Brother, I think this is a way to place a spell on your child.'

What reply could one make to such a remark?

Before she had a chance to frame an answer, the Conte asked her, 'So you believe we pray to the same God?' He held out his hand for the charm, which Jacopo tossed back to him. The Conte polished the *shadai* on his sleeve.

'It is the same God for both Jew and gentile babies,' Hannah said. 'The mother through her blood provides the red of the baby's skin, flesh, hair, and back of the eye. The father provides through his seed the white parts — bones, sinews, nails, whites of the eyes, and the white matter of the brain. But God, and only God, breathes life and spirit into a child. That is the part that makes the child human.'

Jacopo opened his mouth to speak, but she continued, 'It is the partnership of man and woman and God that creates a new life.'

'Yes, I believe you are right.' The Conte appeared exhausted. 'But you have not vouchsafed a reply to my earlier question. May I borrow your *shadai*?'

It would be dangerous to leave it in this household with Giovanna and Jacopo, she knew. But she had an uneasy feeling that the child needed protection. 'Yes, you may have the loan of it.'

'Please give me directions for its use,' said the Conte.

'Tuck it into your child's blankets and keep it with him at all times. Now is the period of greatest peril. The amulet will do its part, but you must perform yours. The child should be kept inside at all times, the windows to his bedchamber shuttered against the night air. The circle of salt that you see here around your wife's bed? Place a similar circle around his cradle. Replenish it daily — not the servants, but you. This will protect against Lilith. Most important, all strangers must be kept away, especially . . . '

The word on the tip of her tongue had been *Christians*, but to her relief the word *strangers* sprang to her mind and she seized upon it instead. She wanted to add that the child should be bathed in warm water from time to time and rubbed with a cloth, but she knew she would make better use of her breath by using it to cool her soup on the Sabbath.

Giovanna sat rocking the child, so relaxed that Hannah feared she would lose her hold and drop him to the terrazzo floor. The woman looked as though she was about to make a comment but had thought better of it.

As though cradling a mourning dove, the Conte di Padovani enclosed the amulet between his hands. He rose from Lucia's bed and moved to Giovanna. Gently, he placed the hammered silver on the baby's chest. The child twitched in response, dropped Giovanna's nipple, and gave a little cry.

'See the bubbles of milk forming on his lips?

Che tesoro. He is a marvel,' he said.

'An angel with the devil's kiss on his forehead,' said Jacopo, indicating the red marks left by the birthing spoons.

'Nonsense, Jacopo, it is the goodbye kiss from the Angel of Death. She knows she has been thwarted.'

The Conte reached into his breeches and took out a gold ducat. 'Here, Giovanna, for your good work. You must tell no one what you witnessed tonight. Do I have your word?'

'Of course, Master.' Giovanna shifted the baby to one side and dropped the gold piece into her apron pocket.

Then the Conte turned to Hannah, reached into his shirt and took out a purse, and counted out two hundred ducats. Handing them to her, he said, 'You have earned not only my money tonight, Hannah, but my gratitude as well. No one but you could have saved my wife and baby.'

Hannah heard Giovanna give a low grumble of discontent. She would worry about her later.

Hannah felt her face growing warm under his praise.

'You risked your life and the lives of your people,' he continued. 'You have repaid me well by giving me something more precious than gold ducats.'

Maybe it was because she was fatigued, or maybe it was the effect of the Conte's kind words, but in that instant Hannah felt like a new mother herself. She had gambled everything to earn this money, just as Isaac had risked everything to sail to the Levant. If only he were as fortunate as she.

'Now you have the means to save your husband,' the Conte said. 'Go home. You are tired.' He went out to the corridor and retrieved his cloak, which was in a heap on the floor, and returned with it. 'You have loaned me your amulet; let me loan you this cloak against the cold air of dawn. My gondolier will see you safely home. Forgive me for not accompanying you myself, but the rest of the family is waiting downstairs for the news.' He arranged the heavy cloak around Hannah's shoulders and once again she felt the heft of it weighing her down.

Hannah slipped the ducats into the pocket of her *cioppà*. Not even Isaac had ever earned such a sum. Her heart rejoiced. She would have her husband back. Whatever rift she and Isaac had experienced could be mended.

'What will you name your son?' she asked. She knew that Christians did not wait forty days before naming a child. They drew attention to helpless infants by christening them immediately so everyone, including the Angel of Death, knew their names.

'Bruno, after my favourite uncle. A sturdy, healthy man who at age sixty-four has recently taken a second wife.' The Conte must have noticed her look, for he said, 'Your face is the looking-glass of your thoughts, Hannah. You do not care for the name?'

'It is a fine name. It is just that to name a child after a living person, is that wise? The Angel of Death could become confused, seeking out your uncle, who is old, but taking the baby instead.'

He thought a moment. 'I will name him Matteo, then, in honour of my late father.'

If ever Hannah bore a son, she and Isaac had decided to name him Samuel. It was the name of her paternal grandfather, who had been a dealer in second-hand goods, a violinist, and a respected scholar.

'When will you leave for Malta?'

She had not had time to consider the matter. She must pack her few clothes, bid farewell to friends and family, and find a ship to take her to Isaac. She had no notion of how to accomplish any of it, but replied, 'As soon as I find passage.'

'Go to my friend Marco Lunari, who lives in Dorsoduro. His ship, the *Balbiana*, sails to Constantinople soon. It will be docking in Malta to take on fresh water and provisions. I will give you a letter of introduction.'

For a Christian to take such pains for a Jewess was beyond her experience. 'You are a nobleman in every sense of the word,' she said. Last night, when he had come for her with his brother, she had thought him so consumed with his own difficulties that he had no concern for others. She had misjudged him.

'God will protect you, my dear.' He patted her shoulder and turned to Giovanna, gazed down at the baby once again, and ran a finger down the child's cheek. 'My brother Niccolò is downstairs waiting to see the child. I will fetch him so you can meet him before you go.'

The Conte left the room, and to Hannah's relief, Jacopo rose and followed him.

When they were alone, Giovanna looked up

94

from nursing Matteo. 'I did not tell the Conte about that device of yours and how you tortured my poor mistress with it. The Inquisitor would be glad to learn of such an instrument.'

At Giovanna's words, Hannah felt her joy ebbing. 'My device saved the baby's life. Surely you can see that? Would you have preferred me to cut open the Contessa?'

'You have marked this baby for the devil. It will be a simple matter to slip a note into the Lion's Mouth in the Doge's palace,' she sniffed. 'It would give me great pleasure.'

The memory of a Sephardic woman named Ezster, a woman from the Ghetto Vecchio, came to Hannah. Ezster had been walking home from buying fish at the docks when she heard the screams of a little girl who had wandered away from her nursemaid and fallen into the Rio della Sensa. The child, unable to swim, had panicked and was choking on the filthy canal water, crying and flailing about. Ezster grabbed an oar from an empty gondola and fished the child out. She dried her and led the sobbing girl back to her house. The next day, the girl was dead of canal fever. The girl's mother, convinced Ezster was a witch, denounced her to the Inquisition. Ezster was taken away by two men from the Office of the Inquisition and never seen again. How easily such a thing could happen to Hannah.

Giovanna said, 'So what will you do with all that money the Conte gave you?'

'Is it the money that has made you hate me?'

'I hate you because I saw what you did — that contrivance you shoved into my mistress, like a shovel into the soil. Who knows why Jews do what they do? Maybe killing our Lord was not enough for you. Maybe you want to kill this baby as well.'

Hannah crossed the room and scooped Matteo out of Giovanna's arms. She kissed him, inhaling his milky smell. Cupping her hand under his head, she drank in the sight of him, stamping it onto her memory. She would see him only once again, when she came to collect her mother's amulet. The thought saddened her. She would not follow his progress through life — see him crawl, toddle, learn to fasten his buttons, and make his covenant with God at thirteen — as she did the babies of the ghetto. This child's life would be a mystery to her, and he was dearer to her because of it.

'Grow into a fine man, little Matteo,' she whispered. To Giovanna, she said, 'We have worked together to save your mistress and her child. We should rejoice together.' She tried to put her hand on Giovanna's sleeve, but the woman pulled back, crossed herself, and kissed her thumb.

Hannah ignored this. She and her birthing spoons had done the impossible, and soon she would be on a ship bound for Isaac, who would exult with her. She handed Matteo to Giovanna. The baby began to wail.

Niccolò, bleary-eyed, smelling of sour wine, entered the room, nodding at Hannah. Jacopo, accompanying him, surprised Hannah by hovering close to Lucia's bed and giving it a little bump. Lucia winced. Jacopo did not seem to notice.

Strange that they both had been up all night, awaiting their nephew's birth. It was not something a father often did, much less the uncles. But here they were, standing at Giovanna's side, yawning and red-eyed. The two of them were now dressed in black silk waistcoats, their elbows close to their sides, reminding Hannah of two vultures waiting for the life to drain out of a newborn lamb.

Niccolò rubbed his hands together, cupped them and blew on them, even though it was warm in the bedchamber, and gave the infant a tickle under the chin. 'Such a handsome baby he is. You have made our family very happy. I thank you, Hannah. You have done well.'

She nodded and tried to look pleased, but she was unsettled by the expression on his face for reasons that she could not articulate.

'Goodbye, *cara*,' she said as she approached Lucia's bedside. 'I am taking my leave.' Lucia groped for her hand. Hannah brought it to her lips. 'You are lucky to have such a healthy baby and such a fine husband. May your strength return to you soon so that you can enjoy both of them.'

A footman entered and picked up Hannah's linen bag and escorted her down the wide stone staircase and toward the canal, where a gondola sat moored, lines holding it fast to the striped mooring pole. The manservant handed her bag to the gondolier, who bid her *buon giorno*.

Hannah stood on the dock for a moment, collecting her thoughts. Venice was awakening. Morning sun glinted on the water, infusing it with the luminescent colours of Murano glass. The canal was filled with boats jostling for right-of-way. Barges spilling over with apples and pomegranates, round and succulent, lumbered toward the Rialto market. A fishmonger on the opposite side of the canal held up snapper and tilapia, their scales pearly white in the first light of dawn. The shops along the *strazi* teemed with early morning shoppers. Water sellers trudged back from the wellhead in the piazzetta, their buckets sloshing.

The gondolier, dressed in the livery of the di Padovani family, offered his forearm and handed her into the boat. From the grin on his face, she knew he had heard the news of the birth.

Once she was settled in the draped cabin, he passed her her bag, but when she took it in her hand it felt curiously light. Shaking it, she listened for the familiar jangle of silver spoons, but she heard nothing. She peered into it, fumbling around in its depth.

Finally, she dumped everything onto the seat next to her: iron knife, gauze, vial of almond oil, silk string to tie the birth cord, herbs, Anatolian cream, and a corked flask of cayenne pepper. She grabbed the candle from the sconce on the wall of the *felze* and held it aloft to see more clearly.

Her birthing spoons were gone.

7

Valletta, Malta
1575

The cart bounced along the coast road from the Convent of St. Ursula into town. Often the wheels fell into ruts, and as Isaac struggled to heave it out, Assunta, sweat dripping down her face and wimple soaked, would shout instructions on the best way to budge the oak-wheeled cart. No one on the road offered assistance, although a couple of the drovers came by with teams of plodding horses, herding their bony cattle to market. They nodded to Assunta, but when they noticed the iron circle on Isaac's ankle, they clucked to their teams and moved on.

Isaac's back burned from hoisting the cart. His legs ached from the fresh blows he had received yesterday from the guard. Before they filled with pus, he must bathe them in sea water. The air was so dusty, his saliva was brown when he spit.

With every jolt of the cart, it seemed an axle would break. Deep furrows in the road made it difficult to determine where the road ended and began. Several times Isaac turned onto a path that ended up leading nowhere.

The sheepskin, thrown into a corner of the cart, began to attract flies in the heat. Isaac was about to ask Assunta to hurl it into the bushes when he decided that it might be useful as padding for the yoke. He asked her to pass it to him, and folded it up and thrust it under the stiff leather of his harness. Now the flies collected around his face and buzzed in his ears, but at least he managed to pull the cart out of the rut.

At last, the fortification of St. Elmo appeared in the distance, a tower surrounded by massive walls. As Assunta and Isaac neared the sun-baked military encampment, the thorough-fare became more crowded with donkey carts, peddlers struggling along with their wares on their backs, and a Knight of St. John, wearing the habit of a monk but carrying a cutlass. The road wound along the sea.

They passed through the gates of the town and saw, wandering the streets, a number of other slaves who, like Isaac, wore leg irons. Most were Moors from North Africa or Turks from the Levant.

'Stop and take a rest, Isaac. I want to deliver you to Joseph alive.'

He shrugged off the harness and clambered back into the cart, sat on the floor, and then, feeling faint, let his head drop between his knees. He had to put his plan of escape into effect before he lost all his strength. But for that he needed food.

Assunta handed him a flask of water and he drank deeply. The cool water trickled down his neck and dripped onto his torn shirt.

A few minutes later, heading toward the harbour, away from the rocking cart, he spied a wagon a few paces away piled high with rutabagas speckled with soil. He was about to steal one off the back and devour it raw. The driver's attention was on beating his poor spavined horse.

Just then Assunta announced, 'I think this is the best place to find Joseph. He always stops here about this time of day.' She pointed to the courtyard of the tavern, where men sat drinking and jostling one another on long, narrow benches. Isaac dragged the cart into the courtyard and hung the harness on the limb of a tree. While the sun beat down on them, Assunta scanned the road for Joseph.

Before long, Joseph and another man approached leading a horse dragging a travois heaped with canvas and oak casks. The Sister strode in their direction, pulling Isaac along behind her. Joseph, stocky, his gold tooth again catching the light of the sun, appeared mellower than the cocky bully Isaac had encountered at the auction yesterday.

He was talking to his companion. 'Giorgio, I want her, but she does not know I am alive.'

The man leading the horse looked enough like Joseph to be his brother. He wore rough breeches and a stained cotton shirt; his hair was matted and hardly a spot of him was not covered in dirt and candle grease.

Giorgio muttered to Joseph, 'You are bewitched. Do you not know that one female is very like another? This one is turning you into a love-struck calf.'

Joseph clutched a basket of grapes and oranges under one arm. The smell of sun-warmed oranges drifted over to Isaac. The grapes

101

were a deep purple with a blush of wild yeast. Joseph was a swine, a killer of slaves, a boor, a lout, and a *Judenfresser*, but Isaac had never wanted anything so much as he wanted that basket of fruit. He longed to sink his teeth into an orange, pull it apart section by section, and feel the juice run down his chin. He wanted to bite the grapes and separate the seeds from the skin with his lips and tongue and taste the sweetness.

Joseph looked at Isaac and then at Assunta. A slow grin spread over his face. 'So the Jew is not so easily converted, Sister? What will you do with him now? Take him to the water's edge and feed him to the frigate birds?'

'Sell him back to you. I need my fifteen *scudi*.'

Joseph laughed. 'No chance of that. Besides, my memory tells me it was ten.'

'Ten from me and five from that woman in the crowd.'

'You are too late. I took your advice and bought that Nubian you recommended. I have already resold him to the captain of the *Madre de Dios*, embarking today for Cyrus. I made a handsome profit.'

'Well, someone must buy this man. The convent needs its money back.'

'Try that tavern keeper over there.' Joseph gestured to a wooden sign that read RENIERA E SODERINA. 'Maybe he can swab vomit from the floor under the patrons and pour out the wine, though he looks barely strong enough to push a mop. I am too busy for this nonsense. These' — he pointed to the loaded travois — 'are a set

102

of spare sails for the *Salvatorre* over there.' He lifted his chin in the direction of a three-masted galleon in the nearby harbour.

The dock was crowded with merchant ships, galleons, even a Dutch *fluyt*. Assunta watched the activity and was distracted. Now was Isaac's opportunity to run and hide. Then, when darkness fell, he could steal aboard one of the ships, tuck himself behind a water cask. A passage from the Psalms came to his mind: *Oh, that I had wings like a dove, for then I would fly away, and be at rest.*

But if he bolted now, one shout from Assunta and a crowd eager for the entertainment of tearing a man limb from limb would descend upon him. The courtyard of the tavern teemed with rough-looking sailors determined to get as drunk as possible before they were called back to their ships.

Sister Assunta pushed back her wimple to show more of her broad forehead. 'Show him some charity,' she said to Joseph. 'He has suffered a great deal.'

Giorgio put in, 'I am suffering, too — from a terrible thirst, which only a flagon of malmsey wine can quench.'

Isaac stared at the fruit Joseph held in the basket. 'One orange, and I will help you with your goods.' He gestured to the travois. 'I will load this canvas onto the *Salvatorre* while you enjoy a drink.' Isaac sniffed the air. The man smelled no better than the last time he had seen him, at the auction.

'You look too starved to lift anything heavier

than a baby's rattle,' said Joseph.

'Or a sack of horse feathers,' said his brother, and then convulsed with laughter at his own wit.

Louts. Illiterate swine. Then Isaac had an idea. 'I am not too puny to lift a quill.'

Joseph frowned. Giorgio's face assumed a puzzled expression common to the none-too-bright.

'I could not help overhearing you,' said Isaac. 'I can read and write. Shall I pen a letter for you to your lady? Give me an orange and I will give you the benefit of my experience in matters of the heart.'

'You insulted me at the auction in front of a crowd of men and now you want to write love letters in exchange for oranges? What kind of a fool do you take me for?' Joseph took Giorgio's arm and started to yank him in the direction of the tavern. 'This basket is for the captain of the *Salvatorre*.'

Assunta put a hand on Joseph's arm. 'A slave who can read and write would be useful in your business. He can also reckon and keep books of account.' She grabbed the bridle of Joseph's horse, which was shifting its weight uneasily from one hoof to the other. 'Fifteen *scudi* and he is yours. If you do not like him, then sell him to someone else.'

'Take him away before he steals our fruit,' Giorgio said. 'You think my brother wants an infidel any more than you do?'

'He is an infidel with a special talent,' said Assunta.

'Tell me,' Isaac said, 'what are the circumstances of your courtship?'

Giorgio spoke up with unexpected spirit. 'My brother has asked for the hand of a woman in marriage, but she will not have him.'

Joseph shot his brother a look.

'A delicate undertaking, wooing a woman, as I know only too well,' said Isaac. His fatigue suddenly lessened. 'My own wife, may her name be exalted, was a hard-won prize. Our courtship required many letters.' This was a lie, but he had a developed gift for dissembling. 'In fact, all successful courtships involve letters.'

The two men and Sister Assunta stared at him.

Joseph whirled on Giorgio. 'Why do you blab my business to everyone within earshot?' To Isaac he said, 'Keep your nose out of my porridge. It is none of your business.'

'Of course it is my business. Are we not both men? Do we all not require wives to bear us children and please us in bed?' He thought of Hannah and wished for both their sakes that she had fulfilled the first condition as well as she had the second. 'Let me guess the reason for your rejection. The lady in question thinks you too poor? She does not like your character? She finds you idle?' Isaac took a breath. 'Or perhaps she finds your person offensive?'

There was a long pause, and then Giorgio nudged Joseph in the ribs. 'Answer him. Maybe he can help.'

'I have another enterprise in addition to providing labour for galleys,' Joseph said. 'Apart from furnishing ships with slaves, I am also a maker of canvas cloth for sails. To treat the cloth,

105

I use sheep piss. She claims I reek of it. Her eye is on a carpenter. A puny whelp with a huge head.' He wobbled his own head back and forth to illustrate. 'Everybody's got to stink of something. He stinks of wood shavings and rabbit-skin glue. You, Sister' — he looked at Assunta — 'no disrespect, but you have about you the odour of onions and sheep hides. It is normal. We all reek of our trade.'

Just then the breeze shifted; Isaac felt his eyes burn and his bile rise. It was like walking into the arsehole of a camel. 'Stench should be no impediment to your love,' he declared, then paused, conscious especially of Assunta's eyes on him. 'There is an expression, you may have heard it: 'The more the ram stinks, the more the ewe loves him.''

Giorgio and Assunta chuckled.

'But not in the case of this woman, it seems, whose name is . . . ?' prompted Isaac.

'Gertrudis.' Joseph breathed the name with a reverent sigh, as though speaking of the Holy Virgin.

Assunta caught Isaac's eye and shook her head in a way that seemed to ask, 'Have you taken leave of your senses?'

A donkey cart clattered by, stacked with timber pilings.

Isaac turned to Joseph. 'Give Sister Assunta her fifteen *scudi* and I will write a letter that will thaw the coldest heart.'

'You talk rubbish,' Joseph said, but he rested his basket of fruit on the travois.

Isaac did not hesitate. 'You will see. The fair

106

Gertrudis will come to love you ardently.'

Assunta motioned Isaac out of Joseph's earshot. Leaning over, she whispered in his ear, 'Our friend Joseph has as much chance of winning this woman's hand as a baboon has of standing on his hind legs and whistling a sea chanty. She is the handsome widow who gave me five *scudi* yesterday.'

'My benefactress, but yes.' Isaac grimaced. 'I see what you mean, Sister.'

They returned to Joseph and his brother.

Giorgio tugged at Joseph's sleeve. 'Come, I need some refreshment to settle the dust in my throat. Gertrudis is a high-flying bird of paradise, well beyond your reach.'

Joseph reached into the waistband of his breeches and extracted a tattered leather purse. He handed three coins over to Assunta, averting his eyes as though he could not bear to see them pass from his possession to hers.

'I hope I do not regret this transaction, Sister. If he dies, I will have wasted my money.'

Assunta placed the coins in the pocket of her serge habit. 'Goodbye, Isaac. I wish you luck. If Joseph treats you badly, and he will, come back to the convent and we will discuss the salvation of your soul.' She turned and started toward the docks, and calling over her shoulder, she added, 'Joseph, treat him gently. Even an infidel is one of God's creatures.

'One more thing, Isaac,' Assunta said, motioning him over. 'The man who represents your society for the ransom of captives is named Hector — a tall man, with a head that would be handsome if attached to a horse. You will find him near the dock most days or hovering around the cells beneath the Grand Master's palace. He wears breeches too short for him.'

'It is he who is charged with arranging my ransom?'

Assunta pinched his thin upper arm so hard he flinched. 'If you do not starve first.'

Hector. A felicitous name. A strong name. Isaac felt ready to write a dozen letters, tan a dozen sheets of parchment. If only he could keep alive for a few weeks, and receive Hector's assistance, his rescue was assured.

He walked over to where Joseph and Giorgio were standing and clapped Joseph on the back. Isaac wasted no time. 'Come, Joseph, and let us get started. You must tell me all about your lady love.' Isaac shuddered inwardly. 'Together, we will plot the quickest way to her heart.'

'I warn you, Isaac. If you do not succeed in winning her for me, then — you see that galley ship?' Joseph pointed to the harbour, where a sleek vessel about forty *braccio* in length bobbed on its lines. 'That is your destiny.' He jabbed a hard finger into Isaac's chest.

Isaac nodded, a queasy feeling coming to his stomach that had nothing to do with the fact he had not eaten a morsel since the sliver of apple in Assunta's kitchen that morning.

'Pen your words well, my friend. You have a month to win Gertrudis. If not, that galley casts off with you tied to an oar.' Joseph tossed him an orange.

'And if I succeed in winning her heart, you

108

shall grant me my freedom?'

Joseph looked thoughtful for a moment, or as thoughtful as a man like him was capable of looking. 'It is only fair,' he acknowledged. Then he grasped the horse's bridle and he and Giorgio continued down the road.

Isaac could pluck words from the air as easily as a conjurer could pluck an egg from behind the ear of a child. But would his words be sufficient to win the heart of the handsome Gertrudis for this oaf of a man?

He peeled the skin off the orange. The oil made his fingers slick. He broke off a section of the fruit and popped it in his mouth, but the flesh tasted bitter and he took no pleasure from it.

8

Venice,
1575

Hannah pushed aside the curtain of the *felze* and peered out into the grey fog. The gondola was nearing the Rio di Ghetto. She slung her bag over her shoulder and considered what to do about the missing birthing spoons. She had no wish to return to the palazzo. If Giovanna had taken them, the Conte, who had been so sympathetic and kind to her, would compel her to give them back when he sent her to return Hannah's *shadai*. It would be a simple matter, she told herself, trying not to think of other possible outcomes.

The gondolier pulled alongside the pier just outside the ghetto. He wound a line around the mooring pole and then handed her onto the dock.

As Hannah walked along, careful to avoid bundles of decaying refuse and the tossed contents of chamber pots on the Fondamenta, she thought she heard the voice she had been forbidden to listen to, forbidden even to think of, a voice the Rabbi had declared no longer existed — Jessica's. She was certain it was her younger sister, singing a madrigal, melodious as a lute in the soft air of dawn. Hannah had often seen Jessica from a distance on the Calle della Masena, just outside the ghetto gates, but they had not dared to speak to or acknowledge each other.

The hair on Hannah's arms stood up as she listened to the voice. Perhaps the dense fog was deceiving her. She had not slept in hours; fatigue blurred her vision and addled her mind. But there, it came again. Louder this time, and closer, and she could not help but rush toward it.

The voice was identical to Jessica's, but the singing figure before her was a young boy dressed in a sapphire-coloured waistcoat, embroidered breeches, and a cap of blue velvet. He wore a plain black *morello* made of papier mâché to cover his eyes and nose.

As Hannah drew closer, she said, 'Please excuse me. I mistook you for someone else.'

She was about to step away when the boy caught her arm.

'Hannah? Do you not recognize me?'

This time there could be no doubt. It was Jessica's voice, with its slight lisp. Hannah watched as the slender form reached up and snatched off the blue cap with a quick motion, releasing a flood of dark hair. Then, she removed her mask.

'Do you not know your own sister? Have I made such a good job of my disguise? You, my darling Hannah, are instantly recognizable in your blue *cioppà* with a scarf over your pretty hair.' Jessica smiled, displaying a dimple as delicate as the tip of an angel's wing.

Suddenly Hannah felt rested enough to face the future, to deliver a dozen more babies, to stay up a dozen more nights. She hugged her sister, younger by five years than her, burying her nose in Jessica's hair.

'Not a day passes that I do not think of you and wonder how you are.' She wanted to say, *I love you, Jessica. I always have, even when you ran away from the ghetto.* She longed to tell Jessica everything that had happened to her that night, but she held her tongue. Instead, she asked, 'Why are you dressed as a page?'

'I'm returning from a party at a palazzo on the Grand Canal and am on my way home.'

Hannah had heard of costume parties where Christians dressed like the characters from the Commedia dell'Arte — Pulcinello, Pedrolino, Harlequin, and Brighella. Was Jessica now so Christian that she enjoyed such diversions? It seemed impossible, yet here she was, her satin breeches catching the glow of the lantern.

'It was a masquerade?'

'Not exactly,' said Jessica. 'I was the only woman in costume. Some older men adore young boys. Many prefer them to pretty young women.'

Hannah nodded, but without comprehension.

Jessica lowered her voice and drew Hannah into the shadow of a building. 'The men fear the sodomy laws.'

'I do not understand.' *Sodomy.* Hannah had only a vague notion of what the word meant.

'I am a *cortigiana*, Hannah. You must have heard. There are thousands like me in Venice competing for the same wealthy protectors. We all need a speciality, and dressing as a handsome youth in tight breeches is mine.' She hooked her

112

thumbs in the lapels of her satin jacket and gave a little bow. 'I permit men to have the pleasure of the experience without the commission of the crime. The penalty for sodomy is fifty ducats for the first charge, if you are a *cittidini*. If you are noble, then it is . . . ' Jessica made a sweeping motion with two fingers across her throat. 'You can find me listed in *Il Catalogo*, should you care to look — my address, prices, and specialities — along with all the other honest courtesans in Venice. There is even a flattering miniature of me in tempera.' She gave her sister a sly grin, but Hannah looked away. 'You are very poor at concealing your emotions. I can see that my talk pains you.'

Of course she had known Jessica was a courtesan, but not the details of her occupation. The thought of her having to please men by performing acts that should be done only between husband and wife made Hannah blush. 'There is no need to speak of this.'

'I am a courtesan, not a whore,' Jessica responded. 'I do not stroll the *calli* of Castello letting men take me against the wall of the Alms House.'

It took an act of will for Hannah not to put her hands to her ears.

'*Dio mio*,' Jessica said, fanning herself. 'I have drunk too much wine.' Unbuttoning her waistcoat, she revealed a shirt underneath, cut low to expose her breasts, between which hung a gold crucifix.

Hannah did not know what shocked her more, the mention of Jessica's profession or the cross

113

around her sister's neck.

'How do you expect me to keep myself, Hannah?' She winked. 'Someday, when my waist thickens and no one desires me, I will live as I please. I will not end up destitute like so many others of my kind. I have properties in Castello and a pile of gemstones.' She paused. 'I could even marry if I wanted. A substantial dowry goes a long way in making a good match.'

Hannah opened her mouth to reply, but Jessica went on, 'Do not worry about me. I have planned my future like a general amassing a war chest.'

'Isaac took me without a dowry,' Hannah said. 'Without anything except my wooden *cassone* packed with a pair of candlesticks and a lace coverlet from Aunt Zeta.' As soon as the words left her mouth, she regretted them.

A look of irritation passed over Jessica's face. 'Isaac is a rare creature. Generous, a head for business, handsome . . . '

Hannah pressed her hand to her mouth in an effort to stop her tears.

'Hannah, what is wrong? And what on earth are you doing here in the early hours of the morning? Venice is filled with ruffians, lumbering pigs, all of whom would be eager to undo you.' Jessica wiped Hannah's cheek with the back of her hand.

'Isaac has been taken as a slave. He is in Malta.'

'I had not heard. Oh, Anni, I am so sorry.' She touched the cross at her throat. 'May God return him to your bed soon, healthy and whole.'

Hannah then told Jessica about her lonely nights and her anxiety about Isaac. She wished they were somewhere private instead of standing on the Fondamenta, where any early morning passer-by could spot them. She drew Jessica by the arm into a nearby doorway.

'Every gossip in the ghetto knows some terrible story of a Jew who perished in Malta and cannot wait to tell me the details. I am out of my mind with worry.'

'I have heard the stories too, but take heart — Isaac is a resourceful man. Quick of tongue, and clever.'

Hannah's shoulders shook with sobs. 'He will make an enemy of everyone he meets. It is his nature to be quick-tempered.'

'Except with you,' Jessica said.

'No, to me as well. We fought in the week before he left. I begged him not to leave for the Levant. I said nothing good would come of it.' She drew the Conte's cloak closer around her.

'Listen to me. Isaac adores you. I used to see him waiting for you to emerge from bathing in the *mikvah*, all clean and pure and ready for his caresses. He knows that you love him. You proved it every day of your marriage.' She gave Hannah a hug and whispered, 'Men forgive everything in bed. When you are snuggled in his arms, he will replace those ugly words with sweet and tender ones.'

'Not if I get to Malta and find him dead.' The dawn was so cold Hannah could see her breath in the air. 'After you left to study for your conversion, I languished in bed for fourteen days

115

and fourteen nights without eating.'

Jessica stroked her hand. 'At the House of Catechumens, each morning the nuns wrung out my pillow, soaked with tears from longing for you. I even missed Rabbi Ibraiham and his foul herring breath. That is how lonesome I was.' She pointed to the hem of Hannah's dress showing under the Conte's cloak. 'You have not told me what brings you out so early. And . . . there is blood on your clothing.'

Hannah pulled Jessica by the sleeve of her waistcoat deeper into the shelter of the doorway and whispered, 'A confinement, in a palazzo on the Grand Canal.'

'A Christian confinement? You are jesting!' A look of amazement came over her features. 'You? The little ghetto mouse? You tell me you have violated a Papal Edict? You could be brought before the Court of the Inquisition!'

'For the love of God, keep your voice down!' Hannah said. 'It was to earn Isaac's ransom and for no other purpose.'

'My God, necessity has made the two of us brave.' Jessica twisted her curls into a knot and shoved them back up under her boy's cap.

Hannah protested, 'It is hardly the same.'

'Of course it is. We both do things we would rather not do for money. You, in the end, will have Isaac back, and I will have velvet gowns and my revenue houses, which no man can take from me.'

Hannah's eyes kept lighting on the crucifix around Jessica's neck. 'Are you truly a Christian? Surely you still observe Shabbat?'

116

Jessica said, 'I have left all of that behind.'

'No blessing of the candles on Friday night, no *challah*?'

'I do not even celebrate Passover. I hang an enormous greasy ham in my window so everyone who passes my house knows me for a Christian.'

A gentile life, free of rules, free of constraint. Not only was Jessica estranged from her past, cut off from the people who had loved her, but she had lost her religion as well. Hannah felt anger rise in her. 'So it seems you lead a life of selfishness, thinking only of the luxuries that money can buy.'

'You think *me* selfish? *You* are the one who is selfish. You have endangered the entire ghetto by attending a Christian travail.'

'I did it for *Isaac*.'

'You did it for yourself so that you could have your husband back in your arms. You are ruled by men — the Rabbi, Isaac, our father when he was alive. You are a little ghetto mouse and will never be anything else.'

Hannah was shocked by the hardness in Jessica's voice.

'I am sorry I asked for your help that night years ago,' Jessica said. 'I hoped you cared enough for me that you would defy that ill-tempered old goat of a Rabbi and help your only sister give birth to her first child, but I was mistaken.'

Hannah wanted to ask her about the baby but could not bring herself to do so.

'I screamed your name throughout the night and sent a girl to fetch you. I wanted you, and only you, to steady me on the birthing stool. Instead a clumsy Christian midwife from San Marcuola parish attended me.' Jessica's voice broke. 'My baby was born dead. Suffocated in the birth passage.'

Dear God. Hannah had not known.

'You say you love me, but you abandoned me when I needed you most.'

'That is not fair. I had to obey the Rabbi.'

'Well, you certainly did not obey him when you went to this noblewoman's travail. A pity you were not as brave when I needed you.'

Hannah felt a pain under her breast and a tearing sensation, as though her heart had come loose from its moorings. In her mind's eye, she covered the mirror and rent her clothing. These were not the empty gestures prescribed by the Rabbi years ago, but heartfelt this time. *Shiva* was complete. Now, Jessica was truly dead to her.

Without a further glance at her sister, she picked up her bag and headed for the gates of the ghetto. Her earlier joy in saving the Contessa and her baby had vanished like ripples from a passing gondola.

As she strode away, Hannah heard Jessica call, 'Run back to your suffocating ghetto! I may be immoral in your eyes, but you have broken the law. You have welcomed disaster not only on yourself but on the entire ghetto you profess to love so much.'

9

Hannah had no choice. She must return to the ca' di Padovani, with its hard, bright surfaces of marble, gilt, and silver, its cavernous rooms and enigmatic Christians. For over forty days she had waited in vain for Giovanna to return the birthing spoons.

In preparation for her journey to Malta, she now sat on the roof, the only place to dry the apples the Rabbi had given her. The fruit, fresh from the lagoon island of Turcello, was a luxury she could not have afforded. When he handed her the basket in the morning, looking as pleased as if he had grown them himself, he had said, 'Take these and be well. If there are any remaining by the time you get to Malta, give them to Isaac.' Hannah accepted them with thanks. From anyone else, the gift would have been an offering of peace. But from the Rabbi, who could tell?

This year the apples were so red and succulent that Hannah could have boiled the skins to dye flax. Sitting cross-legged on the boards of the roof, she sliced one into crescents, scooped out the core with the tip of her knife, and placed the sections, cut side up, on an old linen sheet to dry.

The sun beat down, filling her nostrils with the smell of pitch melting between the boards of the roof. In a few hours the apples would be shrivelled and ready to be wrapped in cloth strips and packed in bags along with her other food. The sheet bore the stains of previous preparations for her voyage — dried strips of lamb and beef, coins of carrots and rutabagas.

The day after tomorrow, when the tides in the lagoon provided the strongest current to open water, she would be on the *Balbiana* sailing to Malta, a passage the Conte's friend, Captain Marco Lunari, said was likely to take two months, depending on the weather and the will of God. For days she had been able to sip only chicken broth, her stomach in knots from anticipation.

She wiped her hands on her apron and glanced from the roof down to the *campo* below. A familiar-looking figure bustled past the shops of the moneylenders, butchers, and bakers, and headed across the square. His high shoes elevated him above the mud, which made his gait unsteady. As he drew closer, Hannah recognized Jacopo.

Hannah dropped her paring knife. For a moment she wondered if Matteo had taken ill and if Jacopo was summoning her for help. But no, more likely the Conte had sent Jacopo to return her birthing spoons — though with a household of servants, why would he be charged with such a task? She watched as he asked directions of an old woman who pointed to the roof. There was no time for Hannah to do anything but fling a cloth over her head and await his arrival. Better to meet him here than in the *campo*, where no conversation could be conducted in private.

Just as she was about to walk over to the stairs, the trap door of the roof clattered open and Jacopo emerged from the stairwell wearing silk tights, his cheeks pink from the climb up four flights. The buttons on his sleeved jacket were covered in embroidered silk. What could it signify when a man was so hairless he looked as though he had been immersed in a vat of lye to remove even the slightest fuzz? Jews, from the Rabbi to the *shochet*, the ritual slaughterer, were hairy men with flowing beards, shaggy chests, and *peyas* dangling on either side of their jaws. The ears of the old men sprouted hair.

Panting, Jacopo looked curiously around the roof, a space barely big enough to contain the two of them, the sheet glistening crimson with slices of apple. Hannah wiped the perspiration off her face with a corner of the apron in her hands, and rose to greet him.

'Good morning, Signore. Catch your breath.'

'Yes, one of your neighbours told me I would find you here.'

If they both sat, they would not be seen by the people in the *campo* below, but she had no chair to offer him. She noted with disappointment that he did not appear to be carrying anything, but he had an embroidered cloak slung over his shoulder.

He stood well away from the low guard railing of the roof, and for a moment gazed at the sagging clothesline hung with bedding jammed in the corner and a barrel of washing water buzzing with flies. 'So this is how it is in the

121

ghetto. How high above the *campo* you are. It makes me quite dizzy.'

'Matteo is well?' Hannah asked a little anxiously.

'Healthy as a tick, and eating like a stone mason.'

'And the Contessa? How does she fare?'

'Coughing every night. Fever. Colour so high you would think she had just come back from a walk in the country. She cannot catch her breath. Plucks the covers, talks like a woman possessed by the devil. I hear the Conte in her room some nights, propping her upright so she can breathe, holding the basin for her.'

'I am sorry to hear that.'

Surely he had not come to give her a report on the family's health. She waited. Finally she asked, 'To what do I owe the pleasure of your visit?'

'My brother sent me,' Jacopo said. 'You are to come tonight for dinner and collect your amulet.'

Hannah was speechless for a moment. It was unusual for Jews and Christians to dine together. Her work at the palazzo was finished. It was not a social relationship she had with the family but a working arrangement, much like a tutor or perhaps a trusted ladies' maid.

But when she recovered her wits, she said, 'It would be an honour.' She was about to add, *There is another matter that concerns me* — but she decided that the subject of the birthing spoons could wait until tonight.

Jacopo shielded his eyes from the glare of the

sun. 'Such an interesting part of the city. Look, I can see the stalls of the moneylenders, and the butcher shop. I feel like a bird up this high.' He put his hands on his hips and studied the fruit spread on the cloth. 'You will need to turn them in a couple of hours — otherwise the sun cannot reach them and they will spoil.'

She waited for him to state his business, which was not to discuss the picturesque nature of the ghetto or to give her advice on drying apples. Whatever he had come to say seemed to be causing him some discomfiture. Finally, she said, 'It is a great honour for me to be invited for a meal.'

'I am delivering this invitation myself because I wished to have a word with you. Do not look so surprised. I found something which I believe belongs to you. Along with your amulet you left behind a curious contraption.'

He reached under the cloak draped over his shoulder. She caught a flash of the familiar silver.

'Oh, thank you.' Hannah held out her hand, relief flooding over her, but Jacopo did not proffer the birthing spoons.

'I found it under the Contessa's bed when I stooped to retrieve a handkerchief. I assume you used this device in the delivery of my nephew?'

'Yes, but — '

'Very careless of you to leave it behind. You must realize how dangerous something like this could be in the hands of certain people. Not me, I hasten to add. I feel as grateful to you as the Conte does. You saved my nephew. I would like to ensure that no harm befalls you as a result of that generous deed.'

'That is very kind of you. I thought, perhaps . . . '

'Any of the servants could have found it. A Jewess delivering a Christian baby, using an unlawful device? It would not look well to an investigating magistrate, would it?'

'I am grateful to you,' Hannah said, wishing he would hand the spoons to her and be on his way.

'For my part, I would like nothing more than to give the device back to you this very instant, but there is something we must discuss first. My brother, the Conte, paid you handsomely for your attendance at the Contessa's travail. Two hundred ducats, if I am not mistaken.'

'Money I earned fairly. The Contessa was more dead than alive when I arrived at your palazzo.'

'Do not misunderstand. I do not dispute the value of your service. It is your use of witchcraft that troubles me. I have an obligation to report you. You know that, do you not?'

'I could no more use witchcraft than I could sprout wings and fly off this roof to the *campo* below.'

'So you say.'

'I speak the truth.'

'I have no wish to see you prosecuted, Hannah. It would serve no purpose. So I am willing to ignore my responsibility — but the price of my dereliction is two hundred ducats. If you wish your device returned, I suggest that you bring the money with you tonight. Our gondola will call for you at sundown.' Jacopo made a show of moving toward the stairs, then placed a foot on the first step, about to descend. He turned. 'Do we understand each other?'

'Those ducats are to buy my husband's life.'

'The ducats will not be of much use to you or to him if you are arrested and tortured to death.' He tapped his polished nails on the buttons of his waistcoat.

As if reading her thoughts, he said, 'Do not think that you can avoid me by sailing off to Malta. The captain of the *Balbiana* transports a great deal of cargo for our family. A word from me and he will withdraw his offer of passage.'

She wanted to spring at him. She was overcome with a sense of despair, but she had no choice but to nod. Jacopo continued down the stairs.

Hannah needed time to think. Returning to the blanket of apple slices, she sat hunched, rocking back and forth. As she fanned away flies, the afternoon shadows lengthened.

Back in her *loghetto*, when it was nearly sunset, she washed her face in the basin and slipped on her only good dress, a red velvet gown with a square-cut bodice and full skirt with silk insets on the sides. Without the aid of a looking-glass, she used her reflection in the basin of washing water to arrange her hair. Her hands were shaking so, she dropped her hairpins and comb and had to crawl under the bed to retrieve them. Then she pinned a snood over her chignon and left her room.

When she entered the *campo* it was dark, and the black-and-red sign that read BANCO ROSSO

125

— the 'paupers' bank,' as it was called — was barely visible under the *sotoportego*. At first she thought Signore Rosso had left for the day, but her eyes made out a flicker of candlelight in the rear of the bank. She knocked on the door until Rosso, an elderly man pale as the Rabbi but with eyes crinkled at the corners, unlocked the grille covering the door and admitted her.

'Hannah, my dear, I was wondering when you would come to collect your ducats.' He handed her a small hessian sack and wished her a good journey. 'You look pale. Are you unwell?'

'Just a little tired.'

'May these ducats be used to purchase Isaac's freedom.'

An impulse seized her to throw herself into the arms of this kindly man whom she had known since her girlhood and ask for his counsel. She knew her choices. It was simple: she could pay the money to Jacopo or be arrested as a witch. Tonight she must use Isaac's ransom money to buy her own life. She said goodbye to Signore Rosso as she tucked the sack of ducats into her bag and marched across the *campo* to the massive gates leading to the Rio della Misericordia, where the Conte's gondola waited.

Her only hope was to confide in the Conte and tell him of his brother's deceit. But why would he take her word against Jacopo's? She was of no significance, just a Jewess from the ghetto.

Isaac was lost to her.

10

By the time the *Marangona* in Piazza San Marco chimed seven times, Hannah was pulling the bell cord at the entranceway of the ca' di Padovani. The Conte's cloak was draped over her arm, her bag slung over her shoulder. At the sound of the bell, a cry of recognition issued from one of the upper windows and Lucia leaned out, clutching a kitten, waving and calling. The sight reminded Hannah of the story she had recounted to the Contessa during her travail to illustrate how poorly wedged the baby was within her. Now the Contessa was planted in the middle of the window, not to one side as Hannah had explained the baby was. A few moments later, Lucia was at the entranceway smiling and extending her arms. She wore a green silk dress; her red hair fell around her shoulders.

'I am so happy to see you, Hannah. I am grateful you were able to take time from your travel preparations to come and dine with us.'

Hannah felt a surge of affection for this woman she had saved from the Angel of Death, though at the thought of how near she had come to murdering her, Hannah shuddered.

Lucia said, 'Come in. I think of you every day and wonder how you are. I wanted to thank you for all you did for me and Matteo. Without you and your gifted hands, we would both be dead. The Conte will not stop singing your praises. I know that he wishes to thank you as well.'

'I am pleased to see you, too.' But Hannah could not in good conscience tell the Contessa she looked well. Lucia had a pale, ethereal look. Dark circles smudged the skin under her eyes. Her hands trembled.

Lucia glanced over her shoulder as though hoping the Conte would materialize behind her. 'Alas, my husband has been at our villa in Maser checking on his figs. He fancies himself a farmer, except' — she laughed — 'when the grasshoppers swarm. Then he turns the whole disaster over to the estate manager. He will return tonight because tomorrow at first light we leave for Ferrara. My father is sick and the doctors fear he is dying. I wish to see him one last time.'

'I am so sorry to hear of your father's illness. May God come to his aid,' Hannah said.

The Contessa acknowledged her words and explained, 'He is not young — past sixty. He has enjoyed a long life.'

Lucia told one of the servants to let them know when dinner was ready. And as they climbed the main staircase to the *piano nobile*, the principle floor, past the familiar fresco of nymphs in green and gold, she slipped her arm through Hannah's as though they were intimates rather than two women separated by the chasm of class and religion.

They entered Lucia's bedroom. It did not seem possible that this was the same room that only a few weeks ago had been redolent with the smell of blood and had echoed with the screams of childbirth. Now, she heard only the

128

high-pitched wail of a healthy infant. Lucia's bed was draped in brocade, and in the corner stood Matteo's cradle, adorned with four pillars supporting a splendid *padiglione* of striped silk. The night of Matteo's birth, Hannah had been intimidated by the splendour of the room. Now, with the chandeliers lit and light bouncing from looking-glass to terrazzo floor, it felt warm, luxurious, and inviting.

'Matteo is a darling, a perfect little being.' Lucia kissed the black-and-white kitten she held in her arms, and motioned Hannah toward the cradle. 'There is not another baby half so sweet in all the world.'

Good, the path of salt still encircled the baby's bed to keep away Lilith. Hannah approached, stepping over the salt, and then bent to pick up Matteo. He had lost the scrunched red look of the newborn. His face was smooth, his cheeks rounded, his blue eyes alert as they tried to focus on her. She brushed back the curls on his forehead. The red marks left by her birthing spoons had healed without a trace.

'*Che meraviglia!*' She had never seen such a beautiful child. Wrapped around him was a white receiving blanket with the family crest embroidered in gold silk thread. She tucked the blanket more tightly around him and felt the outline of her amulet on his chest.

He cried, tossing his head from side to side, searching for a nipple. Hannah felt a tingling in her own breasts. Lucia must have experienced the same sensation, for she placed the kitten on the coverlet, climbed onto the high bed, and

129

unlaced the front of her gown. She gestured for Hannah to pass her the infant.

'Maybe my milk will flow better today.' She exposed her breasts to Hannah, who winced in sympathy, so painful was it to see the deep fissures scoring her nipples. In the ghetto a woman would not expose herself in this way, nor would she treat a guest with such informality, yet Hannah felt herself relaxing and enjoying the sisterly camaraderie.

Most patrician women hired wet nurses so they could be at liberty to entertain and enjoy themselves, and Lucia was far too ill to be nursing Matteo.

'Apply some almond oil. That should help. Perhaps wait a few days and allow them to heal before you try nursing again.'

But Lucia did not appear to be listening, and coaxed the crying baby to her breast. Hannah took a small vial of almond oil from her bag and handed it to Lucia.

'I am endeavouring to feed him myself. My milk is better suited to Matteo than any wet nurse's.'

'Does the Conte not want Giovanna to nurse Matteo to save you from the pain?'

'The truth is that my husband is so afraid of . . . of this child joining the rest of our babies in the family crypt that he is determined that I be the only one to nurse him.'

'Your husband is a devoted father.' Hannah was touched by the thought of the Conte's being interested in the particulars of suckling a newborn. In her experience, fathers rarely paid

130

attention to their offspring until they began to speak. Perhaps she could have a word with the Conte and convince him to allow Giovanna to nurse the child.

The nursing was not going well, and Hannah took the child from Lucia and jiggled him in her arms as his wailing reached a crescendo. The baby was plump, the creases in the fat of his forearms like bracelets. Whatever his feeding regimen, he was not starving. Perhaps Giovanna was feeding Matteo notwithstanding the Conte's wishes.

Lucia stretched out her arms. 'Please give him back to me,' she said. 'The doctor says my lungs are poor and there is nothing to be done. I will enjoy him as long as I can.'

How could she discourage a dying mother from nursing her child? She passed Matteo, still wailing, to Lucia.

Lucia patted a spot on the bed next to her, indicating that Hannah should join her. 'Tell me what you think of my treasure,' she said as though she were speaking to her friend, not her midwife.

The kitten sauntered over and sniffed at Matteo's cloths; Hannah wished Lucia would shoo it away. It was not healthy to allow cats in the presence of infants.

'I have never seen a prettier babe.' Hannah glanced at the devotional painting of the Madonna and Child over Lucia's bed. The baby in the painting resembled Matteo. Hair reddish-blond and eyes blue, Matteo was the very image of the Christ child.

'He has the di Padovani eyes, but other than

that, I do not see a resemblance to either Paolo or me.' She held the crying Matteo in one hand and with the other turned the kitten upside down and tickled its belly. Matteo spit out her nipple and began to wail. 'I must confess, Hannah, that since his birth, worry consumes me. My mind buzzes, desperate for a place to light.' She watched as Matteo became redder in the face. 'I try to be a good mother to him. But I might as well be giving suck to a lion's cub with sharp milk teeth.'

This was not the first time Hannah had encountered a mother who became overwrought after childbirth. 'You had such a difficult confinement. You might try herbs — fenugreek and blessed chisel are known to help the supply of milk.' Hannah wondered if Lucia was still bleeding. Perhaps she should suggest that she insert cotton wadding, which sometimes helped staunch the flow after childbirth, a flow heavier than the monthly courses.

Lucia began to cry quietly herself. Hannah propped a pillow under her arm, tucking the blanket away from the baby's face so he could breathe more easily. But Matteo continued to scream, his tiny body thrashing from side to side.

'Oh, Matteo, after all I went through to give birth to you.' She finally handed him to Hannah. 'I will summon Giovanna to change him in a moment.'

Hannah settled into a chair by Lucia's bed and rocked him in her arms. God be praised, he eventually cried himself to sleep, his translucent fingers curved to his cheek.

This was the last time she would see Matteo, she was sure, so she savoured the moment, committing to memory his woolly, milky smell, the way he arched his strong back when he was hungry, and the bits of sleep that collected in the corners of his eyes.

Hannah said, 'I will change his cloths.'

She placed the sleeping baby on a table near Lucia's bed and removed his wrappings, saw the amulet rising and falling on his chest. His penis rested like a tiny hooded worm between his legs. It was a strange sight on a child of two months. Jewish babies were circumcised on the eighth day after birth. When she had wrapped him in fresh cloth, Hannah nestled him into his cradle.

'What a relief. Thank you for quieting him.' Lucia smoothed her gown. 'I am so tired.' Two bright red spots had appeared on her cheeks. Then she clasped and unclasped her hands in the manner of a consumptive. 'What will happen to Matteo after I am gone?'

'Contessa, try to think happy thoughts. It cannot be healthy for your head to be filled with gloomy ones.' But Hannah shared her anxiety. Jacopo was no friend to the child. Perhaps his other uncle, Niccolò, posed a danger as well.

'Matteo will remain here with Giovanna when we leave for Ferrara tomorrow. He is not old enough for such an expedition. It is a hard journey, several days.'

'You could not take both Giovanna and Matteo?' If she had a child, she would not leave him for any reason.

'Why impose that ordeal on an infant?' said

133

Lucia. A fragile look overcame her face. 'Hannah, I am never sure how frankly I can speak,' she said, tugging so hard at the rope of pearls around her neck that Hannah was afraid she would break the strand and send the beads bouncing to the terrazzo floor. 'But I feel I can be truthful with you.'

Hannah sat once more at Lucia's side and squeezed her hand. 'The experience of a confinement brings women together.'

'They say you forget the torture of childbirth. But I was in such agony.' Her hands began working at the coverlet, plucking at the velvet pile. 'After you left me, the fevers came and then delirium. Giovanna told me I was calling out all manner of nonsense. She said I did not even recognize my own dear husband and kept calling out for my brother-in-law Niccolò.' She took her rosary from the bedside table and held it to her lips.

'But just think — for your pains you have a beautiful and healthy boy. A son, your heart's desire.'

'I should be grateful, but all I can think is that if he were dead, he would be in the arms of the Lord, safe from all danger.'

Hannah was uncertain how to reply. A memory came to her unbidden. The young wife of the silversmith in the ghetto, unsettled in her mind after a difficult travail, had placed a pillow over her infant's face, smothering him. When questioned by the authorities, she said she had done it to keep him safe from all harm. Surely the Contessa was not contemplating such an act?

'He is being watched over by the Lord now. That is why he survived his birth. You have nothing to worry about.'

'They say that with summer approaching, the plague will return to Venice. Suppose, after all my pain and struggle, he dies of it?'

Hannah remembered when the plague had struck two years before. Because the ghetto, unaccountably, had been spared, many Christians accused the Jews of bringing the pestilence to Venice.

'Matteo will be fine,' said Hannah. 'And so will you. You are weak and troubled in your mind. You need rest.'

Lucia's lips pressed together in an anxious line. 'I often wrestle with burdensome thoughts. I summon the priest to make confessions, but after he arrives, I cannot find the will.' She gestured to the leather-bound prayer book resting on the prie-dieu in the corner. 'Sometimes I pray alone for hours.'

Hannah knew nothing of the rite of confession, nor of what this pale woman might have to confess.

'Tell me about your plans, Hannah. You leave soon for Malta?'

'In a few days.' A feeling of dread came over Hannah at the thought of Jacopo. 'God willing.'

Matteo stirred and sighed in his sleep.

'I will take my amulet, Lucia. Matteo seems well out of danger. If I manage to board my ship, the amulet will protect me against stormy seas and pirates.'

'It has served him well, your Jewish charm,' said Lucia.

135

Hannah went to the crib, slipped a hand into Matteo's swaddling cloths, and withdrew the amulet carefully. It seemed almost lifelike, still warm from the child's body, as she adjusted it around her neck.

There was a knock at the door and a maid put her head in. 'The Conte is returned from Maser. Dinner will be served shortly.'

'We will be down in a moment,' said Lucia.

The maid curtsied and withdrew.

'Dress me. We will go down to dinner. My brothers-in-law are dining with us tonight.' She reached for her looking-glass on the night table and brushed her red hair.

Giovanna entered the room, smiled insincerely at Hannah, and then scooped Matteo from his cradle, where he was beginning to stir. Hannah rose from the bed and approached them, planting a goodbye kiss on Matteo's forehead.

'May God watch over you and keep you safe,' she whispered as Giovanna, holding him upright so his round face peeked over her shoulder, swept him from the room.

Hannah gathered her bag and the Conte's cloak from the chair where she had placed them. The gold ducats felt heavy. Such a lot of money, enough for Isaac's ransom and her passage to Malta. It was both the money and the dream of having Isaac back that Jacopo threatened to steal from her tonight.

'The Conte will need his cloak for your trip to Ferrara.'

'I will see that he gets it.' Lucia eased herself out of bed and disappeared behind a dressing screen. She emerged minutes later wearing a yellow silk dress inset with panels of green velvet. She turned her back so Hannah could lace her up. The dress was a poor choice — the yellow drew all the colour from her cheeks. The tight bodice emphasized her stomach, still slack from childbirth. But Lucia's carriage was graceful for a woman of her age. Her back was straight and her chin held high. Her pearls gleamed against her throat. Hannah could only guess at the effort required for Lucia to slip on high shoes and act as though all were perfectly well.

Hannah made her way down the wide staircase holding the Contessa's arm so Lucia would not trip on her treacherous shoes. Hannah placed her feet, shod in thin-soled sandals, firmly on each stair.

Near the bottom, she halted mid-step. Under the multifoil arch leading into the dining room, wearing an embroidered frock coat so tightly fitted it could not conceal a marble, never mind an object as large as her birthing spoons, stood Jacopo. With an abrupt jerk of his head he signalled for her to follow him into a small reception room.

Lucia shot Hannah a puzzled look as Hannah excused herself and walked toward Jacopo.

When she joined him, Jacopo closed the door. 'Have you my money?' he asked. He advanced toward her.

'Where are my spoons?' she countered. She had no experience in dealing with men like Jacopo.

'We will make the exchange after dinner. I

warn you — any word of this to the Conte and I will denounce you.'

Jacopo's head was so close to her that she could see the bristles on his chin and the scurf in his hair and on his satin shoulders.

What would Isaac counsel? How she longed for her clever husband, who always knew what to do.

11

Lucia chatted and laughed as they resumed their walk along the central hallway, the portego, which ran from the façade of the palazzo on the Grand Canal to the *calle* in the back. Still shocked by her conversation with Jacopo, Hannah did not hear a word Lucia said. Lucia, with her arm looped through Hannah's for support, seemed unaware of her inattention.

As they entered the opulent dining room, Hannah slowed her pace to match Lucia's. Jacopo crowded behind them so close that he nearly trod on the hem of their gowns. Then he darted around them and took a chair next to Niccolò's.

On the dining table sat a centrepiece, a perfect golden replica of the *bucintoro*, the Doge's ceremonial barge, which once a year carried the leader of the Republic to the lagoon for the ritual wedding of *La Serenessima*, Venice's marriage to the sea. From the golden deck spilled strawberries, figs, grapes, and apples. All the porcelain and silverware bore the crest of the di Padovani family — warring stags with locked horns. Nothing here was makeshift. Nothing here had been designed with one purpose and ended up as something else. In her *loghetto*, Hannah employed a discarded glassmaker's pincers to arrange the charcoal in her brazier. The chipped plate on which she ate had started life as a dinner platter.

The Conte and Niccolò lounged at the table, talking, their heads together, Jacopo's bald and tonsured with a wisp of brown hair, and Niccolò's adorned with a mop of tumbling curls that dripped with water like those of a spaniel just emerging from a lake.

The Conte rose to greet them and said, 'Hannah, my dear, thank you for coming. You have retrieved your amulet, I see.' He nodded at the silver charm hanging on the red cord around her neck. He kissed her hand and smiled so warmly that for an instant she forgot Jacopo's threat.

'Ah, yes,' Jacopo said. 'How kind of you to come.'

Niccolò stepped forward to greet Lucia, his dark eyes looking as though he had just woken up from a particularly satisfying sleep. He wore a coarse linen waistcoat smudged with mud. He kissed Lucia's cheek. Then, turning to Hannah, he said, 'Will you take some wine?' Without waiting for a reply, he signalled to a servant, who stepped forward with a crystal glass filled with wine that appeared black as canal water and placed it on the table in front of them.

Hannah and Lucia sat down on armless chairs and arranged their skirts, the men across from them on the other side of the table. Hannah felt stiff and awkward. Her shoulders always crept high around her ears when she was nervous. In the ghetto, men and women did not eat together. The women served the men, then withdrew until the men had finished. Only afterward did they serve themselves. Hannah was discomfited by

140

the liveried servant who stood behind her chair, anticipating her every move and every want.

And only at Seder dinners had Hannah tasted wine. Grasping the glass by the fragile stem, she raised it to her mouth and took a sip. It tasted so sour her lips puckered as though she had sucked a lemon. She replaced it on the carved table in front of her. The Conte, without comment, took a pitcher of water and poured a measure into Hannah's glass, turning the wine a watery pink. Hannah acknowledged his gesture with a nod. He was trying to put her at ease, but his ministrations and solicitous looks only make her more tense.

The Conte turned to his wife. 'And you, Lucia — are you better tonight? No more coughing?' He bent and lifted a tendril of her hair from her face. 'Have a fig. I brought them back from the villa. They are sweet this year and very sticky.' He reached into the *bucintoro* and tore apart a small brown fig. 'Eat,' he said, offering her the fruit. 'It will give you strength.'

'You must not worry about me so much,' said Lucia. 'I am much restored.'

But Hannah could see, and so could the Conte, how Lucia's hands trembled and how her veins, in the fading light from the windows, showed blue above the bodice of her yellow dress.

The Conte popped an entire fig into his mouth. 'We are lucky Hannah was able to visit us before she leaves for Malta.'

Jacopo pursed his lips. 'And what, pray tell, are we serving our honoured Jewish guest? A difficult point of etiquette, since Christians do not eat with Jews, and servants do not eat with nobility.'

Lucia gave the Conte a look that said, *Say something to your brother. Admonish him.*

Comments such as Jacopo's fell frequently from the lips of Christians. To mock Jews was a tradition in Venice. Every year at Eastertide a number of Jewish men, leaders of the ghetto, were forced to run a footrace naked through Venice, their buttocks turning red under the willow switches of the jeering crowds. Hannah wished she were anywhere but in this fine palace with its hard reflective surfaces that looked as though they would shatter at any moment.

'We will dine on peacocks,' the Conte replied to his brother, adding, 'And, Jacopo, that is quite enough.'

Hannah was reassured. The Conte had defended her.

'We are grateful for your presence at our table, Hannah,' the Conte said. 'And now we will enjoy our meal together, rather a splendid luxury. A succulent bird made irresistible by a rich cream sauce of pomegranate seeds.'

Lucia laughed. ''Splendid luxury?' You hated the shrill squawks of those birds. Once you commented that they were like beautiful courtesans with the voices of fishwives.'

The Conte looked sheepish. 'It is true that one curiously stupid cock invaded my orangery and then settled his wide arse on my fruit trees, crushing them. So, yes, I was delighted to see him hanging by his feet in the larder.'

Two servants entered, carrying between them an enormous platter of roasted peacock, its braised tongue surrounded by a mound of pâté in the shape of a star. Following behind them came more servants bearing platters. Soon, calves' brains, liver and onions, *fegato alla Veneziano*, beef hearts, and truffles from the lagoon island of Burano covered the table. There were fish dishes, too: *bisato su l'ara*, eels in vinegar; *seppie al nero*, cuttlefish in its own ink; and tiny artichokes.

The Conte inclined his head at a servant to commence carving.

Hannah could not conceive of a more repellent display — meat that had not been ritually slaughtered, vegetables cooked in the same pots that had once held meat and milk, beef glistening with butter sauce. She felt her gorge rise as she stared at the clotted cream forming a border around the pâté.

'Try a slice of the breast, Hannah. It is the most tender,' said the Conte. He motioned for the servant to place a slice on her plate.

She could not offend this man who had been so kind. She made a pretense of cutting up the meat and then helped herself to artichokes and a slice of bread. She was not the only one at the table picking at her food. Lucia, seated on her right, cut her meat into smaller and smaller pieces until each was no bigger than one of the pearls around her neck.

Lucia broke the silence that had descended upon the table. 'The other night in bed, when Matteo was in your arms, I had an idea.'

'Yes, my dear?' the Conte prompted, accepting a helping of *bisato su l'ara* and bread.

'To thank God for sparing my life and the life of your son, I wish you to commission an artist to paint a triptych of the Madonna and Child. We will donate it to the Church of St. Samuele as an altarpiece.'

'We often do the same,' Hannah said, relieved to have something to contribute to the conversation. 'To thank God for a piece of good fortune, we make a donation to one of the benevolent societies in the ghetto. Or sometimes women embroider an altar cloth for one of the synagogues.' She took a bite of artichokes. They tasted crunchy and hot in her mouth. If her stomach had not been in knots, she would have savoured the flavour of garlic.

'Lucia,' Jacopo said, 'perhaps in tribute to your revered midwife, you should instead donate a silver chalice to the *Scuola dei Tedeshi* in the Ghetto Nuovo?' He motioned a liveried servant to give him a portion of *seppie al nero*, a brackish dish of squid cooked in its own ink.

A Christian donating a religious object to a synagogue was unthinkable, as he well knew. Hannah watched Jacopo devour the cuttlefish. The ink stained his tongue and teeth black. She glanced away.

Holding a silk cloth to her mouth, Lucia was overtaken by a fit of coughing. The Conte helped her to a standing position, and as she bent double gasping for breath, he patted her back between her thin shoulder blades. A servant reached for her bloodstained cloth and hid it

144

away, discreetly slipping her a clean one. When the coughing subsided, the Conte helped Lucia to be seated once again.

The Conte leaned over his wife and quietly offered her a tidbit of meat from his plate. Lucia and the Conte seemed to enjoy that same rare quality that she and Isaac shared — happiness and contentment in each other's company. And yet, she remembered her conversation with the Conte in the gondola the night she came to the palazzo, when he had instructed her to sacrifice the Contessa's life if necessary. If she were to tell the Conte his brother was extorting money from her, could she rely on him to come to her aid?

After Isaac left for the Levant, Hannah had sensed his presence watching over her in the same way that she watched over him. She could summon the picture of his dark eyes alight with intelligence and his angular face, and feel comforted. Often she carried on imaginary conversations with him, asking his opinion, receiving his advice. She longed for him, but tonight, when she needed him the most, here in the midst of this noble family and their servants, she could not call him to mind.

Hannah picked up her knife and cut a slice of melon from the *bucintoro*. A young servant moved to replenish her wine, but she shook her head. He then offered the carafe to Jacopo and Niccolò.

She turned to the Conte and spoke in a low voice. 'There is something I must discuss with you.'

'You may speak freely. We are all family here.'

145

The Conte made an expansive gesture with his hand as Jacopo and Niccolò watched.

'I would sooner talk to you alone.'

The Conte shook his head and continued chewing on a piece of artichoke. Hannah had no choice. She would not be able to address the Conte in private.

After Niccolò finished telling a story about hunting deer and the Conte paused from discussing his latest shipment of nutmeg, she cleared her throat and said, in a voice louder than she intended, 'I have lost something precious to me and of no use to anyone else. I believe I left it here when I was attending the Contessa the night of Matteo's birth.'

The room fell silent. All eyes looked at her. It was so quiet she could hear the gurgling of Jacopo's stomach.

Finally, the Conte broke the silence. 'What are you referring to?'

Her words came out in a rush. 'My birthing spoons. They are of great assistance to me in helping babies and their mothers.' She wished she could spring up and stand by the door, ready to run if Jacopo pounced on her, but she forced herself to remain still. The faces around the table looked blankly at her. 'They are like this.' She reached into the bowl of *risotto* and withdrew two silver serving spoons. She arranged them on the table in the shape of the letter X. 'With a small hinge to hold them together.' She blushed to discuss the details of so intimate an object at the table. Jacopo added to her discomfort by pretending not to understand, thus forcing her to

146

describe their function in detail.

The Conte speared a piece of meat from the platter in front of him. 'An important instrument for a woman in your profession.' He looked at his wife. 'Lucia? Have you any idea what Hannah is talking about?'

Lucia shook her head. Of course she would not know. She had been unconscious when Hannah used them.

Hannah glanced at Jacopo, who was now white with anger.

'This really is too much. Are you accusing a member of the di Padovani family of taking something of yours? You accept our hospitality and then make this allegation?'

'No, of course not. It is nothing like that. I did not mean to give offence,' Hannah stammered. 'It is just that I thought I had them in my bag when I left the palazzo the night of Matteo's birth, but then when I reached the gondola, they were gone. Perhaps I dropped them.'

The Conte snapped his fingers. 'Fetch Giovanna,' he said to one of the servants. 'Do not worry, my dear,' he said to Hannah. 'If they are here, we will find them.'

Jacopo rose to his feet.

'Do not trouble yourself, Jacopo.' The Conte signalled his brother to sit. 'This is why we have servants.' His tone was that of an adult speaking to a child.

A few moments later Giovanna entered the room, a servant trailing behind her. She was wiping her hands on her apron. The bodice of her dress had been hastily laced. Good, thought

Hannah, she has been nursing Matteo. No wonder the child is thriving. He would never obtain sufficient nourishment from poor Lucia.

Jacopo addressed Giovanna. 'A problem has arisen. The midwife claims she has misplaced her birthing spoons. Find them, will you?'

Giovanna glanced at Jacopo. 'I am not sure where they are, sir. The last time I saw them — '

Jacopo interrupted. 'I hope *you* did not take them, Giovanna?'

'I did not. I think you know that.' Giovanna shifted uneasily from one foot to the other, refusing to meet the Conte's gaze. 'The last time I saw them, Master Jacopo had them.'

'That is ridiculous, Giovanna,' Jacopo said. 'What possible use would I have for such an apparatus?'

'That is enough!' the Conte said. 'Jacopo, go with Giovanna. Find this birthing device and bring it here. Good God, man, what earthly use is it to you?'

Jacopo stomped out of the dining room, his mouth set in a thin line, Giovanna behind him. Hannah wondered what would transpire between the two of them when they were out of the Conte's earshot.

Lucia shook her head, clearly embarrassed. 'I cannot imagine what is going on, can you?'

'Yes, I can. All too well,' said the Conte.

'An innocent misunderstanding,' said Niccolò, taking a sip of wine. 'Nothing more, I'm sure.'

An ashen-faced Giovanna returned a few minutes later with Jacopo by her side. She held the spoons wrapped in a cloth and lifted a corner to show the Conte. The spoons were still caked with mucus and blood from the birth. The Conte gestured for her to give them to Hannah, who dropped them into her bag, which had been resting at her feet. They fell with a clunk on top of her ducats. Relief flooded her. She now had the spoons and the ducats. If she could keep both, she would sail to Malta and arrive in time to rescue Isaac. The Conte had lifted a great weight from her shoulders.

The Conte said, 'Giovanna, you may go.' She left the room, her eyes downcast, her expression sullen. They finished the meal in silence.

A new servant entered the dining room and whispered something into the Conte's ear. The Conte nodded and got to his feet.

'Our plans have changed, we must leave now. The tides are propitious. Our boat is packed and ready. We will be gone a few days or perhaps a few weeks, depending on the health of Lucia's father. Jacopo, Niccolò, I expect to return to a peaceful household. Is that understood?'

Both brothers nodded.

Surely, Jacopo would not try to take away her ducats now, Hannah thought.

The Conte placed a hand on Hannah's shoulder. 'I apologize for what transpired this evening. I thank you for coming. A servant will see you home after we leave.' He offered his arm to Lucia. 'Come, my dear. Are you ready?'

Hannah grabbed her bag and followed the couple to the main entranceway leading to the canal, where their gondola bobbed at its mooring lines. The servants heaved valises onto the boat. She would probably never see either of them again, or their beautiful son.

'I thank you for everything,' she said to the Conte.

'You will visit us again when you return from Malta?'

'Yes,' said Hannah, but in her heart she doubted she would. 'I have a favour to ask. I would like to bid a last farewell to Matteo.'

'Of course. Just go upstairs,' said Lucia. 'He is in his cradle in my bedchamber.' Lucia touched Hannah on the cheek. 'I think you are as fond of Matteo as I am.'

'He is a lovely babe,' Hannah replied.

The Contessa kissed her on the cheek. 'Go to our son. Give him a kiss, and have a safe voyage to Malta.'

'May you live and be well,' said Hannah.

She stood on the dock and waved as the couple got on the boat and the gondolier cast off from the mooring pole and moved away. It would be a long trip on water and then another three days overland. Perhaps they were wise to leave Matteo safe at home.

When Hannah walked back inside the palazzo, the brothers were nowhere to be seen. She clutched her bag close to her chest and heard the reassuring clinking of her ducats. From the dining room, she heard the clatter of silver and plates as the servants cleared the table.

She hurried up the stairs, remembering how timidly she had approached them the night of Matteo's birth. This time, she placed one foot after another firmly in the middle of each stair.

At the top, she proceeded along the corridor to Lucia's bedchamber at the end of the hall. The heavy carpets muffled her footsteps. Entering the room, Hannah glanced toward Lucia's empty bed, which was as clean and neatly made as if the Contessa had not struggled on it for two days and a night to give birth. A fresh coverlet of red silk draped the bed and a matching silk curtain fell from the canopy.

She tiptoed toward the cradle draped with a *padiglione* woven in the di Padovani colours. This would be her final goodbye to a child she had brought into the world. Already the thought of never seeing him again pained her. Better she should quit this palazzo now, but she could not without one last look at him. The window was open, she noticed. Too much air would not benefit the baby. She pulled it closed. Then, carefully stepping over the protective circle of salt, she pushed the curtains aside and bent down, ready to plant a kiss on Matteo's cheek.

The cradle was empty.

12

Valletta, Malta
1575

In the past week Isaac's fortunes had, if not soared — for how could anyone describe the eating of mouldy bread and half-rotten fish as soaring? — at least improved. He now had victuals, shelter, and an occupation of sorts. He slept in Joseph's stable at night, next to wagons and carts and horses that munched their hay all night relentlessly. And if the rats nibbled his toes before he was finally able to sink into the arms of Morpheus, what of it? That could happen anywhere, even in Venice. At least he was not eating the leather from his own shoes.

As part of the bargain, Isaac had convinced Joseph that he, Isaac, could earn more money writing letters in the square than he could rowing on a slave galley. So Isaac became a scribe. Two-thirds of his meagre fees, whether paid in coin or in kind, went straight into Joseph's greasy pocket; the other third went to Isaac. But — and this was the important part of the deal — if he could win the heart of the widow Gertrudis for Joseph, Isaac would be granted his freedom. Everything depended on his persuasive tongue and his nimble mind.

On Friday, which was market day, and again on Monday and Thursday, Isaac sat on his fleshless behind in the main square. No matter how he shifted on the ground, it was painful. He wrote letters and drafted contracts for the honest citizens of Valletta, who were, for the most part, innocent of the written word. Most could not even recognize their own names written in dust on the side of a wagon. But the astonishing transactions they engaged in! The pig had a firm grip on the Christian imagination. Last week, one of his customers, a farmer from Gozo, directed Isaac to pen a letter to his wife instructing her to give his favourite sow a brisk going-over with a twig brush while he was away. In the course of the past week, Isaac had drafted several contracts for the purchase and sale of sows. He had copied out recipes for head cheese, roast suckling pig, and a stew called *trumpo* made of pig snout and rutabaga. The very thought of such a dish made him bilious.

Business arrangements that men had previously sealed with a handshake and a bottle of malmsey wine were now codified in Isaac's meticulous script, writing so tiny that Isaac himself could not read it, even after the ink had dried. But neither could anyone else. This did not prevent his customers from nodding solemnly over Isaac's parchment and swearing they had never gazed upon a finer hand. The remainder of the week Isaac laboured for Joseph, sizing canvas and sewing sails.

So three days a week, in the square, installed under an olive tree, a plank across his knees for a desk, Isaac dealt with hearty men reeking of cow shit. Some were generous and thanked him with gifts of potatoes, carrots, and even figs. One man for whom Isaac had written a marriage contract presented him with a not-too-badly-worn pair of breeches.

Isaac recited to his customers what was to become a well-honed speech. 'This parchment does not come easily to me,' he would say. 'The Knights in Valletta — may carbuncles cover their asses — refused me paper, so by my own industry I have converted a sheepskin to parchment. I provide a full broadsheet for the verbose, a quarto for the moderately loquacious, and an octavo, an eighth of a sheet, for the succinct. For the inarticulate, I offer odds and ends made from scraps of the hind legs.' He would then wave the various sizes of parchment in front the customer's nose. Sometimes Isaac would add, 'Let my bleeding hands be your incentive to brevity.'

The church bells rang out at noon. It was the appointed hour. Soon Joseph would appear standing over him, blotting out the sun, to collect the letter that would shoot Cupid's arrow squarely into Gertrudis's heart. Better to be a purveyor of love potions, like the crones in the market, Isaac thought. Why had he laboured over — no, *agonized* over — his composition when he could more easily have concocted a stew of bat guano, toad's wart, and fennel, and enjoyed just as great a chance of success?

Isaac had glimpsed Gertrudis several times from a distance as she hurried through the street, sketch paper under her arm, the hungry eyes of every man upon her. His heart sank every time he watched her graceful form picking its way through the idlers in front of the tavern. On several occasions, on her way to the shop of the apothecary who compounded her paint pigments and provided her with linseed oil, she looked across the square at Isaac and smiled.

Oh, Joseph, Isaac thought, you are flying too close to the sun and you will crash to the earth, taking me with you. You are a man who does not desire what is within your grasp, and longs only for what you cannot attain. The island is full of stout peasant girls who would keep you warm in the winter and shade you in the summer.

Isaac remembered that yearning for love, that hunger that could be satisfied by only one woman. But here in Malta he had come to realize that his belly was a more insistent organ than his prick.

His dreams left him in no doubt of that. The same dream had come to him every night since he was taken prisoner months ago. Hannah stood before him dressed in a white camisole, her nipples pushing through the thin fabric, dark hair cascading around her shoulders. She implored him to make love to her. When he embraced her, her arms stretched longer and longer until they entwined him in a vinous embrace, binding his limbs to his torso. When he sucked her nipples, they became clusters of grapes. When he ran his hands over her belly, it turned into a ripe melon. When he kissed her, her lips became persimmons. Entering her was like severing a moist fig in two. During his waking hours, it was the thought of Hannah's baked kugel, which was like eating a cloud, that made him grow tumescent.

Last night when he dreamt of Hannah, she was wearing the blue robes of the Madonna in the painting of the Annunciation he had seen through the church doors of St. Zaccaria. She spoke to him, whispering words of love. When he awoke, Hannah's dream words were fresh in his mind, and he feverishly transcribed them. When he reread what he'd written, he knew that this was the love letter that would melt ice, never mind the female heart.

Now, as he set up in the square, Isaac tried to wash away the memory of the dream. He bit into a lump of bread he had tucked in his shirt. Afraid of breaking off a tooth, he crumbled it with his fingers and sucked the crumbs until they were soft enough to swallow. The letter, securely tucked under the waistband of his new breeches, crinkled and stabbed at his belly. As he arranged his writing material — ink, quill, and parchment — he glanced around, hoping to catch sight of Hector, the local agent for the Society for the Release of Captives and the man who held his fate in his hands.

In the past week, in exchange for a few coins he could use to buy gruel, stale bread, and the occasional piece of fruit, Isaac had hauled canvas, delivered provisions to the ships at dock, and watched Joseph sell slaves down at the wharf to the galley captains. But not once had he set eyes on Hector.

Now, Joseph appeared out of nowhere before him, rubbing his temples and looking worried.

156

'Have you got my letter? I must have it *now*.'

Isaac extracted it from his waistband and made a ceremony of blowing away the dust and brushing off a few crawling ants. Then he handed it to Joseph with a flourish.

Like many illiterate men, Joseph was cowed by the sight of the written word. Gingerly he accepted the missive, opened it, and pretended to read it while Isaac waited. A seagull flew overhead and narrowly missed depositing a consignment of excrement on Joseph's head. The letter said everything a lover could say to his intended. It said what Isaac would say to Hannah if he ever saw her again.

'Shall I read your masterpiece?' he asked, taking it back from Joseph.

Joseph nodded, looked at the ground, and hitched up breeches stained yellow with sheep's piss, a gesture that unleashed an acrid smell. His mare moved nearer, her ears twitching like crows on a branch.

Isaac customarily read aloud in a singsong cadence more suited to the reading of a bill of lading than a love letter, but this time he drew on his experience as an occasional cantor in *shul* and sang out in a high, clear voice: *'Dearest Gertrudis.'*

By the time Isaac finished, tears had formed in Joseph's eyes. 'A very fine letter. I could not have written better myself.' He blew his nose on a rag, producing an alarming honk like the call of a gander. Then he opened the cloth to peer inside, as though searching for pearls or rubies.

There was one sentence — and one sentence

only — in the whole missive that was not complete and perfect. Isaac said, 'There is a small detail you must supply. What colour are Gertrudis's eyes?' Isaac had almost written *black*, because that was the colour of Hannah's eyes.

'Damn me if I ever noticed,' Joseph said. 'What colour are most women's eyes?' Shifting a coil of hemp rope from one shoulder to the other, he said, 'Brown, I guess.' He swivelled his head to look at his mare. 'Same colour as old Cosma's here. And another thing I just remembered — she has eyelashes.'

Was there no limit to the idiocy of this man who held Isaac's life in his hands? Isaac inserted the word *brown* in the final sentence, sprinkled sand on the writing, and when it was dry, held the letter out to Joseph.

Isaac gestured to the bottom of the page. Joseph pressed to the parchment a thumb so dirty it was not necessary to first coat it with ink. Isaac sprinkled Joseph's print with more sand, set it in the sun to dry for a moment, and then folded the letter into a rectangle. He dripped candle wax to seal it. When the wax was almost dry, he sealed it with his own thumb.

'Take the letter to her and then prepare yourself. She will swoon in your arms.'

'We will see what she has to say.'

Isaac patted the letter and gave it to Joseph.

'You may live to see Venice again, my friend,' Joseph said. Then he grasped his horse by its bridle, and that familiar gesture seemed to make him revert to his previous self. 'Get over to my shop now. I have work for you.' Then Joseph, his

158

mare's head bobbing over on his shoulder, headed in the direction of the harbour, presumably to deliver the letter to Gertrudis.

It pained Isaac to see Joseph disappearing down the road with a letter that was meant for Hannah.

Isaac sighed and wrapped his pot of ink, parchment, and quill into a square of linen and knotted the corners. So lost in thought was he that he was startled to see, through the sulphurous smoke from the ship-repair yards, a lanky, horse-faced man tying his mare to a post. The man advanced toward him, proceeding in a half trot that made Isaac wonder why the man had bothered with a horse in the first place. It must be Hector. Assunta had said that Hector had an equine look about him. This man wore breeches so short that, had he been a Venetian, they could have been explained only by the expectation of a high tide. It was as though he were wearing the clothes of a shorter, stouter brother. Over his chest, he wore a close-fitting jerkin of black wool.

The *Esecutori contro la Bestemmia* would find no silk, no rings, and no golden chains on this man — no violation of the Sumptuary Laws at all. And yet, there was a certain foppishness to his aspect — something in the way he folded his neck piece. And the smooth appearance of his shirt suggested the application of a hot iron, or at the very least the pressing between two boards.

He came to a halt in front of Isaac, casting a dark stripe of shadow on Isaac's knees and torn breeches. 'Hello, Signore, you must be Isaac Levi.'

'Hector, I presume?' Isaac scrambled to his feet and shook his hand. 'Isaac Levi, at your service.'

Hector gave Isaac's hand a shake. 'So you are managing to survive?' He glanced at the quill protruding from the tied bundle of linen. 'Writing letters for local people?'

Hector's voice was high-pitched but kind. He smelled pleasantly of woodsmoke and lemons.

'Joseph, the man who owns me, has agreed I can write the odd letter here and there as long as I give him two-thirds of my fees.' To hide his nervousness, Isaac gabbled on. 'I am a one-eyed man in the country of the blind.' He grinned. 'But enough of my poor ramblings. What is the news from Venice?' Isaac clasped Hector's arm and helped him to be seated on a fallen log, trying to conceal his excitement, willing himself to act as calmly as if he were at his desk in the ghetto. When they were both seated, Isaac asked, 'Is there any news of my wife, Hannah?'

'The Society writes me that she is well.'

There was something about his eye-shifting manner that made Isaac apprehensive. 'Is that all? She is well?'

When Hector said nothing more and the silence grew worryingly long, Isaac said, 'What of my fate? Have you fixed on the price of my freedom? What value do the Knights place on the head of this homesick merchant?'

'I should warn you that there has been a difficulty.' Hector waved his hands, slim with long tapered fingers, as though to fan himself, although the day was not warm. 'Allow me to

160

begin by saying that the Society is most sympathetic to your suffering.'

Isaac nodded.

'However, this past winter,' Hector continued, 'a shipload of seventy-five Jews, men, women, and children, were captured while sailing to Salonika. The Society ransomed and returned each and every one to their families.'

Isaac's knee had taken on a life of its own and would not stop bobbing up and down. He clasped his hands around it to steady it. 'I am happy to hear it.' But he was not happy. He was wondering why Hector's eyes refused to meet his. 'The Society is carrying out its duties, as it should. But what of my own release?'

'Before we get to that . . . ' Hector withdrew from under his arm a blue velvet sack embroidered with Hebrew letters and handed it to Isaac. 'I have brought you a prayer shawl, a yarmulke, and phylacteries. Use them well. They were difficult to obtain.'

'Thank you, Hector. You are kind. But what I really want is to leave this island. Do I have a chance?' He had bathed in the sea yesterday to rid his body of lice so at least he would not get his new *tallis* lousy.

'I will put it as plainly as I know how. The treasury of the Society is empty. There is not a *scudo* for your release. The Salonika incident was without precedent.'

Isaac wished Hector would look at him so he could read his face. 'Yes, I understand — more delays. But when will negotiations begin? What is the convention? I presume buying the life of a

Jew is no different from buying a bolt of silk or a sack of pepper. You ask the Knights their price. You pretend to be outraged. They reduce their price a little, then dicker, dicker, dicker, back and forth and' — Isaac snapped his fingers — 'soon an amount is agreed upon that makes both parties wretched.'

'I do not think you comprehend my meaning. There can be no negotiating if there is no money.' Hector looked at him now. 'Quite simply, the milk cow is dry.'

Isaac tried to still his mind. 'But a cow can be freshened. The Society is experiencing a temporary shortage of funds. I understand. But every merchant pays a tariff into the Society's coffers every time a ship leaves the port of Venice with Jews aboard. In time, the ducats will accrue.'

Hector leaned over and placed a hand on Isaac's shoulder. 'Yes, that is how the Society is funded, but it will be several years before it has the money to pay your ransom.' Hector picked up a willow twig from the ground, evidently reluctant to say more.

'Of course I knew my release would not happen overnight, but I did not expect this.' Isaac rose to his feet. 'Hector, look at me. I am sitting on the bones of my arse. For the moment, I have managed to persuade my owner not to send me to my death as a galley slave. The Society is my only hope of getting off this godforsaken island. I have managed to keep myself alive through my tongue, my wits, and my pen, but I have no reserves of flesh and grow

162

weaker every day.' Isaac cast his eyes around the bleak square in which they sat, horse- and mule-driven carts kicking up dust, leaving steaming piles of excrement behind. 'Although its coffers may be empty, maybe the Society can find other sources. I am not without friends. Perhaps a private benefactor could be persuaded to help.' Isaac waited for Hector's reply.

Sympathy softened Hector's face. 'I have inquired, but I am told it is not possible.' He toyed with a stick, scratching it in the ground. Hector knew more than he was revealing, Isaac thought.

'*Mio bueno amico*, getting information from you is like my wife's work, dragging unwilling babies from their mothers' wombs.' He wished Hector would cease tormenting the ground with his willow stick. It made a nasty sound. 'Who are you dealing with at the Society? Mordacai Modena, my fellow Ashkenazi?' Modena was a peasant fit for nothing but raising carp in tubs of stagnant water. Isaac tried to stop talking so Hector could speak, but he found that while desperation may have broken his spirit, it had also loosened his tongue. 'Is he putting up obstacles?'

'It is not Modena.' Hector glanced at his horse, munching grass a few feet away, as though he would like to be on his way. 'It is a cruel fact. There is no more money and will not be for years. I am sorry for you.' Hector rose and brushed his hat before placing it on his head. 'I will bring you food from time to time. I will come again to visit you. It is the best I can offer.'

He straightened his breeches and adjusted the front of his shirt. 'I will be off. Will you help me onto my horse?'

They walked over to the mare. Flies had gathered around her eyes. Isaac bent, laced his hands together, and offered them to Hector, who placed a foot in Isaac's hand. With an upward thrust, Isaac gave Hector a boost up onto the horse's back. Hector settled himself in the saddle. He slid his narrow feet into the stirrups and gathered up his reins.

'Goodbye, Isaac.'

'Thank you for your visit,' Isaac muttered, as Hector rode away.

When the man and his mare were out of sight, Isaac gave himself over to rage, cursing the God who had abandoned him. His last hope was gone. He might as well throw himself into the sea. Better a fast death than a slow starvation. If he failed to deliver Gertrudis's heart to Joseph, he would be on the next galley to leave port. Even if he succeeded in wooing the woman for that oaf, what was gained? He would have his freedom but no passage off the island.

He paced the square, picking up rocks at random and hurling them at a tree. When one ricocheted and hit him in the leg, Isaac decided to strap on the phylacteries. Facing toward Jerusalem, he bowed back and forth, davening in prayer. It was all he had left. What was the point of railing at God?

13

Venice,
1575

There was no need for Hannah's heart to be pounding so. Jacopo and Niccolò would not harm the child. In this palazzo, each room bigger than any *loghetto* in the ghetto, staffed by dozens of servants, Matteo was safe. The only peril this cosseted noble child faced was from being overindulged.

But where in this vast palace could he be? She went to the window to see if the di Padovani gondola was still in sight. It was no longer there. She would search for him on the ground floor. Perhaps Giovanna had taken him. Or perhaps a cook or a housemaid was giving Matteo suck to give Giovanna respite. Hannah would find the child, assure herself that all was well, and then quickly take her leave to avoid running into the two brothers.

A terrible thought occurred to her. Had Lucia's mind become so unhinged that she had harmed the child? Hannah thought of the incident of the silversmith's wife who smothered her baby. She dismissed the thought from her mind. Lucia was ill and weak, but not mad.

Hannah had paused, about to descend the stairs, when she heard footsteps and the low murmur of male voices. Two figures appeared at the far end of the hallway. She thought of racing down the stairs herself, but realized she could not reach the bottom before they spotted her.

There was a niche midway along the corridor, just before the staircase, where a pair of heavy damask curtains hung. Slipping into the semicircular alcove, she pulled the drapery closed, waiting for the men to pass. In the alcove was a statue of the Virgin and Child. The Virgin's knee pressed into Hannah's hip as she tried to make herself smaller. She wriggled behind the statue, closer to the wall, but no matter how she squirmed, her hip protruded into the hallway, outlined by the damask curtain. There was no helping it. Into the folded hands of the Virgin, she thrust her bag with the birthing spoons and ducats. Taking a deep breath, she clasped the statue around the waist, curved her body to squeeze behind it, and pressed her face into the Madonna's marble lap. The marble was as cold as canal water in winter; she shivered and fought the impulse to pull away, but she could not without exposing herself to view.

Through a slight parting of the curtains, she watched Jacopo and Niccolò sneak along the corridor. Niccolò was holding a bundle in his arms. He stumbled, cursed quietly, and nearly dropped what he was carrying. Before they reached her recess, she nudged the drapes into place with her knee. As they passed, she could smell Jacopo's eau de cologne and Niccolò's sweat. Her heart beat so loudly she was afraid they would hear. She listened as they descended the staircase.

When she could no longer hear their footsteps, she grabbed her bag from the Virgin's hands, pushed her way out from behind the statue, and began to make her way down the stairs, clutching the stone balustrade to steady herself. As she hurried, Hannah listened for the sound of a baby's wail, but all she heard was her own harsh breathing and the sound of their retreating footsteps.

When she reached the ground floor, which comprised the warehouse for the family business, she lost sight of the two men. She peered into the darkness, unsure which way to go. Then she heard a squeal. She recognized the noise — the terrified shriek of a baby.

The cry came from the other end of the warehouse, where the boats unloaded cargo for storage. A pine torch in a holder on the wall hissed and sputtered. Silhouetted against the rectangular opening to the loading dock was a familiar dark, cloaked figure. She squatted behind a barrel for fear he would spot her. But he turned toward the doorway to the canal and adjusted his purchase on the bundle in his arms. Several barrels lined the side of the wall. She crouched behind one and then another and then another, working her way closer. There was no sign of Jacopo.

Though dusk had fallen and the light was receding, there was just enough illumination to make out the prominent nose and curly hair of Niccolò. He was making ready to get into a gondola. The bundle in his arms began to cry, and Niccolò placed his open hand over the child's nose and mouth and held it there, then

167

stepped into the gondola. As the boat listed under his weight, he placed Matteo in the cabin. Then he took up the oar and pushed the boat away from the loading dock.

Hannah looked around, hoping to see a manservant, but there was no one, not even a night porter. And there was no time to race upstairs to summon help. Who was left to help her anyway, with the Conte and Contessa gone? The boat glided over the dark water toward the middle of the Grand Canal. Niccolò was leaving with the child!

She felt a stab of fear. It was dangerous for a Jew to be abroad after sunset. It was even more hazardous for a woman alone. But she had to act. Running out of the palazzo, she turned toward the canal, hoping to intercept the gondola. But by the time she reached the *calle*, the boat was disappearing into the distance, Niccolò at the stern.

Hitching up her skirts, she darted after the gondola, shoving aside the few passers-by still on the streets. The tide was high; the street sloshed with water. Her sandals grew soggy and heavy. Stopping for a moment, she wrenched them off, thrust them into her bag, and resumed her chase. A barge pulled out in front of Niccolò's gondola, forcing him to put up his oar for a moment, allowing her to shorten the distance that separated them. She ran on, the sweat trickling off her body, sidestepping a handcart carrying fruit. Now the gondola was in motion again, moving effortlessly along the Grand Canal fifty paces ahead of her. After the bend in the canal, it turned north into the Rio San Marcuola. If the gondola continued in this direction, she did not have a hope of catching it. Niccolò would reach the open waters of the lagoon and the islands of Murano, Burano, and Torcello.

The Fondamenta was slippery with refuse and water, and she had to slow her pace or risk skidding to her knees. She tried to guess his destination. Could he be heading to the Arsenale, the enormous ship-building yard? Or the Castello docks, the poor area populated by ship workers? But no, both of those places lay in the opposite direction. Then, just as she was about to give up hope in her foot chase, the gondola slowed in front of the Church of San Marcuola. It veered and Niccolò ducked his head as his boat passed under a bridge. She was near enough now to have heard the baby's cry echoing across the water, but she heard nothing.

Niccolò turned west at the Rio di San Girolamo, and then at the Calle Ormesini, where he docked the gondola and tossed a line around a mooring pole. Hannah ducked behind a pillar as he disembarked.

Night fog was settling over Venice, making it impossible for Hannah to see if Matteo was concealed under Niccolò's cloak or if he had left the baby in the gondola. Niccolò strode along the *calle*. Hannah let him get several paces ahead of her before she set off.

By now Matteo should have whimpered from hunger or a soiled diaper, but no sound issued from beneath Niccolò's cloak. She drew closer. Just as she convinced herself that the baby

169

was abandoned on the boat or dead, Niccolò stumbled on a mooring cleat, cursed, and fell to one knee. The jostling must have startled Matteo, for a tiny foot slipped out from under his blanket and she heard a cry.

During the daytime, the spectacle of a nobleman carrying a baby would be remarked upon. But now the streets were deserted except for a rare passer-by too anxious to return to the safety of his home to notice. A passing funeral gondola draped in black curtains caused the water of the canal to splash against the steps leading to a *traghetto* landing. Hannah's bare feet were numb with cold.

Niccolò veered down the Calle Farnese, and Hannah realized his destination with a sick feeling in the pit of her stomach. When he mounted the steps of the Ponte dei Ghetto, there could be no mistake. This bridge led to only one place: the Jewish ghetto.

Hannah walked to the crest of the bridge, where she could see Vicente sleeping in his makeshift shelter, a half-empty bottle of wine by his side. Most nights Vicente would have lowered the iron bar across the heavy wooden gates and shoved the deadbolts in place, but he had received his wages today and that meant he had had the money to buy several flagons of wine. The gates were ajar, allowing anyone to sneak through. Vicente did not awaken when Niccolò slipped past him. He would not budge when Hannah passed by either, but nonetheless, she pulled her head scarf higher around her face and hurried on.

Niccolò crossed the *campo*, passed under the *sotoportego*, past the closed and shuttered Banco Rosso, past the empty shops of the moneylenders where Isaac had once laboured next to the other bearded, swarthy men, hump-backed from bending over their brass scales, their faces contorted with the effort of keeping their loupes in place.

The *campo* was so quiet that she could hear the splashing of someone on the floor above her urinating into a chamber pot. Niccolò strode ahead, moving with purpose. She forged on, her eyes fixed on his broad back, afraid to let him get more than a few paces ahead of her.

He passed the *Scuola Italiana* and, a few steps later, the *Midrash* where the Rabbi in the mornings gave Hebrew lessons.

Niccolò turned down a lane flapping with drying clothes, hardly wide enough for the passage of a broad-shouldered man. She knew it ended without warning at the Rio di San Girolamo.

Niccolò carried the child at an awkward angle, the better to squeeze between the tilting walls of the buildings. At the end of the alley, three steps led down to the rio. Her relief at keeping him in sight gave way to alarm. Did he intend to hurl Matteo into the water? She held back, pressing against the door of the bakery, afraid to enter the alley. There was no place for concealment in that narrow passage, no recessed doors, no convenient spaces between buildings; Niccolò had only to turn around to spot her.

There was one shop in the alley, the abattoir

located at the very end, positioned on the edge of the canal so that entrails, gristle, and fat could be easily disposed of. The *shochet*, the ritual slaughterer, Israel Foà, would have many hours ago slit the throat of his last pullet for Shabbat, closed up the shop at sunset, and gone home to eat his evening meal with his wife and children.

Niccolò halted in front of the abattoir and placed Matteo on the ground. He took a step back and charged the door, ramming it with his shoulder. A couple of hard thrusts and the door gave way. He tumbled in and then returned to pick up the baby and bring him inside. Hannah inched her way down the narrow passageway, skidding on the mud and seeping effluvia from the abattoir. The premises' sole window was shuttered, but through the cracks she could see the flicker of a candle.

Matteo lay motionless on a scarred table in the centre of the small shop. She watched while Niccolò unwound Matteo's swaddling bands, exposing his chubby legs, his fat, archless feet. His feet did not kick at the air; his hands, as pale as stars, did not wave at the light of the candle. On the table next to him sprawled the honeycombed tripe of a cow's stomach, spongy and white. Niccolò reached for the *shochet's* knife hanging on the wall behind him.

Ignoring everything except the knife in Niccolò's hand, Hannah ran and flung open the door. She wanted to hurl her body over Matteo's. She screamed, 'Stop, for the love of God! What are you doing?' The dizzying smell of the rancid tripe and entrails scattered on the

172

floor made her reel and nearly collapse to her knees.

Niccolò's eyes widened and he froze holding the knife in mid-air. Finally, he spoke. 'You dared to follow me?' His voice was calm, but the muscles around his mouth and chin were white from tension. 'Perhaps it is for the best. If I kill both the baby and you, it will look as though *you* killed him.'

'Why is he so still? What have you done to him?' Bile rose in her throat. She forced herself to swallow and to ignore the ringing in her ears. She would be no help to Matteo if she fainted. She wanted to snatch him up and run from this foul room. Matteo's chest rose and fell in shallow fits and starts. A leg twitched, then an arm. At least he was still alive.

'Stand away from him,' Niccolò ordered.

'Surely you do not mean to kill him. What harm has Matteo ever done to you?'

'The greatest harm you can imagine,' said Niccolò, still holding the knife. He walked to the door, closed it, and jammed a rickety chair under the handle to block her exit.

Hannah could feel the heat radiating off his body. 'Why bring him here, to the ghetto?' And then the answer dawned on her. 'You want Matteo's murder to look like the work of Jews.'

'I will not be upset if the moneylenders get what they deserve. They have been swindling Christians for decades.'

Hannah willed her breathing to slow. If she could remain calm, perhaps she could reason with this man who held the knife. It was her only hope. She could not overpower him. He stood a head taller than she, and was stronger, too.

'But no one will believe the Jews could do anything so evil.'

He laughed. 'Are you so naive? Of course they will. Especially when they find his flayed corpse nailed to the ghetto gates.'

Blood libel, the belief that Jews killed Christian babies and used their blood for ritual purposes, was an accusation that had been levelled against Jews for hundreds of years. The *Prosecuti* would care only that Matteo's body was found in the ghetto. It was the only evidence needed to implicate the Jews. Hannah's thoughts were racing. Niccolò must have drugged the child, for Matteo lay still, his head lolling to one side.

Niccolò stood over the table, his feet planted apart. He said, 'This child has cheated me and Jacopo out of everything we have waited for for so long. It is only right that we should deprive him of his life.' He spoke without looking at the baby.

'So you kill Matteo to inherit the Conte's money?'

'And his estates, and his precious palazzo, and his warehouses of silk and spices, and his title.'

A thought struck her as she watched Niccolò averting his eyes from the child. She lowered her voice. 'I have seen the *shochet* at work many times. The killing of one of God's creatures must be done with respect and compassion. Slaughter is not just about killing; it is about avoiding needless pain and bringing sanctity to death.'

Hannah looked at the knife in his hand. 'Once as a child I watched Israel Foà in this very slaughterhouse, holding a lamb between his knees. The poor creature struggled, so that Israel's knife slipped and instead of severing the throat with one quick, decisive stroke, he merely nicked it. The terrified lamb broke free of his grasp and ran bleating out the door and down the alley. Israel had no trouble following its trail of blood into the square, where he put the creature out of its misery with a blow of the knife. If you do not kill him right, the child will scream so loud it will bring half the ghetto down upon you.' She looked him straight in the eye. If he was moved by her story, he concealed it well. 'It should not be a hard thing to kill such a small creature. I have killed chickens and game birds.'

'You are talking nonsense.'

'You are going to kill me anyway. Let the child's murder be on *my* head rather than yours. Give me the knife.' She held out her hand.

Matteo's eyelids twitched as he slept.

Niccolò said, 'You must think me a fool.' Then he lunged for her, holding the knife over her head. She backed away from him, trying to keep her footing. He came at her, about to plunge the knife into her chest, when his jacket caught on the corner of the table and he stumbled. Taking advantage of his imbalance, Hannah gave him a shove, sending him skidding. Trying to regain his footing, he came at her again. He slipped but caught himself on the wall.

The knife fell from his grip and careened a few paces away. Hannah bent down and grabbed it by the blade, feeling the cold iron press into her fingers.

She straightened, the hand holding the knife at her side. Niccolò, tight with anger, pulled himself to his feet and scrambled over to the table. He grabbed Matteo and held him high above his head.

'I will have my knife back.' Bits of offal clung to his breeches where he had fallen. 'Or I will dash him to the floor. That will do the job as quickly as the knife.'

'Give him to me. Better for him to be killed by a hand that loves him than by your indifferent one.' Matteo was quiet, taking only shallow breaths, not crying, seemingly unaware of what was happening. 'You do not have the stomach for the task. I can tell by your face.'

'Place the knife on the table in front of me!' He continued to hold Matteo aloft. 'You Jews with your endless talk. Quick as a lawyer you are, arguing this point, arguing that, hoping to find my weak spot.' Niccolò's face was obscured by shadows.

Hannah stood with her feet apart and, leaning over, placed the knife on the table in front of him.

He lowered the baby to the level of his waist. In the dim light, Matteo appeared so white he seemed to glow. His stomach started to gurgle, and then, whether from a sleeping draught, the stink of the abattoir, or the rough handling from Niccolò, he began to vomit. Copious amounts of greenish bile spewed from his throat and landed on Niccolò's shirt front.

Niccolò grimaced in disgust, placed him on the table, and reached for a cloth hanging on a hook behind him. He wiped at his chest. 'For God's sake, let us get this over with. You insist on making this a ritual killing? Fine. You can guide me and tell me how to do this right.' He watched her, his body tense, alert for sudden movements.

'Of course. I do not know what Christian prayer would be fitting, so a Jewish one will have to do,' said Hannah. 'I will say a *brokhe*, a blessing, even though he is a gentile.' Hannah pulled her head scarf higher. Her mind was racing so fast she could not summon the blessing to mind. She lifted her hands over the baby's head, closed her eyes, and intoned, ''Blessed are you, Lord our God, King of the Universe.''

Niccolò said, 'You are taking too long. The sleeping draught is beginning to wear off.'

Hannah said, 'Quickly, put your hand on his chest to steady him. If he wriggles, your knife will not cut straight and true.'

Matteo stirred. Niccolò held the knife in his right hand and positioned it next to the baby's head. The blade reflected Matteo's tiny fist.

'If you turn him toward me,' Hannah said, 'then you can get a good approach.'

Knife raised, he moved in closer and so did Hannah.

'His neck is very fleshy,' Hannah said. 'You must hit the neck vein so the blood will spurt. Stroke his throat so his head tilts back.'

Niccolò stroked the infant's neck with the dull side of the blade. Matteo moved his head.

Hannah said, 'Now stand back from the child

177

as far as you can without letting go of his chest.'

Niccolò extended his arm, keeping his fingers splayed on the tiny chest, his knife an arm's span from Matteo's throat.

A faint scuffling noise came from the corner, behind a barrel. A rat. Niccolò glanced over, his eyes, for an instant, leaving the baby and Hannah. It was enough. She might not get another chance.

She sprang, grabbing for his knife. The suddenness of her action startled him, and after a brief struggle, he lost his grip on the weapon. She began slashing first at his eyes, then at his shoulder, his chest, his upper arm, any part of him she could reach, driving him away from the table where Matteo lay. Again and again she hacked at him, gripping the knife with both hands and slicing, as blood flowed down his face. Niccolò was so astounded by the suddenness of her attack that for a second he did not react. Then he yelled and rushed at her, grabbing for her. She was too fast and danced out of his reach. The blood coursing down his face blinded him.

The blade hit bone with a crunch, as satisfying a sound as any she had heard. Blood from his arm spurted in an arc and drenched her. Half blinded by it, Hannah slashed and slashed and could not stop. Her knife tore his shirt into strips, revealing his bleeding chest.

Finally, she sliced deep through his side, splintering his ribs where the knife penetrated. He clasped his chest and fell back against the table. 'Holy Mother of God.' He skidded

178

backwards and pulled at the table, struggling to stay upright, but he succeeded only in pulling it on top of himself. Matteo dropped with a thud to the floor, screaming in terror, his face as red as the blood flowing from Niccolò's wounds. Hannah scooped Matteo off the floor and clutched him to her breast.

Perhaps she was possessed. Were these not the actions of a witch? Taking pleasure in wounding? Even with the infant in her arms, even with Niccolò lying motionless, his blood pooling at her feet, she wanted to continue hacking at his flesh.

Matteo's screams brought her to her senses. She forced herself to toss the knife to the floor. Matteo was hysterical, struggling against her grip, sobbing. She placed him on a chair. Then she grabbed Niccolò and dragged him by his heels out the door to the canal. For once, she was glad of the slime coating the cobblestones, which made it easier to slide his body into the water. He fell in with a dull splash. Without waiting to see whether his body sank, she ran back into the shop, snatched up Matteo and her bag, and raced back through the maze of alleys and passageways. Out through the gates of the ghetto she ran, ignoring Vicente's snoring form, until she reached the Ponte dei Ghetto.

She needed to return the child to the palazzo, to tell the Conte of his brothers' actions. She looked down at her dress and at the child. Both of them were covered in blood.

And then she remembered. Her entire body started to shake as though with fever. The Conte

179

and Contessa had already left for Ferrara. There was only Jacopo at the palazzo. She had not saved the child only to deliver him back to one who would finish the job Niccolò had started.

With Matteo in her arms, she hurried back to the shop and found a bucket of water and a clean rag. She wiped the baby's face and hands. As she began washing herself, her legs began to tremble so violently she had to ease herself to a squatting position on the floor. She tried to smooth her hair and fasten it with hairpins, but the pins tumbled from her hand.

As she stared into the bucket of pinkish water in front of her, she asked herself where she could go. Who would take her in? She could not remain in the ghetto with this noble child, in his linen swaddling bands, wrapped in a blood-spattered silk blanket embroidered with the di Padovani crest. If the *Prosecuti* discovered Matteo in her *loghetto*, the *campo* would run red with Jewish blood and Hannah would be as guilty as if she had wielded the knife herself.

She must hide until the Conte and Contessa returned — but where? The only person Hannah knew outside the ghetto would never give her sanctuary — or would she?

14

Hannah stood in front of Jessica's house overlooking the Rio della Sensa pleading in vain with Matteo to cease his hungry wail. She clutched him, jiggling and cooing in a frantic manner that attracted the curiosity of a water carrier struggling along under a yoke of pails. At least she had managed to scrub the blood from Matteo's face. As she had made her way through the streets of Parochia San Alvise, she had stolen an ill-fitting dress and cap from a clothesline and stopped briefly to change into the clean garments, stuffing her bloody *cioppà* into her bag next to the birthing spoons.

She jerked the bell cord of her sister's home. The ring echoed along the Fondamenta della Sensa and throughout the house. Her stolen clothes made her appear Christian — or as Christian as she was capable of looking, given her strong profile and black eyes. Her feet remained bare and they were frozen to the bone. It was fear, her trembling arms and her knees which would not stop shaking, not her foolish clothing, that made her as conspicuous as if she were sitting in the men's section in synagogue.

Matteo continued his crying. She reached inside the neck of her dress, touched the silver amulet, and brought it to her lips. The amulet was warm from her body, and she took comfort from it — but of what use would a *shadai* be now?

The house was pretty, as Jessica had said, with elegant arches in Istrian marble and fine stone tracery giving a lacy appearance to the façade. On the second floor the façade was a bas relief of the Annunciation. Thank God, she thought, the street level has no wall shrine with votive candles and a figure of a scourged Christ, just a ham hung in the window for all to see, a silver cup suspended under it to catch the dripping fat. Backing up a couple of steps and craning her neck, she glimpsed an *altanà* on the roof with a wisteria vine spilling over the rail. Shifting drowsy Matteo to her other arm, she rang the bell again.

When a maid finally opened the door, Hannah said, 'Tell your mistress Anni is here.' This was the nickname Jessica had given her when, as a child, Jessica could not pronounce the letter *H*. The young maid, no doubt suspicious of this bare-footed late-night caller wearing an ill-fitting dress, closed the door and left Hannah standing on the step while she went to speak to her mistress.

Hannah felt the eyes of dozens of homeless men and women passing by, desperate for a doorway to sleep in for the night. They stared at her: the dishevelled woman cowering there, clasping a screaming baby. *Please hurry*, Hannah silently prayed. She looked down and noticed a cut on her wrist that was still bleeding. In her haste she had neglected to bind it with a rag. She licked off the blood. A bloodstain the size and shape of a hummingbird marked Matteo's blanket. She refolded it to conceal the spot. If

Jessica refused to admit her, Hannah might as well surrender herself to the *Prosecuti* now and be executed as a witch.

Hannah's arms ached and she transferred the now-sleeping baby from one arm to the other. Finally, when the bells of San Marco chimed signalling midnight and Hannah was about to steal away, to go God knows where, the maid returned, stared for a moment at Matteo, and ushered them into the house, up the stairs, and into a bedchamber almost as grand as the Contessa's.

Three weeks earlier, when Hannah had seen Jessica on the Grand Canal, it had been dark, lit only by the gondolier's lantern, which had cast deep shadows. Now Jessica sat in the glow of dozens of candles in front of a mirror while her lady's maid arranged her hair in curls. Her dark hair was swept high off her forehead and cascaded down her neck and around her shoulders. Jessica's skin was like the velvety skin of a peach. When Jessica was a child, Hannah had been tempted to take a nibble of one round cheek to see if juice would flow.

Jessica's back was turned to her, her eyes fixed on her own reflection in the mirror behind her dressing table. 'You have come to apologize for your rudeness? It is the only excuse for your visit I can think of.'

Hannah swallowed hard. Matteo lay still in her arms. She carefully placed her bag on the floor in front of her. Then she said, 'I have no place to stay. I am asking you to give me shelter. I know I have no right to ask, but it is for a few days only.'

Jessica fussed with a tiny pot on the table in front of her for so long that Hannah thought she had not heard her. Finally she replied, 'You would not understand the intricacies of a *toilette*. You have never taken any trouble with your appearance, other than to fling on your rumpled clothes from the night before. Do you still hang your entire wardrobe on a single hook behind your door?' She twisted her head to look over her shoulder as the maid applied a beauty mark to her back. 'I would not be seen looking like you. You, with your pale face and oversized dress with the bodice pouching out.' She wriggled a shoulder to test whether the sequin was securely affixed. 'Now you carry a bundle in your arms. Of what? Rags? Is this the new fashion?'

Although Jessica had hardly glanced at her, she seemed to know the minute details of Hannah's appearance. Hannah could think of nothing to say. Her sister's cold confidence always had a way of making her feel foolish. With one look or negligent wave of her hand, she could make Hannah feel clumsy, unable to stand straight, unsure of what to say or do.

'I know my words wounded you. I spoke cruelly, and I apologize,' Hannah said.

'I wonder that you have the audacity to ask anything of me, let alone that I take you in.' The maid, a young girl of about fifteen, teased a tress of her mistress's dark hair, secured it with a pearl on a silk thread, and pretended not to listen. 'Out of curiosity, this costume of yours — what role are you playing? A shepherdess? A penitent on a pilgrimage to Santiago de Compostela? If so, you lack the requisite clamshell around your neck, which can be remedied. I may have one around the house I can give you the loan of.' When Hannah made no reply, Jessica said, 'Oh, of course!' She clapped her hand to her forehead, careful not to disarrange her hair. 'A laundress! That would explain the bundle.' She picked a stray hair from her gown.

Hannah felt a fool in spite of her growing anger. She used to change Jessica's swaddling bands; now she had to beg her little sister, first for forgiveness, and then for shelter.

Matteo whimpered and arched his back, demanding food.

Her sister whirled about in her chair to stare. 'What in God's name was that? Have you managed to bear a child at last?'

'The child is why I am here, Jessica. I come because I have no one else but you to turn to for help.' Hannah was unable to keep her voice steady.

'You despise me and think I am immoral, and now you want my help?'

Jessica waved the maid out of the room and closed the door. She rose from her dressing table and bent over for a look at the baby, lifting the coverlet out of the way. Matteo waved a foot at Jessica. Reddish-blond wisps clung to his head; his eyes were shockingly blue.

'Are you mad? Have you lain with a gentile? This is a Christian child.'

'He is a Christian, but he is not mine.'

Matteo was crying, loudly now, his face red with fury. He waved his fists in the air.

'Was your need for a child so great that you stole him?' Jessica leaned closer to Hannah to be heard over Matteo's screams.

'He is in danger,' Hannah said. 'His uncle was trying to kill him. I need stay only a few days until his parents return.'

'You dare to bring this child to my house? You risk my life!' She peered at the tiny form screaming in Hannah's arms. 'Holy Mother, can you not shut him up? My neighbours will think I am castrating a cat.'

Hannah said, 'This is the newly born di Padovani infant.'

'Sweet Jesus, not just any Christian child but a noble one. I know the family well — two of the sons anyway.'

'His uncle was going to murder him in the ghetto and place the blame on me. The whole of the ghetto would have suffered the consequences. Does that not mean anything to you?'

'I am no longer a Jew,' Jessica said. 'Fortune has smiled on me. I have prospered. I have my pretty house, my patrons. I work hard and am skilful at what I do. I have a wonderful plan for amassing my fortune, but now you show up with a screaming brat to spoil it all.'

As Jessica strode to the window, she tripped on Hannah's bag, which clinked. She paused. 'And what is it you carry in that ratty sack of yours?' Before Hannah could stop her, Jessica reached in and drew out the unclean birthing spoons. 'My God! What are these filthy things?'

Hannah felt the blood rise in her cheeks. She replied, 'A tool of my trade. Birthing spoons.'

186

Seeing her sister's disgust, Hannah explained their purpose in more detail than required.

Jessica gave a shudder and dropped them back into the bag. 'You should have been born a man,' Jessica said. 'You remind me of Papa. Remember his tiny pincers for picking up gemstones?'

Hannah nodded in acknowledgment. Matteo had given up hope of food and fallen silent. Hannah placed him on Jessica's velvet canopied bed, trying not to imagine the acts that had taken place on the red coverlet.

The memory flooded back of Matteo on the *shochet's* table with Niccolò standing above him. 'I saved this child from his uncle. Niccolò had the baby in the ghetto abattoir and was holding a knife to his neck.' Her lower lip began to tremble. 'I killed him, Jessica. I killed a man. I kept stabbing him with the *shochet's* knife. Once I began, I could not stop. Then I dragged him to the canal and dumped his body. Maybe that makes me a witch — but what else could I have done?' She unwrapped Matteo and showed her sister the stain over the embroidered crest. 'This is Niccolò's blood.'

Jessica said, 'Holy Mother of God.'

Matteo began to cry again. Fat, round tears dripped down his cheeks and he held out his arms to Jessica to be comforted.

'Do not cry, my son.' The words seemed to fall naturally from her lips. 'You will be fine.' She wiped his tears away with the hem of her skirt. As Jessica bent over him, rearranging his blanket to bind him more snugly, Matteo grabbed her finger and clung to it. Jessica's face softened.

'You are no witch,' she said, looking up at Hannah. 'You are my sister.' Jessica watched as Matteo tugged her finger into his mouth. 'These two brothers are well known to my colleagues. Mine is as gossip-filled a profession as yours. Niccolò is — was — hot-blooded, always getting into fights. He was easily influenced by the older one. Both are gamblers and have, no doubt, borrowed heavily from the moneylenders in the ghetto. Now it is Jacopo you need to fear. You can wager that he will not give up until you and this child are dead.'

Hannah told her how Jacopo had demanded her two hundred ducats in exchange for the birthing spoons, and how she had managed to escape with her payment stashed in the bottom of her bag.

'The bastard, taking advantage of your desperation. These noble sons are all the same. Vain and reckless. No doubt he owes everyone from his cobbler to his valet.'

'I regret involving you.'

Jessica picked up Matteo and held him to her shoulder, jiggling him for comfort. 'Who else could you have gone to? Neither of us has acted as we should. We have taken turns inflicting deep wounds on each other. Sometimes I have played the tethered bull; sometimes you have. One thing is certain: we have both suffered.'

'What should I do?' Hannah asked.

'Return the baby,' said Jessica. 'Now, before it is too late. Sneak him back into the palazzo.'

'But I cannot. The Conte and the Contessa are in Ferrara.'

'Leave him with his wet nurse and tell her what the uncles have done.'

'Giovanna? If anything happens to Matteo she has promised to denounce me to the Inquisition.' Hannah paused. 'I must wait for the Conte to return so I can explain.'

'Explain what? That his brothers are in league to kill his son and heir? Why would he believe you?' Jessica placed the baby on her bed and began to untie the laces of her chemise. 'I do not have much time. I am meeting a patron. If I do not appear, he will think something is amiss.'

'Please, Jessica. Stay.'

'I cannot. If I do, he will come to the house.' She turned back to her dressing table. 'We will decide what to do as I dress.' Using a glass pipette, she dropped a measure of fragrant oil into a paste and mixed it with a tiny silver knife. 'Make yourself useful. Here — ' She handed Hannah a brush of rabbit's hair.

Dipping the brush into the mixture, Hannah began painting the creamy paste over Jessica's face, collarbones, and décolletage, smoothing it into the hollows of her clavicles and the valley between her breasts. As Hannah worked, her anger toward Jessica ebbed. It must have been the same for Jessica, because Hannah felt the tension leave her sister's shoulders and face; her mouth relaxed and her eyelids seemed to grow heavy. How like Jessica to relax under the caress of Hannah's hands. As a child, one of the few times she would sit motionless was when Hannah brushed her hair in long, steady strokes.

When she had covered Jessica's skin, giving it

a luminous cast, Jessica took the mortar back from her and poured the remaining cream into a tiny alabaster casket. 'I must not waste this. I have crushed a pearl into the mixture.' Then she unfastened the bodice of the garment, shrugged it off, and let it pool around her slim legs. 'Help me dress.' She grimaced. 'Fetch my corset.'

Hannah retrieved it from where it had fallen off her dressing screen and held it outstretched so that Jessica could hold it up by the bodice while Hannah laced it from the back.

'Tighter, for the love of God. Shall I waddle into the theatre as thick around the middle as a milkmaid?'

'Your face is red. I dare not pull you in any more.'

'My maid has never shown me such mercy.'

Hannah pulled again, feeling her own face grow crimson from the exertion. 'How is that? Can you draw breath or are you dead?'

Jessica took an experimental breath. 'Not dead yet, but that is sufficient.' She tugged the corset lower on her torso, exposing the rising mounds of her breasts, nearly exposing her nipples. 'Now, bring me that dress' — she gestured to the corner of the room — 'and hold it like this, over my head.' After a few moments, she was fully dressed. She turned to Hannah, thoughtful. Finally, she said, 'Go to Ferrara. Take the child to them. It is the only way. You can borrow some clothes from me. Leave tomorrow.'

'I cannot. My ship sails from Venice shortly.'

'And if the Conte does not return to Venice in time?' Jessica reached for a small glass bottle with an eyedropper on the dressing table.

'I trust that he will.'

She tilted her head back and pinched a drop of belladonna into each eye. She blinked until the drops dispersed. Her pupils dilated, making her eyes even darker.

'Coming to you is the hardest thing I have ever done. Let me remain with you,' Hannah pleaded. 'Then I will return Matteo, sail to Malta, and never impose on your kindness again.'

'It is just a matter of time before someone tells Jacopo that you are my sister. He knows full well where I live.'

Hannah opened her mouth to speak, but Jessica interrupted. 'And how do you intend to feed the child? Have you a wet nurse who will give him suck?'

'I will feed him pap until I can return him to the palazzo.'

'The cemeteries are filled with pap-fed babies.'

'I have no choice.'

Jessica tried to smile. 'Whatever comes, we will face it together, as sisters must.' She picked up Hannah's bag containing the birthing spoons and ducats and tucked it behind the headboard of her bed. 'It will be safe there,' she said, draping a muslin cloth over it. She slipped on a pair of earrings and grabbed her evening bag, then descended the stairs and left.

From the open bedroom window, Hannah observed Jessica making her way slowly along the Fondamenta, her heels so high that the gondolier had to steady her as she stepped on board. Jessica looked up at Hannah in the window and, after blowing a kiss, settled herself in the *felze*.

It was *acqua alta*. Hannah watched as boats competed for space in the narrow canal, churning up a tumult of crosscurrents. Some of the overloaded boats could not pass under the bridges. When the tide was low, some could not budge because their hulls were stuck fast on the silt and debris of the canal bottom.

And then, as Jessica's boat glided away from the dock, Hannah saw something that made her breath catch. A barge lumbered past with bodies stacked so high that it could barely pass under the bridge. Hannah smelled the decay of bloated bodies bursting from the pressure of their own juices. The boughs of rosemary and juniper covering them did little to mask the stink. She pressed a hand to her nose. During the last epidemic many Venetians had fled to the mainland, but armed peasants who feared contagion had beaten them and driven them back to Venice. She needed to get to Malta now, before the plague made travel impossible. It was likely that tomorrow the servants would flee to the countryside, terrified. Apart from Hannah, her sister, and the baby, the house would be empty. She need survive only another few days and then she would board the *Balbiana*.

She stood at the window gazing out onto the street until the moon rose full and high over the canal. Every creak in the floorboards, the voice of every passing pedestrian, and every splash from the canal made her stiffen.

What would kill them first? Jacopo, who by asking a few questions about town would surely discover that the Jewish midwife was the sister of the beautiful courtesan who lived on the Fondamenta della Sensa? Or the pestilence?

Matteo was sleeping on Jessica's bed, breathing softly, bubbles of saliva collecting in the corners of his mouth, eyelashes brushing his cheeks, tiny hands crossed under the coverlet. The two of them were safe for the present, but Jessica was right. Without a wet nurse Hannah could not keep Matteo alive. Pap-fed babies filled the cemeteries.

15

Valletta, Malta
1575

On the floor of Joseph's sail-making workshop, Isaac sat buried in a pile of canvas. With a curved needle, he was sewing telltales onto a square sail, the long, narrow strips of fabric tangling around his hand. A leather patch strapped to his palm allowed him to drive the needle through the canvas without piercing himself.

Isaac looked up at the sound of light footsteps entering through the front door. It was Gertrudis. Tall and fair, she entered the shop, bringing with her the smell of fresh-baked bread in a basket swinging from her arm. Her hair was bound with a ribbon; she had smudges of blue, brown, and black paint on her dress and a dot of white on her temples, as though she had thrust her hair back from her forehead with a paint-wet hand.

He was so entwined in the sail, he had to wiggle his toes to restore feeling to his legs so that he could rise to his feet. She gazed around the shop, squinting for a moment, her eyes not adjusted from the bright sun on the street outside. She had a familiar-looking letter in her hand. Her eyes settled on Isaac.

In a mellifluous voice, she asked, 'Where might I find Joseph?'

'He is down at the docks, victualling a ship.

Can I be of assistance?' Isaac asked.

She tossed the letter on top of the tangle of canvas. 'You can tell him to stop sending me letters.'

He had not had a good look at her before. Now he could see she was not young, thirty perhaps, but still pretty, with blue eyes and a mouth as sweetly curved as an archer's bow. The longer he scrutinized her, the more his heart sank. Assunta was right. Joseph was the god Tantalus, reaching for a bunch of grapes too far above his head.

'You are the Good Samaritan who donated five *scudi* to Sister Assunta to buy me?' Isaac asked.

'I am, for all the good it did you.'

'Nonetheless, you have my thanks.' Isaac picked up the letter and gently swatted it against the crumpled sail to remove the dust that was coating it. 'May I?' he said, indicating the letter.

Gertrudis nodded.

The letter had not been opened. The red sealing wax flaked and particles dropped onto the canvas. He unfolded it and made a show of reading the familiar words.

'It looks like a very fine letter to me. See how neat and evenly spaced the writing? And the angels above could not have fashioned smoother parchment.'

'Do not pretend you are illiterate. I have seen you scrivening in the square. It is not the quality of the penmanship or the composition that irks me. I do not fancy Joseph and I do not want his letters. Convey that message to him for me.' She

195

turned toward the door, but seemed reluctant to leave.

How could he stir the ember of desire in Gertrudis's heart? If he could only move her to give the man a second glance, Joseph would set him free and he would steal aboard the next ship for Venice.

'Joseph admires you as he admires no one else in the world. You will never find such a man as him. Do not throw away a chance for happiness.'

'And who do you think you are,' she demanded, 'to offer such misguided advice so freely?'

He kicked aside a mountain of canvas and bowed as best he could. 'Just another poor slave washed ashore on this island.' He had been about to say *on this miserable shore* but thought better of it. She was Maltese and must love her birthplace as much as he loved Venice. 'Isaac Levi, at your service.'

'You look half-starved.' She reached into the rush basket she carried over her arm and handed him a loaf of bread. 'I wager Joseph is not as generous in sharing his victuals as he is in tossing about words of love.'

Isaac took the bread gratefully and tore off a hunk with his teeth. The loaf was fresh and fragrant, still warm from the bakery.

She studied him as he ate. 'You are Venetian, are you not? You make our poor Maltese dialect sound almost elegant.'

He nodded, chewing slowly to make the bread last.

She glanced at his prayer shawl. 'You are a Jew?'

Isaac nodded again.

Gertrudis bunched up her long skirt and cast about for a place to sit. She saw a stool in the corner, hooked a foot around it, and dragged it toward her. 'This letter is the product of your bleeding hands, is it not?' Gertrudis gestured toward the letter, which Isaac had placed on the sails.

'I penned it, yes. Joseph's handwriting is not the best because his eyesight is failing him. But the composition is entirely his. A bit florid, but heartfelt, I assure you.' He regretted his lies before they were out of his mouth. Someday God would punish him. Right now he needed Gertrudis's help. He read her the letter.

'Joseph could no more scribe this letter than could one of my pigs. The sentiments expressed are beautiful. Coming from another man I might find them welcome.'

She eyed Isaac with such frankness that he was shamed by his own duplicity. Then she stood and rummaged in a heap of debris in the corner of the workshop. She fished out a scrap of canvas and smoothed it out over a pine board she found lying on the floor and placed on her lap. Then she stared at Isaac for so long, and without the least reticence, that it was as though he was an object rather than a man. She held up her thumb and forefinger, measuring the proportions of his face.

'You have an interesting countenance.'

He felt his face grow hot. He concentrated on eating the bread.

She propped the door open with a stone from

the street and sun flooded into the shop. From her bag, she took out a black-smudged scrap of linen and unrolled it. She retrieved a piece of willow-wood charcoal and began to sketch.

Isaac had seen artists sketch before. Tintoretto's workshop was just outside the gates of the ghetto on the Fondamenta della Sensa. It was common on hot days to see apprentices squatting on the sidewalk, roughing out drawings of biblical scenes on stretched canvas. But never had Isaac seen anyone, never mind a woman, sketch with such sure, rapid strokes.

So absorbed was she in her task that her hand flew over the canvas. From time to time, she paused and scrubbed at her drawing with the scrap of linen. She peered intently from him to her canvas and back again, as though watching a ball being tossed back and forth.

Isaac did not know where to look, so great was his embarrassment. He continued jabbing at the canvas sail with his needle. 'There is no sense in drawing a half-starved slave. Joseph is a handsome man with strong features. He is the one you want to draw, not me.' He strained to see the sketch, but she moved it out of reach.

'I would rather sketch a toad.'

She worked for a few minutes more and then turned the drawing around so he could see the charcoal outline. He saw his own long, serious face — dark eyes with pronounced eyelids, cheeks hollowed out by hunger, a sensual mouth that he did not recognize as his own, and a beard covering his square jaw. In her drawing, Isaac bore an unsettling resemblance to an altarpiece he had glimpsed through the open door of a church in Venice. It was a portrait of a majestic Moses receiving the commandments.

'You flatter me,' he said.

'I have drawn you — a portrait of you exactly as you are. Would you like to have it?'

She took up another scrap of canvas and carefully placed it on top of the first. Careful not to rub the two together, she rolled them up into a scroll. She fiddled with the blue ribbon in her hair until it came unfastened and her hair drifted down her shoulders. Isaac had a fleeting image of her tousled and fragrant from sleep, rising from her bed in the morning. As quickly as the thought came, he willed it from his mind.

She wound the ribbon around the scroll and tied it with a knot. Thrusting the scroll into his hand, she said, 'For you, to remember your sojourn on this island — and,' she added, 'me.' Then she tucked her skirt around her and settled back down on the stool in front of him. 'Now you must do something for me.' She leaned forward. 'I wish you to pen a letter.'

Isaac had a sinking feeling he knew what the letter would be. Once he had arranged his writing materials, he said, 'To whom shall I address the letter?'

'Begin thus: 'Joseph . . . though I am flattered by the honour you pay me by asking for my hand in marriage, I must decline and ask you not to write to me again.''

Isaac raised his quill from the parchment. How could he convince her to love that wretched creature? 'Would it advance Joseph's cause if I

199

told you he is a good man and has a flourishing business making sails and provisioning ships?'

'No.'

'What if I said Joseph is humorous and witty and will keep you merry all the days of your life?'

'I would say that you are a shameless liar.'

'What if I told you he is virile, with the equipment of a young bull?'

'Even if you were as glib as a hawker at the market and described Joseph as a veritable Adonis, your words would not persuade me. If the Virgin descended from the heavens and ordered me to wed Joseph I would refuse. He reeks of sheep piss. There is only one man who might please me,' she continued, 'but he does not appear to be interested.'

Isaac hesitated, wondering whether to say out loud what was on his mind. After all, she was the woman who at the slave auction had stepped out of the crowd and given Sister Assunta the five *scudi* to buy him from Joseph.

'What if I told you my freedom rested on your succumbing to his charms?'

Gertrudis looked at him, searching his face. 'You are jesting.'

'Does a sailor on a storm-tossed sea beseech in jest for God to save him?'

'Do all Jews reply to a question with another question?'

'Is there a reason they should not?'

Gertrudis gave a laugh that seemed to issue from deep within her. She had the longest eyelashes he had ever seen, fringing eyes as blue as the wild berries that grew on the outskirts of

Valletta. How could that lout have thought they were brown?

Isaac swallowed his pride and said, 'I see it is for nothing that I plead Joseph's cause, but for my sake, could you pretend to love him until I am free? Once I am gone, you can throw him in a pot and make soup of him for all I care.'

'Why should your fate matter a whit to me?' She spoke in a teasing, flirty way that made him wish he were anywhere but close to her.

'I have a loving wife waiting for me in Venice. I will do anything within my power to reach her,' he said.

'She must be the envy of many a woman.'

Isaac looked to see if her mouth curved into an ironic smile, but she appeared to be serious. He felt impossibly thin and miserable, but perhaps he had not lost all his looks. He was certain he had jumped to the wrong conclusion, but no, there was that glance from her again.

He hoped he could trust her. 'I understand you cannot pretend to surrender your heart to Joseph — but can you find me a boat? You must know someone with a skiff. You see, with a boat I could row out to one of the ships anchored in the harbour and, under the cloak of night, sneak aboard.'

Gertrudis shook her head. 'Many slaves have tried such a trick, but few have succeeded. Why not wait until you are ransomed?'

He felt the blood rise to his face. He would not admit to her that his fellow Jews could not come to his aid. 'A few *scudi*? And an oar? It is not so much to ask.'

She considered the matter. 'My cousin might have a boat I could lay my hands on, but I have something to ask of you in return.'

'Whatever is in my power, it shall be yours,' he said.

'Pen me a letter so fine it will win the heart of this man I am besotted with. And *if* it is good enough, and *if* I give it to him, and *if* he falls in love with me, then I will find you a sturdy boat. To show I am well and truly grateful, I will pay for your passage on a merchant vessel back to Venice.'

'A very generous offer.' But Isaac was puzzled. 'I now think *you* are jesting. You are far too good for the men of Malta, who as far as I can tell are no better than uncircumcised dogs.'

She grinned, and he cursed himself for mentioning circumcision. It had not occurred to him before, but Christian women must be curious about such things. It was only natural.

'Meet me in a week's time in the little cove south of the harbour. I will bring my cousin's skiff. Bring my letter and I shall give it to the recipient on the spot. Then the moon and the stars and a goatskin of wine will do the rest.'

'May I know the name of this most fortunate of men?'

Gertrudis placed her hand in his and gave it a terrifying squeeze.

16

Venice,
1575

Afternoon shadows stretched across the dining-room table as Hannah and Jessica sat eating turnip soup. A sack of limp lettuce and celery sagged in the corner where Jessica had tossed it when she returned from the market.

Hannah had heard the door creak open at dawn when Jessica arrived home from the theatre. Her sister had wearily collapsed into bed next to her. When Matteo awoke and whimpered from a dream, Jessica reached over and jiggled him until he returned to sleep. The three of them slept fitfully until a neighbour's rooster crowed. Then Jessica had gone out marketing, returning home a while later. Now, from across the table, she gazed at Hannah, as dewy and fresh as though she had slept for hours.

She said, 'There is hardly a house between here and the Rialto market that is untouched by the plague. All households struck must paint the sign of the cross on their doors as a warning to others.'

'So *this* is your brilliant idea? That we paint a cross on the door? You think Jacopo will be deceived by such a ruse?' asked Hannah.

'We must do something other than sit here and fret. Niccolò's disappearance is talked of in the streets. Jacopo will avenge his death,' Jessica said. 'Hurry up and finish your soup. We must prepare ourselves.'

Hannah sipped her soup while trying to ignore the bleating of the goat in the garden outside the window. Last night, when Jessica was at the theatre and Matteo was bawling like a hungry calf, Hannah had run out of the house and stolen a she-goat. If she had not had the good fortune to find the creature, she would have been forced to give pap to Matteo. After dragging the goat home and milking it, she had held a milk-soaked rag to Matteo's lips. He stopped crying, opened his mouth, and began to suck vigorously. When he had drunk his fill a look of contentment played over his face, and she hugged him so fiercely she could feel the sloshing of the milk in his belly. He squirmed and she released her grip, rubbing his back in slow, rhythmic circles until he rewarded her efforts with a loud burp.

Now Jessica turned to the sound of the bleating in the garden. 'I know that things must smell of whatever they must smell of. Canals reek of waste. Chamber pots reek of piss. And so it follows that goats smell like goats, but Mother of God, it is awful.' Jessica set down her bowl and wiped her mouth with a cloth. 'Come, let us be as far from that goat as possible.'

Hannah followed Jessica up the stairs to her bedchamber with Matteo in her arms.

Plaster cherubs peeked down from the ceiling with round, bright eyes as Jessica assembled soot scraped from the hearth, rancid olive oil, turmeric, garlic, and onions. The nanny goat had, without encouragement, provided all the dung required and more. Jessica lined up her array of pots of creams, hair dyes made of lye, unguents, powders, and lotions, all part of her arsenal of professional tools.

Hannah's head was throbbing. 'I will paint the cross, may God not take notice and strike me dead.' The ruse would not succeed, but to occupy herself with a task was preferable to doing nothing while awaiting Jacopo's arrival. She ran downstairs and scrawled a cross on the door with a piece of blackened ember from the hearth. When she returned to her sister's bedchamber, Jessica was sitting on the bed.

Jessica announced, 'We will begin with Matteo.' She picked up the baby and chucked him under his chin. 'I like you better now that you are not crying, but' — Jessica giggled — 'I do not know who smells worse, that goat or this baby.'

'He is soiled. I will remove his swaddling bands.' Hannah took fresh strips of linen from her bag and laid the child on the bed. She loosened the soiled cloth and put it to one side, noting, as she always did, his uncircumcised penis resting like a blind worm between his legs. As she bent over him, the *shadai* dangled from her neck, and he reached for it with waving hands.

Jessica looked over Hannah's shoulder at the naked baby. 'A few more days of goat's milk and his little cheeks will be round again.' She gave Matteo a smile as she gazed down on him. 'If only you do not start bleating like that wretched goat and nibbling my peonies, eh? Will you promise me, you naughty boy?'

'Where shall we start?' asked Hannah.

'Right here. We will experiment.'

Hannah placed a clean cloth under Matteo. His hand curled to his cheek and he gurgled and cooed, moving his freed legs and arms.

Jessica stirred a small pot of liquid with a stick, and then added an oily substance to it, drop by drop. 'This is the pus,' she said, holding up the stirring stick coated with a yellow, viscous fluid. 'Let us hope Jacopo does not get close enough to detect the smell of mustard.'

Hannah wrinkled her nose in disgust. 'I have never seen more convincing, reeking stuff. You are a gifted compounder, better than any apothecary in Venice.' She bent over Matteo. 'I will lift his chin so you can spread your paste on his throat, armpits, and groin.'

As Jessica applied the paste, Hannah recited from the Book of Job:

My flesh is clothed with rottenness and the
    filth of dust,
My skin is withered and drawn together,
In the night my bone is pierced with sor-
    rows —

'For the love of God, be quiet,' Jessica said. 'That is not what I want to hear.'

Using a cloth, she smeared the tiny body. Matteo struggled under Hannah's grip, waving his arms in protest at the cold paste.

Holding his legs apart so Jessica could paint his groin area, Hannah said, 'The smell is enough

206

to drive away the Angel of Death herself.' She angled her head toward the open window to take a breath.

'Now some of the arsenic paste on his face to turn him white.' Jessica brought over a new jar and began working on the child's rosy cheeks. 'Then affix a portion of this eggshell to his armpit. Plaster it to him with this muck. It will resemble the black swelling that typifies the pestilence.' Jessica made soothing noises at Matteo and started to sing a lullaby.

Hannah did as instructed, wiping more ointment on the child, and then stood back to admire her handiwork. Matteo was the very image of the Black Death. She shuddered. She had seen the corpse of such a child once, tossed on a barge floating under the Ponte delle Guglie on its way to Lazaro Island for burial.

Jessica stopped singing. 'Hannah, suppose . . . '

'What?'

Jessica hesitated. 'Suppose that by painting Matteo with buboes we cause him to contract the plague? Suppose the Angel of Death believes Matteo truly has the plague and carries him off?'

'Did you relinquish your brains when you abandoned your religion? You are thinking like a Christian.' Hannah put down the stick she had been using to spread the ointment on Matteo and looked at Jessica. 'The Angel of Death will believe he is already infected and, thinking her work is complete, will pass over him. Besides, the Angel of Death is already satiated. Last night the barges scraped the bottom of the Rio della

Sensa, they were so overloaded with corpses. Why would she trouble herself with one more baby? Worry instead about Jacopo.'

Hannah reached for the pail of goat's milk next to the bed and began to feed Matteo using the now-familiar method of dipping the rag in the pail and then putting it to his lips. When he had had enough, his eyes drifted closed and he snored peacefully, oblivious to his hideous appearance.

'An angel in devil's attire,' she remarked as she drew a blanket over him, careful not to disturb the ointments and eggshell on his groin. 'We need a knife, Jessica. Fetch one.'

Jessica put down her pot and returned a few moments later with a knife, which she handed to her sister. 'Hannah, I have made a lucrative career of pretending emotions I do not feel and saying things I do not believe. But I cannot kill a man.'

Hannah, remembering the sound of knife on bone in the abattoir, trembled. 'I will place the knife under the bed pillow.' Could she do it again? Attack a man like a creature possessed by the devil?

Hannah settled onto a chair near the bed and tried not to grimace as her sister approached carrying a concoction with the viscosity of a raw hen's egg. She said, 'Paint me with your pastes and salves and then leave me to marinate in the stink.' For the first time, she noticed a drapery of red and gold silk behind the bed. 'What is behind that curtain?'

Jessica pushed it back to reveal a door barely

large enough to allow a man to pass through. 'A means of escape for those who value discretion over the convenience of the main staircase.'

'It leads to the Fondamenta?' asked Hannah.

'Yes, to the canal.' Jessica's face took on an expression of concentration. 'First you need a layer of this paste, which will act as a basecoat, like gesso under a fresco. It will harden on your face, so you will not be able to talk without it cracking. This will give me an opportunity to say something I want to say to you. So listen, but don't speak.'

Hannah was not accustomed to taking orders from her younger sister, but it appeared she had no choice.

'Often, Hannah, you do not wish to talk about what needs to be talked about. You hope it will go away of its own accord. But this will not.' Jessica began applying the stiff paste with a wooden stick, the tip as flat as a gondolier's oar. 'This may be my last chance to speak what is in my heart.' First daubing and then blending the cream on Hannah's jaw, Jessica worked rapidly. 'We are each of us wrong to criticize the other. If we do not survive, either because Jacopo kills us or because the *Prosecuti* take us away and torture us, I want you to know I love you.'

Hannah tried to speak, but Jessica held a finger to her lips and smoothed a dot of paste under Hannah's nose and on her throat. She continued, 'In a few days, God willing, you will find Matteo's parents, then sail to Malta to be with your Isaac' — she paused — 'to whom you are so devoted. You are fortunate to have him.

Coupling for me is an act of commerce. I know that you have experienced the kind of pleasure I have not.'

The mask of white paste concealed her feelings, but Hannah wanted to tell her sister that Isaac made her laugh, that he was kind and loving, and that in bed he waited for her to reach her fulfillment first.

Jessica saw her attempt to speak and shushed her. 'Never mind, I know what you want to say.' She rubbed the paste on Hannah's brow. 'Love cannot be explained.' She went on, 'You think I have grown too fond of luxury. You think I have sold my soul for porcelain, lace, inlaid tables, and a pillared bed covered in gold leaf.'

'I — ' Hannah began, but she felt the paste crack.

Jessica kissed her on the top of her head and told her to stay still. She passed Hannah a jar of some foul-smelling, gelatinous unguent. 'We will outwit Jacopo. Apply this to your groin and armpits. It will sting and redden your skin but will not do any lasting harm. To be convincing, you must be nearly naked and appear burning up from fever when he comes.'

Hannah had not considered this part of the plan. She dipped her fingers in the jar and gave an involuntary shiver as she smoothed the greasy mixture as directed.

'Even looking as horrid as you do, I truly love you.' Jessica then took a comb to Hannah's dark hair and teased it into a satanic nimbus.

Hannah spoke through lips only slightly parted, so as not to crack the façade drying on her face. 'Suppose I lie for days like this stewing in this horrid stuff?'

'We will wait together. Our plan may work or it may not work, but it is our only hope. Fretting will not affect the outcome.' Jessica gave a final twirl to a strand of Hannah's hair. Then she backed away from her sister, frowning, studying her pale face, the blackened circles under her eyes, and the boils on her chest and arms. She sniffed the air. 'Yes, I think you will do.' She picked up a looking-glass from the bureau and handed it to Hannah. 'Look for yourself.'

Hannah shivered at her reflection. She looked the very image of pestilence. Glancing at Matteo lying on Jessica's bed, she was grateful he was too young to understand the meaning of the face in the mirror, haggard as that of a witch, covered with suppurating sores, vacant-eyed, with wild hair and a nose distorted beyond recognition. She quickly handed the mirror back to Jessica.

Reaching under her bed, Jessica said, 'One last matter.' She fumbled for a moment and then drew out a packet wrapped in cloth. 'Here is a partridge shell that has been emptied of its contents and then refilled with hen's blood. I have a collection of these close at hand for my patrons who prefer me a virgin. Hold it in your mouth and, when the time is right, bite down on it and let the blood trickle from the corner of your mouth.'

Jessica helped her remove the rest of her clothing and climb into bed, arranging the covers to expose the worst of the swelling and pus. She moved Matteo close to her side.

'Shall we play a game of backgammon to pass the time?'

Hannah shook her head. All she could think was: *Jacopo must come tonight.*

17

Valletta, Malta
1575

Isaac was leaning back against the olive tree in the square, his pine plank straddling his knees, when Hector came along the road on his mare. Hector dismounted and wrapped his reins around the pommel of his saddle so the horse would be free to graze in the square. Isaac was in the midst of penning a letter on behalf of a baker from the town of Zabbar who was seated next to him.

'I will be with you in a moment, *mio amico*,' he called to Hector.

Isaac hurriedly completed the letter and tucked the coin he received into his breeches. The baker slipped his letter into the leather bag over his shoulder and sauntered off in the direction of the tavern across the square.

Isaac rose and shook hands with Hector, even though he was angry that this man from the Society had done nothing to help him, short of offering a prayer shawl. Today there was a sombre look on Hector's face.

'What is the matter, my friend? You have more gloomy business? Let us sit in the shade and you can tell me your news.' He pulled Hector to sit next to him on a stump under the tree.

Hector sat as he had the last time they'd met,

213

and began dragging a stick back and forth in the dust.

'Enough map-drawing, Hector. Speak.'

'It is about your wife, Hannah.' Hector continued to scratch away with the stick.

Isaac felt his heart contract. 'Yes?' he said, struggling to keep the impatience out of his voice.

Hector spoke in a rush now, as though eager to get the words out before he lost his nerve. 'Against the Rabbi's orders, your wife delivered a Christian baby.'

It was as though Hector had punched him in the chest, forcing all the air out of him. After a few moments, he recovered sufficiently to say, 'Hannah would never do such a thing. Not only is it against the law, but it would endanger the entire ghetto.' And yet, even as he spoke, he realized that it would be like her to risk herself for the sake of another. 'Where is she now?'

'She is living with her sister . . . '

Isaac looked at him, confounded.

'I know nothing more,' said Hector.

'You are saying she has left the ghetto? No, I do not believe you. Who tells you this?'

'This is what the Society writes,' Hector continued in a voice meant to be reassuring. 'But do not agitate yourself — all will be well. They say she saved the life of a Conte's child and his wife. The Conte is influential. He will protect her.'

Isaac jumped to his feet and began pacing, mindless of the sharp stones digging into the soles of his feet. 'No, all will not be well.' How

214

could he explain the seriousness of the situation to Hector, a gentile living in this rocky outcropping in the middle of nowhere? 'You must understand that if a sparrow falls from the sky in Venice, it is considered the fault of the Jews.' Isaac's throat tightened with fear for Hannah's welfare.

'You exaggerate, my friend.'

'Once, many years ago,' said Isaac, 'a woman was found dead just outside the gates of the ghetto. She had been violated and murdered. No one knew her identity.'

Hector looked unhappy. 'I fear this story will not be amusing.' He shifted on the stump and pushed his hat farther back on his head.

Isaac gestured for him to be silent. 'The Jews were immediately accused. The priests exhorted the mob, 'Kill the Jews. Spill their blood.' A massacre was a certainty. The crowd was clamouring to enter the ghetto and cut off the heads of the men and disembowel the children. The Jews prepared to flee. The entire community was about to be uprooted, houses lost, businesses abandoned, the ill and elderly left behind.' Isaac paused. 'Suddenly, into the square raced a messenger. 'Do not worry, fellow Jews,' he announced. 'I have wonderful news. The dead woman was Jewish!''

Hector's face creased in an uncomfortable grimace.

Isaac leaned over and squeezed Hector's arm. 'Now do you see? My Hannah might as well be dead.'

'Isaac, there is a way out, if you will listen.'

'How?' Isaac asked.

'The Rabbi has finally been able to raise the

money for your ransom from private benefactors, but it is conditional upon your . . . ' Hector paused.

'Upon what?'

'Divorcing Hannah.'

Had the world gone mad? Isaac grabbed Hector by his collar and fought the impulse to throttle him. 'I would sooner cut off my arm! You can tell the Rabbi that if his help depends on that, he can take his ducats and shove them up the arsehole of a pig!' He released Hector and began coughing on the dust stirred up by his movement.

Hector, recovering his breath, said, 'I am so sorry.' He hesitated, clearly preparing to deliver another blow. 'I am instructed not to enter into any negotiations for your ransom as long as you remain married to Hannah. Your wife mortally offended the Rabbi by — '

'Delivering a Christian child.'

'By disobeying him.'

'Then the Rabbi is as much my enemy as the Knights,' Isaac said.

'No one will defy the Rabbi, Isaac. You must bend to his will. Divorce her and then remarry her.'

'Impossible. Under Jewish law, once divorced, a husband and wife may not remarry.' Once Isaac signed the *get*, the official document of his intention to divorce, it would be served on Hannah, and then the Rabbinical Court, a panel of three Rabbis, would consider the merits of the case and confirm or reject the divorce. With Rabbi Ibraiham presiding, there would be no doubt of the outcome. Isaac rubbed his face. His hand came away wet. Hot, angry tears spilled down his cheeks.

'Your laws are designed to create unhappiness,' said Hector.

Isaac shrugged, too dispirited to argue. 'You are entitled to your opinion. The Rabbi has been urging me to give Hannah the *get* for many years on the grounds of her barrenness. Now, he has me like a lamb in the talons of an eagle. He and I have never agreed on anything, from the price of a barrel of pickled herring to the number of men who will appear at *shul* for morning prayers. But this? He goes too far.'

Isaac smashed his fist into the palm of his hand, and Hector drew back. How satisfying it would be if the Rabbi were sitting here instead of the kindly but useless Hector. Isaac visualized joining his thumbs and pressing them against the Rabbi's Adam's apple until the life departed his desiccated old body. Isaac cracked his knuckles.

'Hector, you are simply a messenger. I am not angry at you.' He paced the rough ground, kicking at dirt with roughened and callused feet. He had never felt so impotent.

Hector stood and took him by the arm. 'Come and sit, Isaac. See what I have in my saddlebag,' he said, walking over to his horse. 'You may change your mind.' He extracted a thick package of papers tied with a ribbon. Leafing through them, he said, 'Ah, yes, here it is. You have heard of the *Provveditore*? This is a receipt for your passage on that vessel. She is expected in a week's time from Constantinople, stopping here to take on fresh water, a load of cowhides, and your hide, too, if you will sign the bill of divorcement.' The papers fluttered in the breeze. 'I also have the funds to pay your ransom, pending your signature on the *get*.'

Isaac eyed Hector and then asked, 'Out of curiosity, who are my benefactors?' His older brother Leon had married into a wealthy family — perhaps he had contributed.

Hector said, 'I am only at liberty to say it was raised by private financing. If you sign, you are free to sail.'

'Never.'

Hector shook his head. 'What good can come of your remaining here in Malta? If you want to help your wife, it would be better to return. Your stubbornness is helping no one, least of all you.'

'I love her.' Isaac's voice broke. 'Should my wife's sorrow be the price of my passage home?'

'It would be a poor world indeed if a woman's unhappiness ruled a man's actions.' Hector stood, brushed the dust off his too-short breeches, and strolled over to his mare, grazing a few feet away. He made an impatient gesture with his hand. 'Slaving for a man such as Joseph is not helping you or your wife. Has hunger clouded your reason?' He rummaged in his saddlebag for a second time. 'I also have a safe *laissez-passer*. It will protect you against another capture on the voyage home. It is signed by the Grand Master, who has impressed it himself with a seal.' Hector looked directly at Isaac. 'This is your last chance. Will you sign?'

'When all the teeth have fallen out of my head

218

and my beard is down to my waist,' Isaac answered.

'Then, my friend, make peace with that harsh God of yours. This island will be your graveyard.'

Hector gestured for Isaac's assistance, and Isaac cupped his hands together and bent down. Hector placed a foot in his hands and then Isaac boosted him into the saddle. Hector clapped his legs against the mare's flanks.

'If you have a change of heart, send for me,' he said, slapping the reins. He rode away leaving a rooster-plume of dust in his wake.

The dust coated Isaac's beard and made him cough. He had no need of this man, he thought. The Society — the whole lot of them, from the Rabbi to that Ashkenazi piece of shit — should gargle with the seed of a donkey.

He would escape the island without help from anyone.

18

Venice,
1575

Venice was unearthly quiet this morning. Everyone with relatives outside the city had long since fled as the plague barges continued to overflow with corpses. Hannah had lain in bed several hours, the gesso cracking her face, various potions melting from the heat of her body and trickling down her legs and arms.

Poor Matteo. From time to time he drew his legs up to his belly and screamed piteously, whether from the unaccustomed goat's milk or from the gesso and smelly ointments was impossible to say.

Jessica entered the bedchamber carrying a tray of fruit.

'Livorna left for the countryside at first light,' she said. 'We are quite alone.'

'I am terrified Jacopo will come and I am terrified he will not,' said Hannah, cuddling Matteo as best she could. 'Niccolò's body may have washed ashore by now. One look and anyone will know he did not die of the plague.'

Before Jessica had a chance to respond, the bell on the front door pealed with shrill insistence, shattering the silence.

Jessica rose and flew to the window. 'I can see only the tops of their heads. On the other side of the Fondamenta are soldiers standing at attention wearing bright blue caps.'

Never had Hannah felt so defenceless. She pulled the bedclothes over her naked body. Morning shadows shrouded the room. She wished herself to be invisible.

Jessica said, 'Should I let them in? What if I simply stay here with you? Perhaps they will give up and go away.'

'They will force their way in.' Hannah visualized the two large casement windows on the main floor. They could smash their way in with little effort. She was terrified. We are stupid to think we can fool anyone, she thought.

'Remember what Isaac used to say? ''Without choice one must mobilize the spirit of courage,'' said Jessica.

Then she left the room, clutching her skirts in one hand so she would not trip on the stairs.

Hannah drew the curtains of the four-poster bed around her, leaving a small gap so she could peek out. She coughed, suffocated by her own stench. Only a single candle guttered on the bedside table. Next to her lay Matteo, a small bundle wrapped in an embroidered shawl. She drew him close, feeling the steady beat of his heart, as delicate as a bird's against her own.

From the entranceway below, the bell pealed again, the cord yanked by the same impatient hand, now four times in rapid succession. Hannah heard the door squeak open.

'Is this the house of Jessica Levi?' demanded a male voice. Jessica replied in words Hannah could not quite make out. The door closed.

Heavy boots scuffled on the stone floor of the foyer.

As she lay in bed, hoping Matteo would not awaken, Hannah heard three sets of footsteps ascending the stairs, two heavy ones and Jessica's light step behind. Jessica was talking too fast, which make her lisp more pronounced.

'You are imperilling your lives by coming here. Did you not see the cross painted on the door?'

The steps grew louder, and Hannah heard Jessica say, 'My sister is afflicted with the plague, sir. Your plague garb will not be sufficient protection.'

They were right outside the door now. In another moment, they would enter her room. She slid her hand under the pillow, groping for the coolness of the knife, careful not to awaken Matteo. Hannah rearranged her covers to reveal the worst of her painted sores and lay waiting with half-closed eyes.

But it was not the portly Jacopo who entered through the door. This man was tall and spare, wearing a beak-like mask over his face and dressed in the attire of a plague doctor. Hannah put her fist to her mouth. Panic seized her so completely that she wanted to spring from the bed and throw herself out the window into the canal below, but her legs had turned to stone. Around the man's neck, resting on his coat, Hannah noticed a silver medallion. It was the Examining Magistrate from the office of the *Prosecuti*.

The Magistrate's black overcoat, which extended to his feet, glistened with animal grease to repel the contagion. A wide-brimmed black hat drawn down over his brow did not permit a patch of skin on neck or head to be exposed. The long beaked mask covered the upper part of his face. In the dim light, his eyes seemed without irises. The man turned toward the bed, seeing Hannah for the first time.

'Look at her. Now do you believe me?' said Jessica. 'As you can see, she is not long for this world. She deserves quiet and peace.'

The Magistrate ignored Jessica and approached the bed, stopping several paces away. Hannah then saw Jacopo at the threshold with a handkerchief pressed to his nose and mouth. With a long cane, the Magistrate thrust aside the bed curtains, took up the candlestick on the night table, and held it aloft. Raising a corner of her coverlet with his cane, he peered at her legs and belly, and then at the child who lay motionless next to her.

It was impossible to say what age the Magistrate was. His shoulders were stooped. He was old, perhaps forty or forty-five years. Hannah's skin prickled in the cold draft from the window and she shivered. This man would not waste time and public money on trials. Executions of the *Prosecuti* were secret, hurried affairs that happened in the dark of night. The Magistrate could order her killed immediately if he wished.

'I have come to investigate the murder of Niccolò di Padovani and the charges of witchcraft against you, Hannah Levi,' he said. 'I am Magistrate Marco Zoccoli.' The Magistrate stared at her with sightless eyes, the enormous beak of

223

his mask poised as if to strike. Then he turned to Jessica. 'And,' he added, 'I am also here to consider charges against you.'

Dear God, not Jessica, too, Hannah thought.

'For what offence?' Jessica asked.

'As an accomplice.'

'Accomplice? No one here has committed a crime.'

'Accomplice,' the Magistrate said, 'for offering Hannah Levi shelter.'

From the doorway, Jacopo said, 'And for kidnapping my nephew and murdering my brother Niccolò.' A handkerchief still held to his face, he was wearing a jacket the colour of crushed cherries. 'It would be my pleasure to watch you both dangle from the *strappado*.'

He stared closely at Hannah for a moment and noted the child at her side. Then he tucked his handkerchief away and clapped his hands. 'A virtuoso performance, ladies.' Giving a mock salute to Hannah, he said, 'The cross on the door was a brilliant touch. But we are not fools.'

Jessica said, 'This is no hoax, sir.'

'I have my jacinth ring to protect me against the pestilence, if you are telling the truth.' Jacopo held up his hand to show a heavy gold ring set with a reddish-orange stone on his thumb. 'And' — he drew a matchlock pistol from his breeches and pointed it in her direction — 'I have this efficient instrument at my disposal should you be lying. I have practised shooting melons off the parapet of ca' di Padovani and I can assure you it is accurate.'

'Put that away,' the Magistrate ordered. 'It

falls to me to decide who is guilty and to mete out punishment.'

Jacopo shrugged and tucked the pistol into the waistband of his breeches. He waved a hand back and forth in front of his face. 'God in heaven, pull the drapes and fling open the windows. The stench is unbearable.'

'The light hurts her poor eyes,' said Jessica.

'Well, the stink of it hurts mine. This woman is not only the murderer of my brother and the kidnapper of my nephew, but also a witch.'

The Magistrate still stood a few paces back from the bed. As the moments passed, Hannah felt the carefully applied buboes on her armpits and neck begin to melt in the heat of the room. Her sweat was beginning to seep through the bed linen and make her itch.

'She looks like a plague victim — a white, almost greenish complexion, blackened eyes and teeth,' said the Magistrate.

'Rubbish,' Jacopo said. 'It is nothing more than the crude paint of a bad actress.'

At that instant, Hannah moaned and bit down on the partridge egg tucked in her cheek. Blood trickled out of her mouth and down her chin, staining her pillow.

Magistrate Zoccoli recoiled. 'Good Lord, if this is an act, she should be on stage at the Teatro Orsini.' He looked at Matteo sleeping in Hannah's arms. 'Is the child similarly stricken?'

Jessica nodded.

The Magistrate glanced in Jacopo's direction. 'Sir, you claim this baby is your brother's child? I will ask you to identify him.' He nodded to

Jessica. 'Hold up the child so we can see it.'

Jessica went to the bed, slid Matteo from Hannah's arms, and held him up. Matteo had a whitish pallor and his limbs twitched. Although free of the plague, he was in truth suffering without the rich, copious milk of Giovanna. The sores and scabs that Jessica had painted on him looked gruesomely real.

'Can you say that this child is, without a doubt, your nephew?'

Jacopo replied, 'He is my own flesh and blood.'

The Magistrate said, 'This infant is so covered in buboes, I cannot tell if it is human or animal. How can you be so certain he is your nephew?'

'By his reddish hair. He takes after his mother, the Contessa,' said Jacopo.

'The child is my sister's,' Jessica blurted out, 'born weeks ago after a long and difficult travail.'

Jessica sounded so convincing that for a moment Hannah's heart leapt. Would the Magistrate believe this?

'You know full well that is a lie,' Jacopo said.

Jessica adjusted the bodice of her dress, tugging it a finger's width lower. 'Hannah has been staying with me since she was stricken. She had no one else to look after her and her child. Her husband is in Malta.'

'You know it is against the law for a Jew to live outside the ghetto,' said the Magistrate.

Jessica tucked Matteo under the covers. 'You are right, sir. She should have obtained official permission, but we are in a desperate situation, as you can see. She will be dead soon enough. As

226

will the infant.' Jessica squeezed Hannah's fingers and a smear of cream mixed with goat excrement came off in her palm. Quickly, she rubbed her hand over the silk coverlet. 'I beg you, sir, let them die in peace.'

'They are liars, the pair of them!' Jacopo said.

'If this Jewess is indeed the child's mother, it will be easy enough to tell.' The Magistrate fingered the medallion around his neck. 'Remove his swaddling bands. If he is circumcised, then I will accept that the child is hers. That will be the end of the matter.'

Jessica bent over the child and began slowly to unwind the swaddling bands, which fell away in yellow-and-black mottled strips.

Hannah wanted to throw herself across the child's body. Soon they would see Matteo's hooded penis. What if she rose from the bed and charged them with the knife? But there were two of them. They would seize the knife from her and kill her in less time than it takes a pack of wolves to hamstring a doe. As Jessica reached down to lift the child, Hannah quickly untied the cord around her neck and pressed the *shadai* onto Matteo. When Jessica held him up for inspection, the amulet in the shape of a baby's hand gleamed against the rise and fall of his small chest.

'What is that?' asked the Magistrate.

'The Jews call this a *shadai*,' said Jessica. 'It is an amulet to hang over the cradle to protect a newborn, for all the good it has done him.' She lifted the amulet and dangled it between her fingers. 'Such a custom is widespread among Jews.'

The Magistrate bent forward to study the Hebrew letters on the *shadai*, but the appalling stench of feces repelled him and discouraged closer inspection.

The Magistrate recoiled and said, 'No one would hang such an abomination around the neck of a Christian child.' He shook his head. 'I see no need to proceed further. Unwrapping him any further will only unleash the vapours of the pestilence.'

'Nonsense,' Jacopo said. 'She is a midwife, not a mother. My brother and I brought her from the ghetto to deliver the child. That amulet is the Jewess's charm — proof that she is a practitioner of the dark arts. She no more gave birth to the baby than I did.'

Hannah watched through half-closed eyes as Jacopo turned pale, realizing what he had just said.

The Magistrate's next words left Jacopo in no doubt of his error. 'You fetched her from the ghetto to assist at your sister-in-law's birth? You know such an attendance is against the law.' In a voice made strangely hollow by the mask, he continued, 'When you seek justice from me, sir, you must come with clean hands. Perhaps I should charge you and the Conte with breaking the law that prohibits Jews from giving medical assistance to Christians.'

The Magistrate turned to Jessica. 'You are the child's aunt. If that is so, you must be a Jew as well. And yet it seems from that ham in your window downstairs and the rosary you are clasping so fervently to your bosom that you are not.'

'The Lord led me to the Church of Rome years ago. I am a New Christian,' Jessica said.

Jacopo moved toward the bed. 'Magistrate, Jews bring the plague on us by poisoning the wells, and then, when the city is in an uproar, bold as rats, they snatch Christian babies from their cradles!' He pointed to Jessica. 'She is as much a Jew as her sister. Do not be deceived by her cheap props.'

'Justice is for me to dispense, not you.' The Magistrate turned to Jessica. 'Now, what do you say to this allegation of Niccolò di Padovani's murder? Were you or your sister involved?'

Jessica was quiet for a moment and then replied, 'Niccolò was set upon by ruffians and killed for his purse when he was reeling home drunk from a party at the ca' Venier.'

'How do you come by this information?'

'Magistrate, in my profession, we are all privy to information about certain nobles in Venice. And the streets have more ears than cobblestones. I am told that Niccolò was so drunk he could not perform. He lurched out into the street. When his friends followed him out to accompany him home, he was nowhere to be found. Everyone knows that thieves and ruffians have free rein of the city at night. My sister had nothing to do with his death.'

'She is a whore and a liar!' said Jacopo. 'My brother was found floating face up in the Rio della Misericordia. Dead of stab wounds inflicted by this Jewess.' He pointed at Hannah.

Jessica turned to face him. 'There are rumours that you and Niccolò are heavily indebted to the moneylenders. Too much time spent at the casinos. How convenient for you if the Jewish moneylenders were all killed.' She paused. 'You use the *Prosecuti* to do your dirty work for you.'

The Magistrate looked at Jacopo. 'Just what is it you are up to? Do you dare to exploit my office?'

'Why would you take the word of a whore over the word of a nobleman?'

'Answer the question. So far this woman's worst crime has been tending to her sick sister and the baby. You, on the other hand, have admitted to breaking the law.'

Jacopo was quiet now and appeared uncertain how to proceed.

'You are treading in dangerous waters, my friend.' Magistrate Zoccoli spoke slowly, as though a scrivener were taking down his words. 'For all I know, it was you, di Padovani, who threw your brother into the canal over some brotherly rivalry. I will settle the matter thus: This woman is too sick now to answer for herself. If she lives, so be it. She will answer to me. Obviously, I cannot take her into custody without spreading the pestilence. My soldiers shall remain outside, guarding the house to make sure neither the sister nor the baby leave. I will return in five days' time. They will either all be dead, in which case that is the end of the matter, or Hannah Levi will be well enough to answer charges and have her evidence tested by the *strappado*.'

Hannah knew that with her arms behind her back, wrists bound together, raised by the strap until her arms popped out of their sockets, she would confess to anything.

'Can you not see through this charade?' Jacopo said.

'My soldiers will be on watch twenty-four hours a day,' said the Magistrate. 'Nothing will be lost by delaying justice for five days.'

'But what if these women manage to slip past your men and leave the city? This one' — he jerked a thumb in Hannah's direction — 'plans to sail to Malta.'

'Venice faces a bigger problem right now than this Jewess. The Doge has decreed that in two days, the city will be in quarantine. No ships will set sail for Malta or anywhere else.' The Magistrate rose to his feet. 'We will take our leave.' He walked to the door, Jacopo trailing behind.

Jessica took a last secret glance at Hannah, a look of relief on her face, and followed them out of the bedroom and down the stairs to the front entrance. Hannah lay rigid, waiting until Jessica ushered the men out.

When she returned to the room, Jessica held her hand out for Hannah to see. 'Look at me shaking. I need a glass of wine.' She glanced at Hannah. 'And so do you.'

'You were magnificent,' Hannah said. 'Nothing they said seemed to confound you in the slightest. I never imagined you would be able to do it. My little sister has more courage than I could ever have predicted.'

Jessica walked to the window, pulled the curtain aside, and peered out. 'The Magistrate is stepping into his gondola.'

'And the soldiers?' asked Hannah.

Leaning farther out the window, Jessica said, 'Yes, there are two of them, on either side of my door, wearing the crest of the *Prosecuti*.' She let the curtain drop and leaned against the wall. 'My God, I am weak as a kitten. I will fetch us that wine. We need it.'

After Jessica had left, Hannah turned to the child. Matteo had sweated in the shawl. The paste and unguents on his face had smeared, giving him the appearance of a wax effigy held too close to a candle. She gave him a gentle kiss on the top of his head and his blue eyes fixed on her face.

Jessica returned with a tray of two glasses and a bowl of almonds and set them on the table next to the bed. Hannah poured from the carafe and handed her sister a half-filled cup. Rising from the bed, she went to the washbasin behind Jessica's dressing screen and began to scrub the concoction off her face and hands. Matteo was sleeping peacefully. She would wash him later.

Jessica said, 'God has given us a reprieve.' She fell into a chair, her legs sprawled out in front of her. She took a sip from her glass. 'But what next? What are we to do now?'

'We will think of something,' Hannah said as she dried her hands on a towel and took a seat on the side of the bed. She was exhausted and could not think. 'We are prisoners in your house just as surely as Isaac is a prisoner in Malta.' She fished a piece of meat from the almond shell with a pick, then glanced at Jessica. 'What is it?

232

You have an idea. I can tell by your face.'

Jessica took a gulp of wine and grinned. 'They are not such an ugly sight.'

'Who?' Hannah asked. 'The *Prosecuti's* soldiers?' She went to the window and gazed down at the soldiers, who were cramming lumps of bread and cheese into their mouths and passing back and forth a goatskin of wine.

Hannah felt the colour rise in her face.

'Look at them stuff their faces, the savages.'

Jessica came behind her and looked out the window. 'Show me how a man behaves at table and I will tell you how he behaves in bed. These two will be quick about it.' Giving Hannah a poke in the ribs, she said, 'It is not that difficult. Just close your eyes and pretend you are rolling out dough for *hamantashen* cookies for Purim. When they are spent and lying open-mouthed and snoring on the divan, we shall flee.'

'I could never,' Hannah whispered, afraid the two soldiers would hear and glance up.

'What does it matter now? Besides, you must do something to escape or this child will not be returned to his mother and the *Balbiana* will sail without you.'

Jessica popped an almond into her mouth just as Matteo began to stir. 'Look, our gorgeous boy is waking up.'

'I love him more each day,' said Hannah. 'I will find it painful to surrender him to his parents.'

The child began to wail.

'Go and fetch the goat's milk. I will feed him.' Hannah rubbed the last bits of caked gesso off her face.

Jessica kicked off her shoes, high wooden-soled ones, fashioned to give her a graceful appearance but not for moving quickly. She walked to the doorway and turned. 'Think about what I said. A rhythmic, stroking motion and then, before you know it . . . '

Hannah heard Jessica's giggles as her sister flew down the stairs in her stocking feet.

Hannah reclined against the cushions of the bed, holding Matteo in front of her as his legs pumped the air. In the three days Matteo had been with her, Hannah had often caught herself daydreaming about what it would be like if he were her own child. She had tried to stop herself from imagining what Matteo would look like when he was older: whether his eyes would remain slate blue or turn dark, whether his hair would remain red, and even whether he would be an able student.

So much time elapsed that Hannah wondered what had detained Jessica. When she heard the blast from downstairs, it sounded like the explosions that sometimes occurred during the fires at the shipyards in the Arsenale. She put Matteo down on the bed and raced downstairs to the ground floor. As she ran past the front door she saw the two soldiers, their blue caps askew, charging down the Fondamenta in pursuit of someone. Hannah flung open the door to the larder.

Jessica lay on the floor, her face pressed against the cupboard door. Blood poured from a hole in her chest, staining the bodice of her velvet dress.

19

Valletta, Malta
1575

Isaac trudged down the road that ran along the shore, eying the *Provveditore* bobbing at its lines. He ignored the ache in his legs and the blisters on his feet. It was no use, he thought, putting one weary foot in front of the other. He was no closer to freedom and returning to Hannah in Venice than he had been when he arrived in Malta earlier. Hector had made it clear that the Society could not help him. His letter-writing efforts on Joseph's behalf had failed miserably. In lusting after Gertrudis, Joseph was the god Icarus, flying with waxen wings too close to the sun, except it was Isaac who would crash to earth.

Gertrudis continued to ignore Joseph, and as a result, Isaac's backside was covered with welts from Joseph's whip. Whatever meagre scraps he had been receiving from Joseph had now dwindled to almost nothing. Any longer and he would be dead of starvation or beatings. His only hope of escape now was Gertrudis, who had agreed to find him a boat so that he might row out to the harbour and steal aboard a ship. If the sentries caught him and threw him overboard as a stowaway, so be it. At least he would die quickly. He was on his way to the beach, but first he had some property to recover.

Isaac had lost every ducat he had to his name when he was captured by the Knights and enslaved. If he managed to make it back to Venice, he had nothing to offer Hannah. So he was going to recover the only thing he owned in the world, though he well knew that to risk his life for a few cocoons, each no bigger than a walnut, was madness.

From his position across the harbour, Isaac could see the sailors, small as mice from this distance, scurrying to hoist the square sails and lash them to the masts. Tomorrow morning, the *Provveditore* would cast off to take advantage of the breezes coming from the south, off the shores of North Africa. With any luck he would be on board.

From the main square, he heard the church bells ring six times. He would go to Assunta's now. He would creep in during vespers, grab his small sack from behind the hearth brick, and steal out before she had time to know he had been in the convent.

His satchel, packed with the few things he had acquired in Malta — a spare shirt, a belt, his quills, and parchment — banged against his shoulder. He entered the convent grounds. Not a soul in the olive orchard, or in the courtyard. Mercifully empty. They were all in the chapel.

He pushed open the door of the convent kitchen and tiptoed toward the massive hearth at the far end of the room. The brick was on the left-hand side, second course from the top.

Keeping a wary eye open for Assunta, he advanced, scuttling along in a half stoop. The brick would slide out easily. He would reach into the space and in a trice have the bag of eggs safely tucked into the bosom of his shirt.

But as he crept toward the hearth, Isaac tripped on a pile of mulberry branches heaped into a mound on the apron of the fireplace. He was about to sidestep the boughs when a series of slight movements caught his eye. He bent to examine a limb.

Masses of writhing, roiling worms were crawling, creeping, jockeying for position, and gorging themselves on bits of twigs and leaves. King of the Universe be praised! The eggs had hatched! She had not fed them to the rooster. He felt like lifting his arms to the heavens and dancing the *hora*. A few of the grubs, their white, cylindrical bodies covered with fine hair, over-whelmed by their gourmandizing, dropped to the ground. Each was about the length of a man's finger; each body had a series of twelve rings around its circumference as though constricted by drawn threads. The area behind their mastica-tors was engorged with food. There was something repulsive yet enthralling in the orgy of twisting, gyrating bodies. The collective sound of their chewing was like the sweet humming of a cantor. He could not tear his eyes away.

But his shoulders slumped and all the joy left him as the realization hit him. He could not take these worms anywhere, much less on a sea voyage. He had no means of concealing them or keeping them fed with fresh mulberry leaves every day. It had been a foolish idea to retrieve them in the first place. Hannah would have to accept him, penniless as the day she stood under the wedding canopy with him.

His foot struck something as he made his way to the door, and he looked down. On the floor sat a basket heaped with several cocoons, as white and fragile as quail eggs. He tore his eyes from the boughs and swung his satchel from his shoulder. The worms she could keep and God bless her. He would thrust the cocoons into his satchel and take his leave.

Just as he bent to drop several into his bag, a voice called from the door, 'Delightful, are they not?'

Isaac whirled around, his hand freezing in mid-air. Sister Assunta strode in, a mulberry branch in her arms. Her wimple was askew, the skirts of her habit rucked up around her knees.

'I heard you clanking in with that leg iron of yours. Come to steal my worms, have you?' She pivoted her torso so she could see beyond her wimple. 'Surprised they have survived? As you can see, with God's guidance, the eggs have hatched. Now I have a frenzy of worms all demanding to be fed.' She set the mulberry on the floor and positioned a few worms on its limbs. 'I have picked till my arms ache, but these creatures give me no peace.'

Isaac sensed a new liveliness about the Sister, a new sense of purpose. She seemed younger, more vibrant. She held herself straighter, swung her arms about, striding through the kitchen shooing the chickens outside, and surveying the

238

worms like a visiting general reviewing troops on parade.

'Left in your care, they would not have hatched. You are a merchant. What do you know of silkworms?'

'You are full of surprises, Sister. When I left my eggs with you, you were contemptuous of the notion of silk. Wool was good enough for everyone on the island, nobleman or peasant, I recall you saying. You flung a sheepskin at my head to illustrate your point.'

'Are we so rich at St. Ursula's that I can squander the opportunity to convert scrubby trees into gold ducats to buy food to feed the poor?'

If she had the grace to feel abashed at the abrupt reversal of her opinion, she concealed it. 'Sister Caterina, one of the novices, told me a story that convinced me these insects are an opportunity sent by God to make our convent prosper.'

'I have no time to hear it.' He sidled toward the basket of cocoons on the floor. 'I must be on my way.' He set his satchel next to it.

'Sit,' she said to Isaac, as though speaking to a dog.

Isaac took a seat on the plank bench. He must leave now if he was going to have time to get to the *Provveditore* before she sailed.

'I will prepare lemon balm tea and you shall hear my plan.'

'Please do not trouble yourself.'

She took a kettle hanging from the arc-shaped bail in the hearth and poured hot water into two mugs, which she plunked on the table. She sat across from him, but kept shifting to see the worms. When one dropped to the floor, she sprang up with a cluck of sympathy and replaced it on a bough.

'Many hundreds of years ago,' Sister Assunta began, 'the Byzantine Emperor Justinian I, jealous of the Chinese domination of the silk industry, sent two monks to China to discover the secrets of the industry. The monks studied the hatching of the eggs, the formation of the chrysalis.' She paused, obviously proud of her use of that word, for him to acknowledge that he understood. 'The chrysalis is a marvel of nature, hard and tough. The monks did their job well and, without a soul suspecting, returned to Constantinople with a number of eggs concealed in their walking staves. In this way they conveyed their cargo from China and introduced silk to the west.' She slapped the table so hard their mugs bounced. 'Good trick, eh?'

She kept speaking before Isaac could interrupt.

'God spoke to me in a dream. He wants me to turn St. Ursula's into a workshop for the making of silk thread. It is a simple process from start to finish, but it requires a large workforce, which, with God's assistance, I have.'

Isaac watched the rooster pecking scraps in the corner. To watch a woman, particularly one as large as Sister Assunta, quivering with excitement embarrassed him. Isaac preferred Assunta's former cantankerousness to this newfound earnestness. 'Sister, allow me to speak. You have

240

done me a great service, but now I must collect my cocoons and be off.'

'To where? Do not tell me you have been ransomed?' She studied him for a moment and then a knowing look came into her eyes. 'Oh, I understand. You have plans to stow away on some ship. They will toss you overboard like the piss in yesterday's piss-pot before you are out of the harbour.'

'Sister — ' On the pretext of bending over to shoo away a hen, Isaac nudged several of the cocoons from the basket into his satchel, which lay open on the floor.

'Isaac, for a Jew, you are a worthy man. I am fond of you. I will not let you risk yourself like this any more than I would let you risk these worms that I carried in a pouch around my neck to keep warm.'

'I must go.' Isaac rose and slung the satchel onto his back, then started in the direction of the door.

Assunta blocked his path. 'If you wish to risk your own welfare on some stinking ship, that is your affair, but you will hand over those cocoons in your satchel first.'

If he simply ran off, she would summon the soldiers and have him arrested. The Knights would have him beaten until his back was raw, and then he would be left to starve in the dungeon below the Grand Master's palace.

'Let us discuss this as reasonable people,' Isaac said.

'There is nothing to discuss,' Assunta said.

'With the greatest of respect, Sister, you are

241

mistaken. With Jews, there is always something to discuss.' The next morning, the *Provveditore* would be casting off, her sails filling with wind, her anchor raised, her beamy stern growing smaller as she disappeared toward the horizon. 'You want to commence a workshop? You are like the fool who sells the lionskin before he has killed the beast. Who will buy your beautiful silk thread to weave into draperies and dress material? You need expertise. And what of markets? The ignorant dogs who live here? They would use your silk to wipe their behinds or muck out their pigsties.'

'I am listening,' she said.

'I have contacts among the weavers in Venice.' A lie, but the nod of her head showed she believed him. 'Sell me your thread, all you can produce, and I will sell it to the artisans of Venice to weave printed silk and velvet.' For all he knew, it might even work. 'So . . . ' He cleared his throat. 'I will take the cocoons. The worms shall stay here to feed your enterprise.'

'How do I know,' Assunta said, 'that you will fulfill your end of the bargain? You could vanish, never to be seen again.'

'So could you. Then where would I buy my thread?' The longer he spoke, improvising as he went, the more he realized he had hit upon a brilliant idea. 'You can produce thread at lower cost here than in the workshops in Venice, or even in Bellagio. Your costs will be low. Your nuns receive God's love as their wages.'

Her broad face relaxed. 'Before you leave we will embrace to seal our bargain.'

242

Isaac was pleased to have her agreement but wary of touching her. A man did not touch a woman to whom he was not related. But Assunta was not a woman. To realize that, one only had to look at her huge feet. He hugged her, saying, 'Shalom, Sister. Live well and prosper.'

'And you. Take care of yourself. I look forward to our long and prosperous union.'

He slung his satchel over his back. 'A more formidable trading partner than you, I could not imagine.' That at least was the truth. Then Isaac raced through the kitchen, through the cloisters where nuns were walking, their rosaries swaying at their waists, toward the harbour.

If, may God be listening, Isaac had the good fortune to be reunited with Hannah, hold her in his arms, and make love to her, he would summon up the image of Assunta just as she had appeared to him this evening in the convent kitchen — muscular arms folded over her wide chest, thick legs spread apart, and jaws clenched. Among Jews, it was well known that the chances of conceiving a male child were enhanced if the husband delayed his moment of climax and waited for his wife to reach fulfillment first. This vision of Assunta would ensure the conception of a son.

He shoved this fanciful thought from his mind as he heard the bell tower in the square chime eight times. Gertrudis and her skiff awaited him. He raced toward the cove.

20

Venice,
1575

Hannah knelt down and took Jessica in her arms, brushing the hair out of her eyes. Blood seeped into Hannah's lap and pooled on the floor. The pistol shot filled the main floor with the smell of gunpowder and smoke so thick Hannah choked, and her eyes streamed with tears so that she could barely make out the figure of Jacopo disappearing down the Fondamenta.

'Take me up to the *altanà*,' Jessica said. 'Then follow the soldiers and chase after that bastard. I have a pistol in the table next to my bed.'

'Jessica, try not to talk.' To chase after Jacopo would be reckless. He would shoot her as well, and then who would care for Matteo? Hannah took a handful of her petticoat, tore off a strip, and pressed it into the wound in Jessica's chest. It did little to staunch the flow of blood, and soon the material had turned into a sodden red ball. 'Do not die, Jessica,' Hannah said. But her sister was losing blood so quickly. 'I love you, Jessica.'

Jessica murmured, her eyes drifting closed, 'You know I always loved you, Hannah, even when I did not. Do you understand?' She struggled to breathe.

'Yes, it is the same for me,' said Hannah.

'Let me go, Hannah,' she whispered. 'It is too late for me. Take Matteo and run. This is your chance. Take it while the soldiers are off chasing Jacopo.'

'I cannot leave you alone.' Hannah's tears fell on her sister's cheeks. She rocked Jessica just as she had rocked her as a child when she was unable to sleep. She held Jessica until the last breath left her sister's body and she became limp in Hannah's arms.

After so many years of estrangement, she had reunited with her sister only to lose her again. It was too painful to think of.

Jessica felt so light. Hannah should wash her, wrap her body in a shroud, and bury her before sundown. She should sit *shiva* — but all she could think about was that Jessica's death was her fault. Jacopo may have pulled the trigger on the pistol, but if Hannah had sought refuge elsewhere, Jessica would still be upstairs laughing and applying her sequins and hanging on to the bedpost as her maid laced her up in her silk gown.

Hannah could not think what to do now except sit on the floor with Jessica's head in her lap, stroking the dark curls away from her face as the heat left her sister's body. She would have sat there for hours, but from upstairs came the sound of Matteo's cries. There was no time. Jessica would understand. She passed a hand over her sister's face, closing her eyelids. Hannah would have to grieve for Jessica later.

From outside she heard the shouting of more soldiers and the clomp of their boots as they raced down the Fondamenta. They would arrive at the door in a matter of moments.

She ran upstairs to Jessica's bedchamber and grabbed the page costume from her *cassone*. Hurriedly, she stuffed her hair under a green *biretta* and bound her breasts. When she emerged several minutes later from behind Jessica's dressing screen and looked at herself in the cheval glass, her hand flew to her mouth. In the reflection she saw a black-eyed boy with a pale oval face. There was a freedom in not being female, in not being Jewish, and in no longer being a little ghetto mouse.

There was no time to wash Matteo. The ointment and buboes still covered his face. Taking him in her arms, she wrapped him well, draping his face with the receiving blanket. Then she grabbed a flagon of goat's milk from the bedside table, and her bag containing her ducats and her birthing spoons, and slipped down the back staircase to the canal below, moving as fast as her satin-slippery legs would carry her.

She hailed a passing gondolier and stepped on board. The man gave her a puzzled look, which at first she interpreted to mean he had penetrated her disguise. On reflection, she realized he was confounded by the sight of a young page with a bundle in his arms, out on the canals at dusk.

As the gondola moved smoothly through the refuse-filled waters of the Rio della Sensa, Hannah drew the curtains of the *felze* around her. Her movements woke Matteo, who was locked in her arms as snugly as a baby is locked under his mother's sharing bones. She had saved

Matteo, but now he had saved her. Without him, she would have been paralyzed by her grief and remained in the larder with Jessica's head on her lap until the soldiers came for her. It was foolish to think of now, but Hannah hoped that Jessica had at least once enjoyed the same pleasure in coupling as she had with Isaac. Hannah had wanted to ask but could not bring herself to. Now it was too late.

Reaching under Matteo's blanket, she stroked his cheek, murmuring, 'You are a handsome boy, Matteo. Will you remember me when you have grown into a fine man, with all the advantages your parents can provide?' In answer, he snatched her finger and jammed it between his lips, mouthing it with his hard pink gums. 'No, of course you will not.' She started to croon, under her breath, an old Hebrew lullaby, but stopped after a couple of verses, her voice breaking. It was a lullaby she used to sing to Jessica when she was a baby.

The gondola pitched and rolled, broadsided by the wake of a flat-bottomed barge laden with produce. Goat's milk splashed on her satin slippers; she did not bother to shift her feet from the puddle.

On the Grand Canal the gondola docked between the familiar green-and-gold mooring posts of the ca' di Padovani. Matteo fussed as the gondolier held him in one arm and, with the other, helped Hannah over the gunwales of the boat. When she was standing on the Fondamenta, the gondolier handed her the baby and the milk, his gaze lingering on Hannah's embroidered waistcoat and the *biretta* pulled low over her eyes.

She said, '*Grazie, signore*. Do not wait for me. I will make my own way home.'

She handed him a gold ducat, hoping that it was enough to buy his silence, and that the *Prosecuti* would not learn of his passenger, the slender page carrying a well-turned-out Christian baby to his breast.

'*Prego*,' he said. A few feet away, a young boar nosed in some garbage. Before casting off, the gondolier lifted his oar out of the *forcòlo* and jabbed the boar in the hindquarters. It lumbered off. Replacing the oar in the oarlock, he called out, '*Buona fortuna*,' and pushed away from shore.

For a few moments, Hannah lingered in front of the palazzo. If the Conte and Contessa were not at home, she had no notion of what she would do with Matteo.

When the gondola was out of sight, she turned, Matteo in one arm, her bag in the other, and said, 'Wait until your mama sees you. How delighted she will be.' When Matteo gurgled and cooed, a tear dropped from Hannah's cheek and rolled into the fat creases of his neck. His painted buboes and his horrible smell did not prevent her from nuzzling her face into his woolly blanket. 'How am I going to explain your appearance to the Conte?' If only she had had the time to wash him.

The setting sun was a dull orange colour and so huge and flat it could have been cut from parchment. Its rays bounced off the windows of the façade. But no illumination came from the warehouse and office on the ground floor. The *fondachi*, where the family conducted business, was dark, the entranceway barred. No signs of life, no chatter, no maids shaking out quilts, no smell of cooking issuing from the middle and upper floors, where the family lived.

Hannah hesitated. A black wreath hung from the door. She reached for the bell cord and pulled before she had time to consider its significance. After a few moments, the door swung open and Giovanna stood facing her. She stared at Hannah for a moment, a bewildered look on her face.

'Giovanna — it is me, Hannah. Thank God someone is here.'

Giovanna studied her a moment before recognition came into her eyes.

'I need to see the Conte immediately.'

Giovanna slowly shook her head. 'You may not see him. Not in this lifetime. The Conte is dead. And my mistress along with him.' She made the sign of the cross and glanced at the wreath on the door. 'The plague. We received word from Ferrara yesterday.'

Hannah used to think that only the poor suffered, that rich and well-born people were sheltered from grief. Now, she knew she was mistaken. Poor Lucia had not lived to hold her son in her arms one last time.

'I am so sorry to hear that. I have brought Matteo back. He was . . . ' She was about to launch into a stumbling explanation as to why she had the child, but she stopped herself.

'Ever since you entered this household, bad luck has befallen the family,' Giovanna said. 'Master Jacopo has disappeared and I fear he is dead. A herring fisherman found Niccolò's body last night floating face down in the lagoon. He was dead of knife wounds.' Giovanna wiped her hands on her apron.

'But the child is alive. What am I to do with him?' Hannah smoothed Matteo's reddish hair and held him up.

Giovanna sniffed and bent over the baby. When she saw the buboes, she gave a scream and retreated back into the doorway.

'Are you mad? Get him away. He has the plague! If I catch it, who will care for my children? Get away from here!'

'Please listen to me. It is not what you think.' Taking a gulp of air, she tried to slow her breathing in spite of the bindings on her chest. 'The child is healthy.'

Giovanna backed away, her hand on the door to close it. 'Leave before I summon the *Prosecuti*,' she said.

Then Giovanna slammed the door. A moment later, Hannah heard the grating noise of the iron bolt sliding into place.

As Hannah stood there, not knowing what to do, Matteo began to whimper. She rocked him in her arms, still standing in front of the bolted door.

Had she risked everything only to see the baby cast off as an orphan? The thought of the devotional portrait in the Contessa's bedchamber came to her, the Virgin Mary with the Christ

250

child on her lap. She felt a stab of grief for the Contessa, who had struggled so valiantly to bring forth Matteo, only to perish of the plague.

The infant, sensing her panic, stared right at her, his brow wrinkled, as if in sympathy. He reached out a hand to touch her face. She loved him, this exotic little creature. She loved his blue eyes and fair skin, so different from the dark babies of the ghetto.

As she bent her head to kiss his cheek, Hannah realized — Matteo was not an orphan. She was his mother as truly as if she had given birth to him. Whatever happened now, she would protect him. Matteo had no one else in the world.

21

Valletta, Malta
1575

Isaac tramped along the waterfront, the stones digging into his callused feet. Gertrudis's sketch was rolled up and tucked against his heart, next to his sack of silkworm cocoons. For good luck, he fingered the blue hair ribbon that held it fast. He held his head low, a *biretta* pulled down on his forehead. He had no desire to attract the interest of patrolling soldiers of the Grand Master, muskets over their shoulders, sniffing the air for contraband and absconding slaves.

Gertrudis's offer of her cousin's pirogue was heaven-sent. She might not have been persuaded to feign love for Joseph, few women could have managed such a feat, but she was kind and, furthermore, a gifted artist. Her likeness of Isaac was so finely done and so flattering that any woman seeing it would consider him handsome. It would be his gift to Hannah when they were reunited.

Yesterday, they had met again at the square, where Isaac was reading over a contract for a merchant with sheep pelts to sell to a ship's captain on his way to the Levant.

Gertrudis sat on the stump, her skirts pulled up to reveal a trim ankle, and waited until Isaac was finished and had pocketed the merchant's five *scudi*. 'So,' she said, 'I will speak quickly. I can see you have a long line of impatient customers.' She was jesting. The square was deserted. The market had closed for the day and the vendors were drinking up their profits at the tavern. 'My cousin's skiff will be waiting for you on the beach tomorrow evening. You are a fool, but a loyal one, and I like that in a man. I will reward your loyalty.' She spoke without rancour, as though she were discussing the terms of a contract. 'The skiff is old but seaworthy. When you reach the ship, give it a good push to shore. The tides will carry it back to the beach, where my cousin will reclaim it.'

To board a vessel anchored far out in the harbour without a skiff was impossible. Isaac was a strong swimmer, but the ships were too far to reach. Neither was it possible to board a ship at dock. Too many stevedores were loading and unloading cargo: oranges, dates, wine, and bark from Sardinia. From Romania alum, lead, and pilgrims' robes. The sweating men, tumplines marking their foreheads, staggered to and fro under their immense burdens. Weaving between the porters, crashing into them, were sailors lurching back to their ships, stupid with drink, whores clinging to their arms. No one could escape detection in such a crowd.

So although Isaac was relieved she had not withdrawn the offer of her cousin's skiff, he sighed with regret as any man would who had gazed on her blue eyes and fair skin.

Isaac continued to walk in the direction of her cousin's boat. The evening was hot, even though the sun had now set; sweat flowed in rivulets down his back and between his buttocks. The moon, suspended like a pearl over the harbour, seemed oddly ripe and female on this island of muskets and swords and battle-ready men eager to use them. The wrights had caulked the decks of a *bertone* newly arrived from Genoa, judging by the flag flying on her foremast, and from the hull the faint odour of pine pitch and wood shavings wafted over him.

The seagulls overhead, fatigued by the heat, had ceased their insistent screeching and perched, wings folded, on the yardarms of a Turkish *caramusal* from Constantinople and on a *fregate* from Genoa. By decree of the Grand Master, guards searched every ship before it cast off, poking and jabbing long poles tipped with iron-clawed instruments into the cargo hold, under decking, and into the nooks and crannies behind ladders and beneath stairs. Any hapless stowaway lucky enough to have found his way aboard would have to be careful not to yelp at the thrust of the grappling hook.

Farther out from shore, at the very entrance to the harbour where the cliffs were at their highest, Isaac saw the *Provveditore*, a high-sided galleon drifting at anchor. She would serve his purposes well. By squinting, he could make out the welcome sight of the flag of Venice, a golden-winged lion on a field of red, rippling from the foremast in the silvery light of the moon. The galleon was a beauty, with a beamy hull and sails reefed in, neatly awaiting her departure. From the way she rode high and proud in the waves, she was not carrying a full cargo. Plenty of room in the hold for a man who was not afraid of a few rats nibbling his toes, or the jab of a hook.

It was much too far for him to swim. If he rowed out in Gertrudis's skiff with the moonlight to guide him, he could haul himself hand over hand up the anchor line and fling himself, nimble as a monkey, over the side. He could creep past the sailor on watch and, provided he did not stumble over the windlass and anchor line, find a snug hidey-hole before dawn broke and all hands surged on deck.

He merely had to find the skiff and oars and be on his way. He quickened his pace toward the cove, several hundred paces south of the harbour, trotting in spite of the feet-cutting stones.

Finally, he reached the cove, as flat and regularly shaped as half a pie. The water glinted, reflecting the pewter light of the moon. The shoreline was bare except for its decaying pine stumps. The trees had long since been harvested for ships' masts. The starkness of the cove made it possible to see for some distance in all directions.

Near a piece of driftwood on the far side of the bay was a small skiff floating just where Gertrudis had promised it would be. Isaac walked toward it, his dismay growing with every step. Half-submerged in the water, the pirogue was the length of a tall man, stove in at the helm, missing a board in the stern. Isaac picked out a pebble from between his toes and left the sack

255

containing the cocoons and Gertrudis's portrait of him above the high-tide mark.

He waded into the sea, the salt stinging his feet. He gripped the boat by the gunwales and rocked it back and forth. Grabbing a frayed rope slimy with algae from the bottom of the boat, he wrapped it around his waist and dragged the craft the few paces toward shore. He heard the whooshing water rushing through the missing ribs of the hull. The skiff landed on the beach with a splintering noise. An oar lay on the sand. Isaac glanced around the cove for something to bail out the water, but there was nothing but rocks and seaweed. Then he remembered: his portrait.

Hannah would have to be content with the gift of himself instead of his sketch. Untying the ribbon from around the charcoal sketch, he made a funnel of the canvas. As he bailed the water from the bottom of the boat, he watched his likeness bleed and dissolve, leaving behind a ghostly outline.

Isaac wrestled the boat hull-side up to inspect the bottom. More water poured onto the beach; a couple of minnows floundered on the sand and curled into quivering crescents. Isaac groaned. Gertrudis could not think this piece of water-logged flotsam would stay afloat long enough to get him out to the *Provveditore.* This must be her revenge for his failure to respond to her charms.

Isaac scooped up the minnows and, without bothering to rinse off the sand, lifted his head to the sky and swallowed them. He turned his attention back to the boat. Maybe it could be repaired, though the bottom was encrusted with barnacles and seaweed. Isaac took a sharp rock and prised off a few of the barnacles, sucking out the salty contents of each one. Someone had once, long ago, caulked the hull with oakum but had done a poor job of it. Bits of the stuff had fallen from between the boards and now floated on top, wriggling like dirty white worms. In its present state, the skiff was as seaworthy as the rib cage of a dead cow.

Just as he was about to rip up his portrait to stuff between the boards, he heard voices and the sound of tromping footsteps east of the cove. He looked up to see two soldiers from the Grand Master's office wearing breeches of unbleached muslin and sash belts, and with muskets slung over their shoulders. They walked toward him between the tree stumps.

Isaac lifted the side of the boat and crawled under. It stank of stagnant water, sodden wood, and dead fish. Sharp rocks dug into his backside. Isaac lay there, breathing as quietly as possible in the salt-thick air, waiting for the men to leave. But the footsteps came nearer, boots scraping along the stony beach.

'Here, Luigi,' said a slurred voice. One of the soldiers slumped onto the hull of the skiff, which took his weight with a creak of protest. 'Have some wine. She will be along any moment.'

'Are you sure?' asked the other soldier.

'Ever know a whore to refuse drink or a few *scudi*?'

The boat hull sagged under the weight of the

first man and then the weight of both soldiers. Isaac worried that at any moment, the wood might splinter.

Soon he heard the sound of a woman giggling, and a voice calling out, 'Hullo?'

'Here she comes. Let us save a swallow of wine. Do not drink it all.'

The one called Luigi said to his companion, 'Go take a walk.'

Isaac felt the ribs of the skiff creak with relief as one soldier stood up and walked away.

'Come here, my darling. Let us see what you have under that pretty frock of yours.'

Isaac curled into a ball under the boat, his hands over his ears, while the whore coaxed Luigi to greater and greater pleasure. The boat trembled with their exertions, and Isaac was sure that the writhing couple would crash through the rotten hull on top of him. But by some miracle the boards held, and after much pleading with Jesus Christ, the Virgin Mary, and St. Ursula, Luigi let out a cry and rolled off the hull, landing with a thud on the sand.

Through a crack in the slats, Isaac could make out the dark beach, although the moon had slipped behind a cloud. There was the flicker of a fire several *brachia* down the beach and the smell of fish drifted over to him. He could almost hear Gertrudis laughing to herself as she witnessed his humiliation.

The second soldier returned and slapped the strumpet on her rump, loudly anticipating his turn. He positioned her on the hull.

King of the Universe, Isaac thought, these

gentiles fuck like feral cats. Soon Isaac's ears rang from the moaning and high keening sounds that issued from above his head. It was as though the second soldier were being tortured by the Chief Inquisitor instead of being serviced by a strumpet.

Suddenly there was the sound of splintering and the hull nearly gave way, tumbling the soldier and his whore, still joined together, onto the jagged rocks. With moist sounds, they uncoupled and, bare-arsed, charged yelping to the sea.

Isaac hoisted up the boat and rolled out from underneath it. Just as he was about to make good his escape, the three returned, laughing and passing a bottle back and forth. Before they could see him, Isaac scuttled crab-like several paces along the beach until he found a boulder to crouch behind. He hunkered there so long his right calf muscle began to spasm. He massaged it, and his leg relaxed. He thought of Gertrudis. How satisfying it would be to wring her lovely, long neck. He forced himself to put this thought aside. His fury would keep.

Isaac looked around the cove. The only skiff was Gertrudis's, now abandoned by the soldiers and their *putà*, who, he could see, were ambling down the beach, heading into town. He had no choice. He ran back to the collapsed skiff. He found the portrait of himself trampled by the soldiers and slammed it against his thigh to remove the sand.

The *Provveditore* would be casting off at dawn. He worked frantically. There was no cover, no welcoming thickets of brush, not even a stand of spindly poplars where he could drag the boat while he worked on it. He tore the sketch into strips and, making a compound of sand, seaweed, and bark from the pine stumps, bound together the pirogue, now more like a raft than a skiff. After a few hours, he was ready to haul it into the water. It wobbled unsteadily. Some water leaked in, but it did not sink. Perhaps it would suffice. Isaac glanced out into the harbour, where the high-decked galleon bobbed on its anchor line, so close but so out of reach, a couple of pine-pitch torches burning from her bow.

The sky grew dark with rain clouds. Soon it began to pour. Wind blew the sand so hard that his mouth was gritty with it. Waves in the harbour swelled as high as the walls of St. Elmo. The moon was nowhere to be seen; it would be only about two hours before first light. Should he risk setting off in this leaky vessel? The words of the philosopher Maimonides rang in his head: *The risk of a wrong decision is preferable to the terror of indecision.* And besides, what choice had he?

As he worried how he could sneak aboard under the watchful eyes of the sentries, an idea occurred to him. Isaac scooped up in his arms a pile of dried seaweed and twigs and tossed them into the bow of the boat, the only place likely to remain dry. When the boat was halfway into the water, he snatched up the oars on the shore and jumped in. He began to row, the muscles of his back heaving with the effort. At first the boat went in circles, but when he slowed down and concentrated on rowing with equal strength on both oars, it followed the course he set toward the *Provveditore*. He struggled for what seemed like hours, making slow progress. To the east, the sun was beginning to make its presence known, casting red light on the water. Dawn was beginning to break. Soon it was light enough to see the crew on the yardarm, setting the sails. How could he steal on board undetected?

Then he heard a sound that filled him with dismay — the clanking, groaning sound of the windlass. The crew of the *Provveditore* were weighing anchor, preparing to cast off. He was too late.

22

At Sea,
1575

Hannah clung to the deck railing of the *Balbiana*, dressed as a Christian in one of Jessica's gowns of blue silk. It was the only one she had been able to find in Jessica's *cassone* that was modestly cut. The dress gave off her sister's familiar scent of lemon and bergamot. It made Hannah want to weep.

After leaving the di Padovani palazzo under cover of night, she had stolen back to Jessica's house. She had thrust into a trunk clothes, her birthing spoons and ducats, and packed food. Of the two hundred ducats the Conte had given her, she had about one hundred and fifty ducats left after she paid her passage to Malta and bought provisions for the trip. Whether this would be sufficient for Isaac's ransom she had no idea.

If only it had been possible to bring the goat onto the ship. She didn't know how she would feed Matteo on this long voyage, which would take weeks depending on the winds. But she had had no time to grieve or to think, only to act. At dawn she found a gondolier who, for a sum substantial enough to ensure his discretion, transported her and Matteo to the docks for the sailing of the *Balbiana*. They were the last to leave the port of Venice. By order of the Council

262

of Ten, the city was now in quarantine.

Milk, she thought, as the deck of the ship rose and fell under her feet — she must find more milk for Matteo. Her dwindling supply of goat's milk would keep him alive for only one more day. He had not cried since they had cast off a short while ago.

If only Jessica were here, she would know what to do. But Jessica would soon lie in a mass grave on Lazzaretto Vecchio, along with hundreds of others who had succumbed to the plague. Here, on the restless deck of this shifting, pitching three-masted galleon, there was no wet nurse, or even a goat, to provide nourishment to a child.

Her fellow passengers, Greeks, Armenians, Turks, Persians, and Jews, as well as Venetians, clustered at the rail watching as the pillars of San Marco disappeared from sight. Standing next to Hannah was an old man, an Armenian, draped in a flowing caftan and coughing from catarrh. Hannah stepped onto a pile of hemp rope to peer over the high sides of the galleon. Holding on to the rail with one hand, Matteo tucked in her arm, she watched as the Basilica di San Marco receded into the distance.

Through the cacophony of people chatting, gulls screaming overhead, and ropes thrumming against the sails, the distant bells of the *Marangona* chimed six o'clock, signalling the beginning of the day. To the east, the fiery ball of the sun began to lift itself from the sea, rising above pinnacles, domes, and towers. Above the tangled finials of San Marco, it paused and winked while the water made clapping sounds. To the west, like the spine of a sea monster, the waves arched and broke over the shores of the Island of Guidecca. The Laguna Veneta, the Venetian lagoon, was choppy. The wind teased the azure water into white wavelets.

Overhead, the *Balbiana*'s three square sails bellied and then fell slack from gusts of wind that began and stopped, came and went, without pattern. The breeze whipped the ends of her red scarf into her mouth. She plucked them out and then, using the advantage of her increased height on the coil of rope, turned to study the crowd.

Matteo whimpered.

'I saved you at your birth, and I saved you from your uncles. Now I wonder if I can save you once again.' He was pale, his legs so thin and his arms so flaccid that they flopped lifelessly when Hannah shifted him from one arm to the other. She transferred the *shadai* from around her neck to his. Had she worked so hard to save him only to lose him to starvation?

Hannah, shielding her eyes from the sun with her hand, scrutinized one woman after another, dismissing each one in turn. And then, on the other side of the deck, she noticed a lady, Venetian judging from her velvet dress and blonde hair done up in twin coronets, who bore a small object in her arms. Hannah let go of the rail, climbed down from the rope, and pushed her way toward her. Just as she was about to place a hand on the woman's arm, she looked more closely at the bundle and realized it was a brown spaniel wrapped in white muslin. She backed away, treading on the feet of another woman, who reached out and grasped Hannah by the shoulder to steady her.

This woman was dressed in a *pelisse*, a floor-length gown of silk, as green and iridescent as a hummingbird's breast. Over her face was a veil that did not permit Hannah to see more than her black eyes.

When Hannah smiled and apologized, the woman replied, '*Maşallah*.' After Hannah had regained her footing and greeted her in turn, the veiled woman bent forward to examine Matteo. She tickled him under his chin. When he did not respond, she said, 'Your child is ill, *hanim effendi*. He hardly moves.'

'I have no milk.'

'May Allah have pity on him. Where is his wet nurse?'

'That is a story that does not bear telling. Suffice to say, I have only some goat's milk growing sour in a bottle. Enough for one more day, no more.'

'A boy?' When Hannah nodded, the woman said, 'Then you have been given a gift.' She gave a slight shrug. 'I, to my regret, have produced only girls. Six beautiful but useless girls.'

'Perhaps next time.' Hannah wondered at the woman's perfect command of Venetian, which she spoke with only the faintest hint of an Ottoman accent.

The woman patted her stomach and shrugged. 'But how does one escape Allah's will?' She bowed her head and said, 'My name is Tarzi.' A gust of wind blew her gown against her body, and Hannah noticed that she was lush in the

265

plump, sensual way of the Turkish women she had glimpsed in one of the markets in Dorsoduro.

'I am Hannah.'

'Forgive me for saying this, Hannah *effendi*, but do you not think you have been reckless to embark on such a trip without a wet nurse?'

'I had little choice in the matter.'

'In his condition, a slight fever or grippe could take him.'

Hannah felt like replying, *Do you think me so simple as not to have thought of this?* Instead she said, 'I was giving him suck until a few days ago and then my milk dried up. By then it was too late to find a suitable nurse to accompany us.' The lie came easily to her. In truth, she had had no time to plan anything other than how to get Matteo onto the *Balbiana* before the *Prosecutis* soldiers returned to Jessica's house and seized both of them.

Tarzi said, 'You were nursing him *yourself*?' She sounded astonished by the thought.

Jessica would have known how to handle a woman such as this one. A mere tap of Jessica's fan on the woman's solid arm and Tarzi would have become less haughty.

'I was brought to bed a month ago with my last daughter, Gülbahar.'

'So you have a wet nurse?'

'Of course,' said Tarzi. 'Hatice is an *ikbal*, a Circassian slave from the mountains. Slender, but tough as a mountain cat.' Tarzi tied the ends of her veil behind her head to keep them from being whipped about by the wind. Above them, the sails gave a thump as the wind filled them.

'My husband gave me Hatice when my eldest daughter was born.'

'You are fortunate,' said Hannah. No one in the ghetto could afford slaves; no one in the ghetto wore jewels of the size and perfection that Tarzi wore.

'You have no time to waste.' Tarzi gazed around at the crowd at the rail. She gestured to a portly man of about fifty years standing a few feet away, talking to an old Armenian man who was coughing phlegm into a piece of cloth. 'The Sultan has appointed my husband to be Governor of the province of Üsküdar. I had no choice but to accompany him on this voyage and bring my daughters with me.'

Hannah could not help noticing that Tarzi had shaped her dark eyebrows into crescents and had outlined her eyelids with kohl. The effect was fetching.

'I desperately need a woman to give suck to my son. Perhaps your wet nurse would be available?'

Tarzi said, 'I am sympathetic, do not misunderstand, but my Gülbahar has a ferocious appetite. If Hatice had to give suck to two babies, both of them would be in jeopardy.'

What inducement could Hannah offer this Pasha's wife in her silk gown, wearing around her neck a ruby the size of a pigeon's egg? Just then the ship broached and Hannah fell against her. Tarzi put her arms around her to steady her. Hannah feared that at any moment she would burst into tears. She had no choice. She pleaded with the woman in front of her.

'Please! I beg you. I cannot stand by and watch my son starve to death.'

'There is nothing to be done for this baby. You will bear other children. Every time my Ahmet and I lie together, as if by magic, a child arrives a few months later.' She patted Hannah's arm. 'That is Allah's way. For my part, I would prefer it to be different.'

'Different in what way?' Hannah asked.

She bent closer to Hannah's ear and lowered her voice. 'I am hoping not to grow big again. My confinements are difficult. Vomiting for months, fatigue, and insomnia. Then the pain of the travail and flooding, which, with the next confinement, my midwife fears she will not be able to staunch. And then who will watch over my girls? Who will see they make suitable marriages if I am gone?'

Hannah looked down at Matteo and fussed with his blanket. Perhaps she had something to offer this woman after all, she reflected. In the ghetto, *coitus interruptus* was called among the women 'winnowing within and threshing without.' It was a poor technique. A specially contrived golden ball inserted in the female passage to seal off the entrance to the womb? Impossible to obtain on the *Balbiana*. Douching with an infusion of guaiac tea? Hardly practical on this pitching galleon. Then there was abstinence. She glanced at Tarzi's husband, who still stood several paces away chatting with the old Armenian. No man wishes to be denied the joys of the marriage bed, especially not one such as

268

this, with his fleshy bottom lip and the thick hillock where his legs joined.

A wave as high as one of the pillars of San Marco threw the ship to one side. A spray of salty water hit Hannah in the face. She staggered, falling to her knees and nearly dropping Matteo. Mopping her face on her sleeve, she decided she would risk offering this woman forbidden knowledge.

'I am a midwife. I know many ways of encouraging conception — from infusions of fenugreek to the ground seeds of wild rue.' *And have tried most of them myself*, she could have added, but instead said, 'But I also know ways to prevent conception.'

Tarzi looked at her and said in a quiet voice, 'If you have a remedy, I will pay you whatever you like.' She placed a hand on her ruby necklace. 'Take this if you like.'

In Hannah's linen bag were herbs for bringing on pangs of birth, for easing the pain, for stopping the prodigious bleeding that sometimes followed birth. She even carried balm of Fatima, an Anatolian cream known to heal the striations of the belly left after a confinement. But she did not have with her any herbs to prevent the formation of a child.

Hannah considered Tarzi's dilemma. She remembered a Bedouin practice from the Negev Desert. 'I can assist. But it will be painful.' Hannah looked at Matteo, his eyelids laced with blue veins and his mouth drooping. 'Your ruby does not interest me. My price is your wet nurse. She must give suck to Matteo.'

'But what of my own baby?'

'I will give your wet nurse some herbs to make her milk flow.'

'As freely as the Sweet Waters of Asia?' Tarzi asked.

Hannah nodded.

Lowering her head to Hannah's ear, Tarzi said, 'I will come to you early tonight. I know my Ahmet and in what manner he will want to celebrate the first night at sea.'

While Hannah was changing Matteo's swaddling bands that evening, in the meagre sleeping area she had carved out for them amidst all the other passengers, she noticed his skin was growing wrinkled and dry from lack of milk. His eyes looked dull; his limbs hung limply. She fed him some boiled water and the last of the goat's milk, even though it had turned sour. A trickle of the milk escaped his mouth. He began to cry. Hannah wiped it off with a corner of the blanket and put Matteo to her own breast hoping that she might provide some comfort, though no nourishment. He gave a few obliging tugs and then fell back in her arms, relaxed, enjoying the security of her embrace.

'Do not give up, son. Help is at hand. Soon you will be drinking the finest mother's milk.'

As the ship pitched and rolled, Hannah found it safer to crawl on her hands and knees around her small space at the base of a ladder than to stand upright and be thrown to her knees when the ship hit a wave. Her stomach rebelled at the movement and she kept a basin nearby in case she became sick. The pitching was as bad on

270

deck, but the air was fresher.

At the appointed hour, Tarzi climbed down the ladder, arriving at Hannah's sleeping pallet as she was enfolding Matteo in his coverlet. As Hannah had quickly learned, there was no privacy on the ship. Passengers, even the wealthy ones, performed their ablutions in full view of others. Men and women trod past Hannah's tiny sleeping area, under the steps joining the upper and lower decks. Hannah had draped a wool blanket over the rope on which she had strung up Matteo's cloths to dry, forming a makeshift triangle of privacy. The hem of it pooled on the deck, growing sticky with pine pitch oozing from between the planks.

'Goodness, this is a mouse hole. And the air!' Tarzi waved a hand in front of her face.

'Little of that precious stuff reaches me down here,' Hannah said.

Tarzi looked apprehensive. 'So what is your plan to prevent all these babies of mine coming unbidden into the world? Let me have your remedy quickly, then I want to bathe and perfume myself for Ahmet.' She gave a sigh and muttered, 'The sooner started, the sooner finished. I have a feeling this will not be agreeable.'

Hannah described what she intended to do. Tarzi looked frightened, but Hannah laid a hand on her arm. 'Do not worry. I have gentle hands. I will not harm you.'

'In my way, I am as desperate as you,' Tarzi said. 'Let us get this unpleasantness over with.'

'Lie over there.' Hannah gestured to her straw pallet. 'And remove your lower garments.'

After shrugging off her billowy pair of drawers and pulling up her chemise, Tarzi positioned herself on the pallet, which served as a bed, her legs crossed in front of her. She used Hannah's valise as a pillow.

'When I am through we will go directly to your wet nurse with Matteo. There is no time to waste.'

Hannah placed Matteo into a hammock made from a shawl that she had strung from an overhead beam. His body felt as slack in her arms as an empty pillowcase. Then she squatted on her heels next to Tarzi and stroked her cheek to relax her. 'You will be brave.' But Hannah suspected that Tarzi would not be brave, would moan and writhe and make this unfamiliar procedure all the more difficult. Hannah washed her hands in a bucket of fresh soapy water. Finding a pebble smooth and small had been easy. She had only to look on the deck to find any number of them jammed between the planks. The stone, about the size of a dried pea, felt smooth between her fingers as she scrubbed it in the water. 'Open up your knees like the petals of a flower.' Hannah spoke with confidence to ease Tarzi's worry.

'You will not hurt me?'

'I will try not to. You must stay calm and breathe through your mouth.'

'And that is what you intend to use?' Tarzi pointed to the pebble. 'I do not understand.'

'Last year, a Sephardic Jew, a trader in cochineal, returned from the Levant. He told my husband the story of Bedouin nomads. They

272

insert a pebble into the matrix of their she-camels to keep them unfruitful during long journeys across the desert.' When Isaac repeated the story to her, Hannah could not fathom why such a thing would work. Now, on reflection, she thought perhaps the pebble in the womb destroyed the male seed by crushing its fragile protective shell in the same way a pestle grinds a peppercorn. Hannah had discussed the Bedouin story with other midwives. None of them had heard of such a technique ever being attempted on a woman.

'But I am not a she-camel,' said Tarzi, starting to pull on her trousers and rise.

'And I am not a Bedouin,' said Hannah, pouring a drop of almond oil into her hands and massaging it into her fingers and onto the pebble. 'Look.' She held the pebble up so Tarzi could see. 'You have pearls bigger than this. Do not fret. This is safe.' Hannah tried to take courage from her own words, but in truth, the insertion of an object where it did not belong, like a cinder in the eye, could cause pain and purulence.

Moreover, since Tarzi had recently given birth, Hannah must be careful that the pebble did not disturb the healing of the womb and result in fresh and copious bleeding. It would have been dangerous to attempt such a procedure on dry land, never mind on this galleon that never ceased plunging up and down. It was as though God himself, pretending to be a clumsy conjuror, were tossing their little ship from hand to hand in a game of exuberant juggling.

Tarzi parted her knees. Hannah slipped two fingers into the woman's passage, feeling for the opening of her womb. Soon she realized that she could not insert the pebble by manipulation alone. She needed to view the passage, see if such a procedure was even possible or if the mouth of the womb was now clamped shut against intrusion. Perhaps the birthing spoons would help. She reached for her linen bag and took them out. She had not even thought to clean them in all that had happened to her since she had retrieved them from Jacopo. The dried fluids from Matteo's birth still adhered to the spoons. She turned her back on Tarzi and swished them clean in the bucket of water, carefully drying them on a clean cloth. She draped a towel across Tarzi's bent knees so the woman would not see the procedure.

After rubbing the spoons with oil, she inserted them into Tarzi's passage and very gently squeezed them open. She could now see that the womb's mouth, a small thing to be grateful for, was still pliable from the birth of Gülbahar.

Footsteps drew close. Tarzi gave a groan. She heard what sounded like a pair of heavy boots hesitate and then climb quickly up the steps. Jessica had been right: men had no interest in the affairs of women. At the thought of Jessica, Hannah felt herself grow teary. It was too much to expect after all these years that she would bear a child, but if someday God smiled and gave her a daughter, she would name her Jessica.

Hannah placed her other hand on Tarzi's belly, trying to gauge the position and size of the fundus of the matrix.

'You have tender hands, Hannah, but still it hurts. Perhaps this is not a wise idea.'

'Try to stay still and remember to breathe.' Hannah was glad she was not trying to stand upright because she could not have kept to her feet on the pitching ship. A sudden heaving of the galleon threw her into the corner, nearly hitting her head on Matteo's hanging hammock. Tarzi gave a yelp of pain. The sudden movement had wrenched Hannah's fingers from the birthing spoons.

It could not be right to thwart God's will by preventing conception. Was this His way of telling her so?

Hannah regained her position, kneeling on one side of Tarzi's upraised knees, her hand between her legs. With the birthing spoons in place, she pinched the pebble between her index and middle fingers and pushed it up the passage, nudging it past the mouth of the matrix and into the womb. Then she eased the birthing spoons out of Tarzi's passage. In less time than it takes to recite the Shabbat prayers, the task was finished.

'Good girl. Lie back and rest.' Hannah washed her hands in the bucket and plunked the spoons in as well — away from Tarzi's line of vision.

'I am so glad it is over.' Tarzi rested a moment, panting slightly, whether in relief or pain Hannah could not tell.

'You are still bleeding a little from Gülbahar's birth, so your organs are supple and the pebble went in well. You must take care that it does not fall out. Lie back and give your body a chance to accustom itself to the pebble. Let us hope your womb does not expel it.'

'Will your magic pebble work?'

'We shall see,' Hannah said.

Flies had gathered around Matteo's eyes, attracted by the moisture. Hannah brushed them away. After a few minutes she said, 'Come, take me to your wet nurse. Matteo must be put to breast while he still has the strength to suckle.' She helped Tarzi get dressed and then picked up Matteo and strapped him to her back using his blanket tied across her breasts as a sling so that she could climb, hand over hand, up the narrow ladder to the deck above. Over her shoulder was her linen bag containing fenugreek and blessed thistle for the wet nurse.

When she reached fresh salt air, she breathed deeply. Tarzi led the way as they walked arm in arm across the deck. They walked over the grating cover of the cargo hold, through which wafted the stink of animal hides and dried fish.

'You must not ask Hatice about her own baby,' said Tarzi. 'He died at birth and she mourns so deeply that she has no tears left.'

A dead baby. The poor woman. To have a child and then to lose it. Was that not worse than never having given birth at all?

Hannah followed Tarzi up a ladder and down a passageway. Tarzi pushed open the polished oak door of her cabin, which had a large porthole to admit air and light. It was furnished with plump cushions and silk carpets. Built into the walls were several sturdy berths for sleeping.

Tarzi said, 'Hatice will have that son of yours

healthy in no time.'

The room smelled of swaddling cloths. In the corner, huddled against a bolster, was a girl. She was small as a ten-year-old. She did not sit up when they entered the room or acknowledge Tarzi's greeting. At first, Hannah thought she was one of Tarzi's daughters, but when Hannah's eyes adjusted to the dim light, she made out the squirming outline of a baby struggling for nourishment at the girl's breast. After a moment of trying without success, the baby spit out the nipple, gave a frustrated cry, but then latched on again. Hatice was fair, like most Circassians, and so pale that she looked as though leeches had been left on her too long.

'Hatice, this is Hannah. She has a difficulty we must help her with. Her baby' — she gestured to the still form on Hannah's back — 'is in need of milk.'

Hatice did not raise her head. She held Tarzi's baby with one hand, the legs and bottom without support, indifferent to whether the infant suckled or not. Hannah sniffed the air, recognizing the odour of vomit in the cabin. Hatice's other hand patted the head of a little girl about two years old who lay drowsing beside her. It seemed the pitching of the ship had affected them all.

Several other girls of various ages sprawled on the luxurious cushions, wedged together so snugly it was not easy to see where the body of one child ended and another's began.

'Hatice,' Tarzi said in a loud voice. When the girl did not look up, Tarzi said, 'She is a lazy girl. I will rouse her.'

'The poor girl is sick herself. The motion of the boat is making her ill.' Hannah went to where Hatice lay and put a hand on her brow. 'She is clammy.' Taking Gülbahar from Hatice's unresisting arms, she held her out to show Tarzi. 'Look, your own child is growing weak.'

'Hatice was healthy this morning when we boarded. She was frolicking with Gülbahar, playing her flute, singing to my other girls.'

'What she needs is a reviving infusion.'

Tarzi picked up a piece of sticky *lokum* from a tray on the floor. She offered a candy to Hatice, and when Hatice did not respond, Tarzi asked Hannah, 'What should we do?'

'We must nurse her back to health.' Hannah opened the porthole. A cool breeze flowed in.

'Poor girl. Here we are, sunset on the first day of the journey, and already there is sickness.' Since there were no men around, Tarzi's veil was draped around her shoulders like a cowl.

Tarzi and Hannah moved Tarzi's children to their own bunks and settled Hatice on a separate berth. Hannah helped Hatice pull off her *feradge* of embroidered silk. 'Tarzi, I have fenugreek and blessed thistle. Take them from my bag and make a tea with hot water. It will give her strength.'

Tarzi returned a few minutes later with a cup of strong-smelling tea. She held it to Hatice's lips. 'Drink, my dear. This will help you regain your health.'

When Hatice had drunk her fill, she fell asleep and remained that way for nearly an hour, while Matteo fussed and Tarzi's girls lay still. When she awoke, she was much restored and the vacant

278

look in her eye was replaced with grateful relief when she saw Hannah. She was ready to feed Matteo. Hannah passed the baby to her. Hatice fumbled with her breast, and after a false try, Matteo gave a few weak sucks but then appeared to fall asleep.

'Come on, do not give up.' Hannah tickled the soles of his feet.

Matteo recommenced, this time getting more of the nipple and areola into his mouth. Hannah bent as close as she dared without disturbing them. A bubble of saliva formed on his lips and his cheeks continued to work in and out, his mouth maintaining a hold on Hatice's nipple. After a few more pulls, Matteo went limp and fell asleep. Hannah was delighted to see a trickle of milk pooling in the corner of his mouth.

23

Valletta, Malta
1575

By the time Isaac's leaky skiff reached the *Provveditore*, dawn was breaking, sending fingers of red light skittering through the morning fog. The stevedores from a large-bottomed barge laboured to off-load their cargo of wheat and timber. Thank God for the delay, thought Isaac. Perhaps my luck is changing. The captain strode along the portside of the ship, watching as the men sweated in the cold air.

Sweat stung Isaac's eyes and he could hardly grasp the oars for the pain of his newly formed blisters. Water leaked into the stern of the skiff, leaving the only dry spot under the bow. Although mist shrouded the harbour in grey light, it was not so dense that he could not be spotted. He headed toward the seaward side of the vessel, as far from the stevedores as possible. If he was quick about it, he might reach the ship before he was observed from the decks above. It was his only chance, since the captain and crew were preoccupied with the loading of the cargo. The stevedores were shouting and cursing as they heaved sacks of wheat and timbers. As often as Isaac had heard the local dialect in the last several months, it still sounded as sibilant as though all the vowels had been worn away.

He pulled so hard on one oar that it splintered into pieces just as he came alongside. With both hands outstretched, he grasped the ship's cladding to prevent the skiff from banging into the side of the *Provveditore*.

The huge vessel dwarfed Isaac's tiny craft. To Isaac she seemed as tall as the Basilica San Marco. From the decks above he must appear as a bit of flotsam. Keeping to the seaward side of the ship, Isaac craned his neck to watch the fore and aft decks crawling with dozens of men, all as busy as ants. A sailor leaning over the side tossed a single crumb to a black-headed gull. The bird grabbed it in mid-air, and then, when no more was forthcoming, flew off to try his luck at a ship anchored farther out in the harbour. Hanging just above his head, and banging against the oak sides of the ship in rhythm to the waves, Isaac spotted a ladder fashioned of barrel staves and rope. If he stood upright, he could just grasp the bottom rung and haul himself up.

But first he must assemble the debris in the bottom of the boat, ensuring enough air would reach all layers of the wood and seaweed. With shaking fingers, he rubbed two sticks together over a few wisps of dead grass. When he was rewarded by the sight of a spark and a column of thin smoke from the grass, he added the desiccated pine cones and fibrous seaweed he had collected from the beach. He waited until it started to smoulder and then blew on it until a thick coil of smoke rose from the damp wood of the hull. When the detritus burst into flame, Isaac gave the skiff a shove with his foot and

281

scrambled up the ladder.

Hand over hand he climbed, his toes smashing against the side of the boat with every rung of the ladder. When he reached the top, crouching so that he was not visible to anyone on deck, Isaac peered down to the waterline. Orange flames rose from the skiff, turning it into a floating torch. From the rigging, he heard a man scream, 'Fire! All hands on deck.'

Men were everywhere. All was confusion. The sailors, who until a moment ago had been occupied flinging sail bags and cargo into the hold, setting the rigging, spicing rope, and mending torn sails with evil-looking curved needles, now raced to the side and peered down at the burning skiff banging against the hull of the *Provveditore*. Two men had the presence of mind to fill buckets and heave the water at the boat.

Soon they formed a brigade and were hurling water over the side at the burning skiff. No one took any notice of him as Isaac hauled himself over the guard rail, scurried across the deck, and lowered himself into the dark cargo hold. Dropping to all fours, he landed on something soft and yielding: the dead body of a rodent. He crawled between the stacked timber and sacks of dried beans, until the familiar smell of the sheep piss used to fortify the fabric directed him to the sail bags. He felt his way over to the largest of the bags, which probably held the replacement for the mainsail, and tugged the mouth of the bag open. He rearranged the sail as best he could by hollowing out a space for himself and then climbed in, gathering the mouth of the bag around his chest. He draped the opening loosely around his head like a cowl. The reeking canvas put him in mind of Joseph.

From the deck above, sailors grunted as they filled more water buckets to dump onto the burning skiff. Some were shouting in Veneziano, some in Maltese.

He checked his pouch, lumpy with cocoons, dangling from around his neck. They were safe and dry. His thoughts turned to more pressing matters. What if he had done his job too well and the ship caught fire? But after several moments of noise and shouting, he heard a boat being loaded with men and the decks above grew strangely quiet. Isaac climbed out of the sail bag and cautiously stuck his head up through the hatch.

The deck was deserted. Hammocks, which should have been filled with resting men, swung empty between the cannons and swing guns on the bow. He crawled to the side and peeked over. The crew was jostling for space in a huge pirogue filled with water casks, which Isaac realized they were taking back to shore to be refilled with fresh drinking water. His plan had worked better than anticipated. The men were going ashore to replenish their water supplies and perhaps to quaff a last quick drink in the tavern before casting off.

He returned to the hold, the dark, cramped space that would be his home for several weeks. The sailors would sleep on deck at night. He must remain in the bag at all times with the overhead hatch cover always closed, otherwise the crew would stumble and fall into the hold when they got up to piss. Not even when the cook came down to fetch provisions would Isaac see a sliver of light, because he would be at the bottom of the sail bag. For the entire journey his days and nights would be spent in darkness.

He propped the hatch cover open with a scrap of wood and took a quick look around his new home. Between bolts of silk, well wrapped in coarse muslin, were wedged containers of cinnamon, pepper, ginger, and nutmeg — all worth more than a seaman's life. From Araby were fragrant ambergris, musk, and attar of roses. Hidden deeper within the hold must be gold, Indian diamonds, Ceylonese pearls, and opiates. Isaac poked his nose into a sack of salt, the insignia of Ibiza stencilled on its side, and took a pinch between his thumb and forefinger. How good it tasted on his tongue, as sharp and briny as a kiss. A sigh of contentment escaped his lips. Perhaps he would survive. Maybe he would live to see Hannah again. He helped himself to another pinch.

As he was about to bring it to his mouth, he heard a scream. At first he thought it was a cormorant caught in the rigging, but then it came again, shriller this time. He edged over to the hatch and craned his neck. All he could see was the top of the mizzenmast.

He climbed a couple of rungs of the ladder of the hold and looked up. The scream came from overhead, below the crow's nest, the round lookout from which, if the voyage succeeded, after many weeks a sailor would shout out, 'Land ahoy!'

A cabin boy, his blond hair whipping in the wind, hugged the outermost end of the yardarm, the mast that ran perpendicular to the mainmast. Isaac saw the boy's terrified expression as he clung, arms hugging the mast, his legs working violently as they kicked into empty space. As he fought to maintain his purchase on the yardarm, a rope wrapped itself around his ankle. The more the boy struggled, the tauter grew the rope.

After struggling for several moments, the boy lost his grip, and he slipped from the yardarm and fell. Isaac gasped, anticipating the sound of a thud on the foredeck. As the boy fell, instead of smashing ten paces to the deck below, the rope on his ankle broke his fall and held him fast. Swinging back and forth, the boy let out a long, keening scream of pain.

Isaac watched with horror as the boy, no more than eleven or twelve years old, swung upside down. With every roll of the ship his head thudded against the mast.

His heart pounding, Isaac glanced around the deck, ready to drop out of sight when one of sentries heard the boy and rushed to his aid. He crouched behind the bilge pump, but not a soul came into sight. The sailor on watch had either passed out from wine or gone ashore with the rest of the crew.

The boy's moans grew fainter, hardly as loud as the whimper of a newborn. One could easily mistake them for a seagull or the whine of the windlass raising the anchor. Isaac knew he should return to his snug sail bag and pull a fold of canvas over his ears to muffle the child's death throes. He had a decent chance of remaining hidden until the ship reached Venice. Should he sacrifice his only chance of freedom for this child who was neither friend nor relative?

The Torah teaches that when you kill a man you murder not only him but all of his heirs and descendants for generations to come. Was the opposite true? By saving the boy would Isaac save all of the boy's progeny? Whatever the answer to this question, Isaac could not return to his sail bag. He walked to the base of the mast. The rigging resembled nothing so much as an elaborate cobweb, ensnaring the boy as a spider holds a fly.

Isaac began to climb using hands and feet and even his teeth to maintain purchase on the rigging. Hand over hand, he scrambled, the rope cutting into his blistered palms and feet. The wind picked up, and in response, the ship rocked to and fro. He continued his ascent, fixing his eyes on the swaying figure of the boy overhead.

Isaac's callused palms grew slippery with sweat and he feared losing his grip and tumbling to the deck far below. His hands and legs trembled from the effort of the climb. There was no way to be invisible. If the pirogue with the crew returned now, he would be as visible to them as the red flag of Venice fluttering above his head.

To look down made Isaac dizzy, so he kept his eyes on the cabin boy struggling against the rope that held his ankle fast. The boy tried to pull himself double by knifing up from the waist and grasping at the rope. Isaac called up, 'Stay still,

Figlio. Do not thrash about.' *Figlio*. Son. The word had fallen naturally from his lips. 'What is your name?' Isaac called to the boy.

'Jorge,' the boy replied, his voice so weak that Isaac could barely hear him over the cawing of the crows.

The boy pivoted toward Isaac, so he could see that blood streamed from his eyes and trickled from his mouth. If he did not reach him soon, Isaac would be risking his life for a corpse.

The boy was on the farthest reach of the yardarm, at least ten paces from the mast. Isaac clambered farther up the rigging and, when he reached the crow's nest, heaved himself in. Secured to the railing was a bamboo cage containing a pair of black crows, land-loving birds that, when released, could be relied upon to navigate the most direct route to shore. The wind was less forceful now, although the mast continued to seesaw back and forth as though trying to rub out the sun.

'Jorge, I want you to be brave,' he called down to the boy. 'We will wait for the ship to list to starboard and then you will be like a pendulum. The rope will swing you to the mast. Then I will haul you up and lift you into the crow's nest. Can you endure another few moments?' Isaac's voice suddenly sounded unnaturally loud in the air. The wind had died.

'All right,' the boy said, his voice hardly audible.

He was tantalizingly near, not more than a few arm's lengths below. Isaac waited for the wind to pick up. Nothing.

As the sun rose in the sky, Isaac thought if he could fling the rope to the boy, the boy could tie it around his torso. The rope, the mast, and the yardarm would form a perfect triangle. Isaac could then haul him up into the crow's nest. Did the boy have the strength for such a manoeuvre?

'Jorge? Can you hear me?'

The boy made no reply. He hung limply from the rope.

There was nothing else to be done. Isaac must crawl out on the yardarm and, pulling the rope hand over hand, heave the unconscious boy into his arms. Then Isaac must hack the rope off from around the boy's ankle. If he could creep back along the yardarm, carrying the boy over his shoulder to the mainmast, it might be accomplished. If the boy panicked and struggled, they would both crash to their deaths on the deck below.

The water was so still he could see several fathoms to the bottom. As he glanced toward the shore, he saw the pirogue, filled with sailors, cutting swiftly through the waves toward the ship. Isaac paused. They would arrive in a few moments. Why not wait and let them rescue the boy? A few more moments would not matter.

The boy moaned and Isaac saw that blood matted even his eyelashes. His bare foot, broken at the ankle and held fast by the rope, was blue. If the rope did not come off immediately, the foot would be lost.

Isaac threw a leg over the railing of the crow's nest, one arm around the mast, and climbed down the rigging. The pirogue bumped against the side of the ship, and Isaac heard the men scramble on board.

He kept going, afraid to look down for more than a moment at the deck crowded with dozens of sailors, some staggering from drink. Just as he arrived at the juncture of the yardarm and the mast, someone from below shouted, 'Look aloft!' and he heard a chorus of voices shouting at him and cheering. It had been a long time since anyone cheered for him, or even noticed his presence. He felt strength flow into his arms and legs and he grinned. He could do this impossible feat. What happened to him afterward did not matter. What mattered was saving the boy.

Glancing down again, Isaac saw sailors racing to starboard. Soon men were leaning backward over the side to maximize the effect of their weight. The ship responded by broaching slightly to starboard. The boy swung toward him. Maddeningly, he still dangled out of Isaac's reach. Isaac extended one arm, and then, gripping the mast between his legs, he stretched his body until the rope holding the boy was within his grasp. He managed to grab the rope with the tips of his fingers and then his hand. He hauled the rope toward him, the boy suspended from it. To his relief, Jorge was slight, hardly heavier than an eight-year-old. When the boy was near enough, Isaac hauled on the rope hand over hand until the top of Jorge's head was level with his own and he could see the fear in the boy's eyes.

'Stay calm and do not struggle. You must climb onto my back like a baby monkey scrambles onto its mother and cling to me as I crawl down.'

The boy groaned but he did as he was told, draping himself over Isaac's back and gripping his neck. With trembling limbs, Isaac shinnied his way down a few paces until his foot made contact with the rigging.

Applause floated up from the deck, along with the sounds of whistling and shouts of encouragement. Fresh energy coursed through Isaac's body. With Jorge still clinging to him, he managed to right himself and climb up the mast until he reached the crow's nest. He clambered over the rail, the boy holding on so tightly that Isaac felt nearly strangled. He reached behind to grasp the boy's ankle. He fumbled with one hand to untie the rope, but it was so deeply buried in the boy's flesh that Isaac could not prise apart the knot. It would have to wait until they reached the deck. The boy hung motionless, still on Isaac's back. Fainted or dead, he could not tell. Isaac whispered the words his own mother had said to him so many years ago, 'When you grow the wings of an angel, *figlio*, all things are possible. Until then, remain on the ground.' Perhaps it was his imagination, but he thought he saw a smile pass over the boy's face.

When the boy's narrow chest rose and fell, relief filled Isaac. He was about to begin his descent when he saw a soldier, a coil of rope draped over his shoulder, advancing up the rigging toward him.

'You are a brave man,' said the soldier, glancing at Isaac's leg iron. 'But a foolish one.

Give the boy to me.' The soldier, who looked barely older than the cabin boy, took Jorge in his arms. 'I am sorry, my friend. My orders are to march you to the cells of the Grand Master.'

'Take care of the boy. He is bleeding badly.'

The soldier draped Jorge over his shoulders and began his descent. Isaac looked away, unable to bear the sight of the bloody head. On the foredeck the other men watched, waiting for him to come down, waiting to watch the soldiers arrest him and throw him in the cells below the Grand Master's palace.

Isaac would disappoint them all. He would disappoint Hannah. He would disappoint God. Never again could he live as a slave. He gazed at the water. The sea was smooth, but even a calm sea could drown a man.

The sea air had dried the sweat on his body to a carapace of salt. The ancient Hebrews salted their dead before placing them in the ground. As he looked out toward the open water, he noticed another galleon pulling in to the harbour flying the familiar flag with the winged lion on a field of red. She rode high in the water, the lateen-rigged sail on the mizzenmast half-bellied out from the wind.

If he waited a few moments, the wake of that elegant galleon would cause Isaac's ship to heel over so that he could hurl himself from the mast and land in the water without smashing himself on the deck. He climbed atop the railing of the crow's nest to await her approach. The soldiers below bellowed at him, ordering him to descend, but he ignored them, watching the galleon slice through the waves, leaving a path of turbulent green foam in its wake.

When the *Balbiana* was a stone's throw to the leeward side, Isaac released his grip on the mast, opened his arms, and jumped. For the first time since he had arrived in Malta, he felt free.

24

Land Ahoy

Some nights the winds blew so fiercely on the *Balbiana* that even the sailors could not keep to their feet. On those nights, Matteo lay in Hannah's arms, her body cushioning his, so the storms could not dash him against the sides of the heaving ship. After the squalls passed, she would lie exhausted on her straw pallet, too seasick to lift a hand to push her hair out of her eyes while she vomited into a basin.

Melancholy stalked her like a phantom and held her in its clammy embrace. That Jessica's death was her fault consumed her. The conviction that Isaac, too, was dead grew and took root in her mind. Some mornings she could barely summon the energy to rise, so weary was she from her nightmares of Isaac's death by starvation, drowning, or hanging. When the *Balbiana* pulled in to Valletta harbour, she was certain she would learn Isaac had been tossed into an unmarked grave and forgotten.

She would lie on her pallet clutching the baby while odd, unconnected thoughts made her think of Jessica. Only Matteo's need for milk forced her from her dank quarters to Tarzi's cabin. Often on these excursions, she glimpsed from the corner of her eye a flash of red silk or a well-shod foot or a small hand gloved in lace tatting. She would move toward it, thinking for the briefest of seconds that Jessica was on board. Then she would remember Jessica bleeding in her arms and, saddened, she would withdraw.

Would her memories always be so painful? she wondered. Or would her yearning for Jessica diminish with time? These thoughts assaulted her most strongly in the morning, when, still tired from a night of nightmares, she flung on one of Jessica's gowns, now grown stiff with salt from the winds but still giving off her scent of jasmine.

Fortunately, life at sea agreed with Matteo. It was as though King Poseidon were his father and Amphrodite his mother. The heaving of the ship, the dull beating of the wind in the sails, the salt-laddened air, and the cry of the birds — all made him scream with laughter. He cooed from the makeshift hammock she had fashioned for him and hung from the ribs of the hull. When she raised her eyes from her pallet, she could see him waving his hand, trying to clutch with his chubby fists at dust motes floating in the air.

Yes, she thought, she had kept Matteo alive. But he had kept her alive, too. His need to be fed, to be cuddled, to be loved was all that prevented her from abandoning hope. And so she clung to him during the interminable voyage as she grew thinner and his cheeks grew fuller and his colour brightened from grey to pink.

After a few weeks at sea, she realized Matteo watched her more intently. He released his grip on her only long enough for Hatice to give him suck. The baby's bright eyes would follow the girls around the cabin and a look of joy would play on his countenance when, one by one, Tarzi's girls bent over to kiss him and tickle his toes. When he had drunk his fill, Hannah would scuttle back with him to her sleeping quarters under the stairs.

As the seas grew calmer and her stomach grew more steady, it amused Hannah to fashion simple toys for him. She found a hank of rope from a coil on the deck and knotted it into the shape of a doll. With charcoal she quickly sketched a face and ears and tied on a rag with strings for an apron. She hid her face behind it, dancing it around on his chest, pretending it was a puppet. The streamers from the apron tickled his cheeks. 'Hello, young man,' she would sing in a high, silly voice. 'Are you a good boy? Are you eating all of your food? What did you have to break fast this morning?' When the puppet was tired it would flop on Matteo's chest, and allow the baby to grab it and thrust it into his mouth.

At last, after many weeks, just when Hannah had given up hope of seeing dry land ever again, she heard the cry of 'Land ahoy' from the crow's nest. She snatched Matteo out of his hammock and joined the other passengers on deck. With the baby in her arms, she leaned against the railing as the other passengers jostled her in their eagerness to glimpse the Valletta harbour. She thought of Isaac as the island grew larger. When the shores of Malta came into view, so bleak and desolate, so devoid of any grace or beauty, they looked like the scraped hide of an animal skin. The *Balbiana* would anchor here for a few days while the chandlers victualled the ship, and Hannah would go ashore to find Isaac.

Tarzi, veil whipping about her face in the afternoon breeze, approached Hannah at the rail and put an arm around her. Her friend had not missed a meal the entire voyage and had grown plump on *lokum* and *dolmasi*.

Tarzi whispered in Hannah's ear, 'I am a good she-camel after all, and you are a brilliant midwife. I am enjoying the pleasures of the marriage bed, yet my monthly courses continue.' She gave Hannah a squeeze. 'Since the time of Beyazit II,' Tarzi said, 'the Ottomans have been good to Jews. Ahmet is a trusted adviser of the Sultan. If you come with me to Constantinople, he will secure you a position as a midwife in the harem in the Sultan's palace. But never mind your pebbles. The Sultan is a man who likes to reap where he has sown.'

'We will speak of my future plans tonight when I return to the ship.' I must know whether I still have a husband, Hannah thought, before I can think of the future.

Tarzi glanced down at Matteo. 'Leave him with me while you go off to search for your Isaac.'

Hannah shook her head. If Isaac was alive, he must meet Matteo. She must know his reaction to the child that fate had thrust in her arms. And if she had to make a choice between Isaac and Matteo? She refused to think about it. If she returned without Isaac, Hannah would tell Tarzi that her husband was dead, no matter what the truth. God forgive me, Hannah thought, but I would prefer to be a widow than to know Isaac no longer loves me.

A light film of perspiration formed on Hannah's upper lip. Tarzi mopped her face with a cloth.

'I wish you the best. This has been a terrible voyage for you. You have borne it bravely.'

'My son would not have survived without your help. I owe you a debt I can never repay,' said Hannah.

Two sailors turned the crank of the windlass and, with a groan and much straining of the hawsers, lowered the anchor. The *Balbiana* drifted leeward until the anchor hit the bottom of the sea. The hawsers tightened, the ship resisted and then shuddered to a halt. A couple of nimble young boys climbed up the rigging, took in the sails from the mainmast and mizzen, and reefed them tightly.

Hannah shaded her eyes, surveying the other ships in the crowded harbour. The masts of a ship from the Levant beat back and forth against the sky, blinding her one moment, leaving her in shadow the next. Most were not elegant galleons like the *Balbiana*, but beamy vessels, three-masted affairs with two decks and plenty of room for cargo and passengers.

A tender pulled alongside to take passengers to shore. Hannah pushed her way to the front of the crowd and handed Matteo and her linen bag to an oarsman who stood up to receive them. Then she climbed down the rope ladder, which slapped against the hull of the ship. She settled on a bench as the rest of the passengers crowded in. Next to her, a sailor so young he had only a fuzzy down on his cheeks was peering through a spyglass at the other ships.

Their tender skimmed through the water, the oarsmen as full of longing for solid ground as the passengers. A few minutes later, she gave a start and almost dropped Matteo when the tender bumped the Valletta dock. The others clambered off, delirious with joy to be standing on a surface that did not pitch and roll. Many fell to the ground and kissed it. A young local man caught the bowline and secured it on a cleat on the dock, and offered his hand to help Hannah disembark.

When she asked him where she should begin her search for a captive named Isaac Levi, he replied, 'Ask for him in the main square, at the slave auction. Sooner or later all slaves end up there.'

Hannah took a horse cart to the square and elbowed her way through the crowd of men watching the buying and selling of slaves.

The ground refused to stay steady under her feet. It seemed to pitch and roll as vigorously as the deck of the *Balbiana*. The crowd pressed in too closely around her, and she felt herself fighting for breath. Lined up on the platform were several men in shackles — Turks, Nubians, and Moors, all of them thin and dull-eyed. Isaac could not be one of these men so wasted in body and spirit that they appeared indifferent to the voice of the auctioneer and the searing heat of the morning sun. She overheard two spectators standing next to her talking of a slave who had leaped into the sea to escape the auctioneer's gavel. Understandable, she thought. I might have done the same.

The guards, whips in hand, led in more slaves, blinking in the sudden light, shackled together in a dispirited coffle. Would she even recognize Isaac if he was among them? She craned her neck, shifting Matteo to the other arm. Near the back was a bearded man wearing a tattered shirt. He was the only one in the group who seemed to have some spirit left in him. His shoulders were thrust back, his chin held high as though daring the guards to lay their whips on him. She rubbed her eyes with the tail of Matteo's swaddling cloth and looked again. Tall and still handsome; thinner, yes, but with black eyes and a strong jaw. Relief flooded over her.

It was Isaac. He was alive.

She screamed, 'Isaac! Isaac!'

The people in the crowd turned and stared at her. Isaac did not turn in her direction. She was too far away. He could not hear her.

Clasping Matteo tightly in one arm, Hannah mounted the stairs of the auction platform. She clutched the stair rail because her legs, accustomed to the heaving of the ship, threatened to give out from underneath her. One of the guards grabbed her arm and tried to restrain her. He said something to her, but the words did not register and she shook him off.

'Please stop the sale!' Turning to the auctioneer, she said, 'I have that man's ransom!' She pointed to Isaac.

Isaac looked around, trying to determine

where the voice was coming from, and then, seeing her, his face dissolved in a look of amazed delight. She tried to climb the last few stairs toward him before the guards yanked her back.

'You may not interrupt the sale, *signora*. This man is not for purchase. We are simply guarding him until his owner comes to reclaim his property. Soldiers fished him out of the harbour this morning trying to escape.' The auctioneer spoke a coarse dialect that she could barely comprehend, but his meaning was clear from the scowl on his face.

'My husband is no one's property!'

'You will have to take that matter up with Joseph. Here he comes now.'

She was so close to Isaac now, just a few paces away, and yet the distance between them seemed great. She would not pause to look at him, not until he was safely delivered from his captors.

The burly, squat man known as Joseph lumbered up to the auctioneer's platform, pushing past Hannah. 'Hand him over,' he said to the auctioneer. 'I know how to treat runaways. There is a galley leaving tomorrow that needs oarsmen. Good riddance to him.'

He turned around to face the woman on the steps below him. Hannah reached forward and put a hand on Joseph's arm. 'He is my husband. I will buy him from you.'

'Not on your life. He has caused me too much trouble already. I will not reward him by selling him to you. I have other plans for him.'

'He has caused me a great deal of trouble, too,' Hannah said. 'This is his nature. Would you

300

not rather be rid of him for a good price?'

'I want him to die slowly and painfully on a galley.'

'So you would cheat yourself of ready cash for the pleasure of seeing him suffer? Surely you are wiser than that. Pause to consider, sir. Would you drink poison and expect your enemy to die?'

Isaac called down, 'Hannah!'

A murmur rose from the crowd.

'Do you hear?' said Joseph. 'Now that he has seen you, his torment will be all the more painful.'

How to deal with this lout? Hannah wanted to throw her purse with all her ducats in the man's face, grab Isaac, and run — but she said, 'What will the galley captain give you for him? I will match his price and then some.'

Joseph scowled and was about to reply when a couple of men from the crowd started heckling him. 'The lady needs a father for that child in her arms, Joseph. Be a gentleman.' Others joined in with similar remarks, until they were united in a chorus of disapproval.

'Give me ten ducats,' said Joseph. 'Even the worst husband is worth that much.'

She still had one hundred and fifty ducats remaining after paying her passage on the *Balbiana*, but she would be damned if she would give this creature a *scudi* more than necessary. 'You have used him harshly, sir. Look how scrawny he has become. When he left Venice he was handsome and had all his teeth.'

'He can still fill your bed, madam, and provide you with a brother for that brat in your arms.'

301

'Offer him no more than two!' a voice called up to her.

Hannah looked down to see a corpulent nun in a brown habit, a white dog tucked under her arm.

Joseph responded, 'Give me five ducats and he is yours.'

Hannah reached into her bag, found the purse of ducats, and fished out five. She tossed him the coins before he could change his mind. He caught them deftly and thrust them into his breeches.

The guards unlocked the manacles around Isaac's neck and wrists, which fell away with a clank. Isaac shuffled unsteadily along the platform toward Hannah. Together they started slowly down the few steps to the ground.

All the things she had meant to say to him, all the speeches she had rehearsed on the many nights when she could not sleep for craving him, all the words of love she had saved up for his ears . . . not a word could she remember.

When they reached the bottom of the stairs, she stood, simply drinking in the sight of him. Isaac turned to her, his dark eyes luminescent with joy. He was grinning so broadly she could see he did still have all his teeth, still strong and white after all the deprivations he must have endured.

He said, 'So you *are* real. I was afraid you might be one of those visions I have from too little food and water.'

They walked over to the quiet corner of the square under the olive tree where he had sat penning letters so many times, and he helped her to sit on the log and then took a seat beside her. He leaned forward and drew back a corner of the blanket.

'A child? How did you come by him?'

Matteo squirmed in her arms.

'Isaac,' Hannah said as his eyes fixed on the baby, 'I have brought you a son.'

'My God, our last night. Did we conceive him then?'

Since Isaac had been away for nearly a year, of course he would assume the child was his. Perhaps it was wisest to let him or she might lose him a second time. But a marriage based on a lie has no more substance than a house built on sand. She took a deep breath.

'I saved his life, but, no, I did not give birth to him.'

'Then who are his parents?' Isaac asked.

'His mother and father are dead.'

Isaac looked as though he wanted to ask another question, but Hannah interrupted him.

'I am not his mother. I could never be unfaithful to you.'

He waited for more.

'Isaac, I have so much to tell you, so much to explain, but before I do, tell me that you will take this child as your own.'

Isaac looked pensive for a moment. 'How did he survive the journey?'

'By fate and God's intervention.'

Isaac fingered the *shadai* hanging from its red cord on Matteo's neck. 'He is a Jewish child?'

'As you will see the first time you view him

without his swaddling bands, he is a gentile.' She paused. 'But we can raise him as we wish. We will make him ours. We shall have him circumcised. We shall immerse ourselves in water, the three of us. Here in Valletta, if you wish, before we depart.' Her voice was firm. 'He has no one else in the world except us.'

He was staring at her with an expression of amazement, whether because of her words or because of the vigour behind them, she did not know. She forced herself to stop talking, willing him to say the words she wanted to hear.

At last, Isaac spoke. 'We have longed for a son, you and I. Perhaps God at last has heard our prayers.' He looked at the child and laughed with delight as Matteo grabbed his thumb and sucked on it. 'He is beautiful.'

He took Matteo from her arms and untied his lace cap, revealing curly wisps of hair. He cupped the child's head in one hand, smoothing the reddish hair off his forehead with the other. Isaac's eyes filled.

'I will raise him as my own. He will be my own son, as though from my own flesh.'

Hannah felt herself relax, the air reaching deep into her lungs, the first full breath in a long time.

'But how did you come to have this child?'

'I will tell you the whole story later,' Hannah said. 'There is no hurry.' She reached into the linen bag at her feet. 'There is something else.' She took out the purse of ducats and showed them to Isaac. 'You married me without a dowry, but I have one now. What we do not have to pay over to the Knights for your ransom will go to starting a new life for us.'

Isaac said, 'The Knights will free me for fifty ducats. I have caused them nothing but headaches since I arrived.'

'The same Isaac. Everywhere you go, a pain in the *tuchas*.'

Isaac tore his eyes from Matteo and looked at her. 'You are not the only one with a treasure.' He passed Matteo to her and then untied a pouch from around his neck and showed her the contents: twenty or so hard white cocoons, smoother and slightly larger than a robin's eggs.

'What are they?'

'Silkworm cocoons from healthy stock. Something to help us make a new life.' Isaac closed the bag and placed it around his neck. 'Silk is beloved everywhere — except,' he said with a laugh, 'on this barren island. Although that may change. The stout nun who spoke to you at the slave auction? Sister Assunta is my new business partner, God help me.'

'The Rabbi said you would be dead before I reached you,' Hannah said.

'And the Society for the Release of Captives offered me my freedom months ago if I signed a divorce. But without you, what was the point of freedom?' He released one hand from the child to caress her face. 'And here you are. No longer my little ghetto mouse.'

Hannah placed her hand on Isaac's. 'We cannot return to Venice.'

'So where shall we start this new ducat-filled life of ours?' Isaac asked.

'Wherever babies are born.' With her birthing

spoons to coax out babies who had grown too contented in their mother's wombs, she could make her way anywhere in the world.

'You are a bringer forth of life, my Hannah.'

'You are talking blasphemy. Only God can do that.' She leaned against him, feeling the heat of his body along her side. She had been so long without him.

'You ask where I wish to go,' she said. 'The Ottomans treat Jews well. In Constantinople we could own any kind of business, not just second-hand clothing or moneylending as in Venice. We could buy land, live in any quarter of the city, work at anything we pleased.'

Isaac considered her words. And then he nodded slowly, an idea growing. 'We could start a weaving workshop . . . ' He told her about the convent and Sister Assunta and her plans for fabricating silk thread.

'In a few days,' said Hannah, 'the *Balbiana* sails for Constantinople. It will mean many more weeks of pitching and rolling, but with you, anything will be bearable.'

'And the child? Who will give him suck?'

'I have kept him alive this long,' Hannah said. 'I will find a way.'

She smiled at him and then lowered her eyes and noticed the lesion on Isaac's ankle from the leg shackle. When they were alone she would rub it with almond oil. It would heal with hardly a scar, just as, in time, her memory of Jessica's death would grow less painful.

It was immodest, but she pulled him closer and kissed him despite the throng of people in the square. As she pressed her body against his, she felt herself grow warm in a way that had nothing to do with the setting sun beating down on her bare head. She felt his hands, once so smooth, now callused and stained with ink. Hannah ran her hand across his ribs.

'Like a washboard. I have my work cut out, getting the meat back on your bones.'

'And you?' he replied. 'Not exactly fat.'

They held the child between them on their laps and he cried now in protest from the pressure of being squeezed. They moved apart, but only slightly. Their hands remained clasped, the three of them forming a tight circle.

GLOSSARY

Altanà — Terrace or sitting area on the roof of a house.

Arsenale — The Venetian naval shipyard in Castello founded in the 12th century.

Bahnaches, or 'cupping' — An ancient medical treatment that relies upon creating a local suction to mobilise blood flow in order to promote healing and relieve pains and aches.

Bastinado, or 'foot whipping' — A form of corporal punishment in which the soles of the feet are beaten with an object such as a cane. Although extremely painful, it leaves few physical marks.

Biretta — A square cap with three or four peaks or horns, sometimes surmounted by a tuft.

Borsella — Pincers used by glassmakers.

Brachia — Unit of measurement: about the length of a man's upper arm, from shoulder to elbow.

Bucintoro — Doge's ceremonial barge.

Ca' — Abbreviation for casa or house.

Calle (pl. calli) — Street.

Campo — Square.

Caramusal — 16th to 19th century Turkish merchant ships, similar to a galleon, carrying four sails and a cargo capacity of up to 900 tons.

Cassone — Chest for storage.

Castello — The district (sestiere) of Venice where the shipyards were located.

Challah — Traditional Sabbath bread.

Cioppà — Loose-fitting dress.

Cittidini — A privileged class of notables in Venice.

Conte — Count.

Cortigiana — Courtesan.

Dolmasi — A stuffed dish, such as stuffed peppers.

Esecutori contro la Bestemmia — Laws against blasphemy and scandalous behaviour.

Fegato — Calf's liver.

Felze — Cabin on a gondola.

Fluyt — A Dutch type of sailing vessel originally designed as a dedicated cargo vessel.

Fondaco — A storehouse or warehouse with a square plan and three levels facing a central courtyard. The façade has, at the lower floor, five large rounded arches which enclose a portico from where goods are unloaded.

Fondamenta — A street parallel to a canal other than Canal Grande and the lagoon (in which case they are called Riva).

Forcòlo — Oarlock of a gondola.

Gesso — A white paint mixture consisting of a binder mixed with chalk, gypsum, pigment, or any combination of these. It is used in artwork as a primer.

Hamantashen (The 'ears of Haman') — Pastries notable for their three-cornered shape, traditionally eaten during the Jewish holiday of Purim. Hamantashen are made with many different fillings, including poppy seeds, prunes, nuts, dates, apricots, apples, fruit preserves, or cherries.

Hora — A traditional Jewish dance.

Huppah — Wedding canopy.

Kugel — Noodle pudding.

Laissez-passer (literally 'let pass') — A travel document to ensure the safety of persons across international borders.

Levatrice — Midwife.

Loghetto — Small, cramped room or apartment in the Venetian Ghetto.

Lokum — Turkish Delight.

Marangona — One of the five bells located in the great campanile in Piazza San Marco.

Masallah — Literally 'what Allah wishes' — Used when admiring or praising something or someone, in recognition that all good things come from God and are blessings from Him.

Mezuzah — Parchment inscribed with verses from Deuteronomy, contained in a small case and affixed to the doorframe of a Jewish house.

Mikvah — Ritual bath.

Mitzvah — A good deed or act of human kindness performed as a religious duty.

Morello — Type of mask.

Niddah — Ritual uncleanness: a woman during menstruation, or a woman who has menstruated but not yet completed the associated requirement of immersion in a mikvah.

Padiglione — Drapery or canopy over a bed.

Parnassim dos Cautivos — Society for the Rescue of Captives.

Parrochia — Church parish.

Pelisse — A garment, half-way between a dress and a coat, and typically calf-length, worn over trousers.

Pessach — The Jewish holiday of Passover, to celebrate Moses leading the Jews out of Egypt.

Piano terra — The ground floor of a Venetian palazzo (palace).

Portego — The long salon-like space of the Venetian home that extended from the front to the back of the house.

Purim — A Jewish holiday that commemorates the deliverance of the Jewish people in the ancient Persian Empire from destruction by Haman, from the Biblical Book of Esther.

Scudo — Small denomination coin of Venice.

Scuola — School.

Seder — The Jewish ritual feast that marks the beginning of the Jewish holiday of Passover.

Sestiere — An administrative district in Venice, of which there are six.

Shabbat — Sabbath, the Jewish day of rest.

Shadai — An amulet or good luck charm.

Shalom aleichem — A Hebrew greeting, literally meaning 'Peace be upon you'. The appropriate response is 'Aleichem shalom', or 'Upon you be peace'.

Shochet — A ritual slaughterer of animals; a religious Jew who is duly licensed and trained to kill animals humanely.

Shul — Synagogue.

Sotoportego — Street that crosses under a building.

Strapado — A form of torture in which the victim's hands are tied behind their back, the person then suspended in the air by means of a rope attached to their wrists, and dropped from a height.

Tallis — A Jewish prayer shawl.

Tefillin, or 'phylacteries' — A pair of small black leather boxes containing scrolls of parchment inscribed with verses from the Torah, which are strapped to the body during prayer.

Traghetto (pl. traghetti) — A gondola ferry in Venice designed to carry passengers across a canal at designated points.

Travois — A type of conveyance for carrying goods, without wheels, consisting of two joined poles dragged by a horse.

Unsoggolo — A nun's wimple.

Veneziano — Dialect of Italian spoken in Venice.

Yarmulke — Head covering worn by Jewish men to fulfill the customary requirement that their head be covered, especially during times of prayer.

AUTHOR'S NOTE

I first came upon the idea of writing about Hannah as I was wandering through Venice. I ended my walk having a *correcto* and *hamantashen* cookies in the Jewish Ghetto Nuovo in Cannaregio. I was struck by how closely this small island resembled a movie set, with its open square, only a wellhead to break the expanse, and narrow, knife-sharp buildings enclosing the *campo* on three sides.

In the 1500s, as more and more Jews arrived from northern Europe, Spain, and Portugal, the tiny apartments shrank even more as they were partitioned into cramped living quarters, rather like a cake sliced into small and smaller pieces as unexpected guests arrive. Floors were added, and eventually the city government permitted the Jews to expand to two additional islands, Ghetto Vecchio and Ghetto Novissimo.

In trying to imagine what day-to-day life must have been like, I thought of women raising large families in overcrowded conditions. This led to thoughts of midwifery and, from there, to the notion of birthing spoons. I then had to imagine how these birthing spoons would be used and who would be wielding them. And so the idea of *The Midwife of Venice* was born.

Did such a midwife exist? I like to think so, although in my research I never came across a reference to such a woman. This is no doubt because the history of women, their fortitude and accomplishments, is written in water.

If you are interested in further exploring this fascinating era of history, I include a list of readable and interesting books from my research.

ACKNOWLEDGEMENTS

The Midwife of Venice has been a labour of love. I wish to thank all of the many people who have helped through its conception, long labour, and birth:

To my wonderful agent, Bev Slopen, who has been a source of encouragement and advice for many years. I thank her for her persistence, wisdom, and insight.

To Nita Pronovost for being the kind of old-fashioned literary editor whom I thought had gone the way of books with marbled endpapers and hand-set type. She smacked this manuscript on the bottom not once but many times until she got it to breathe and turn pink. Instead of birthing spoons, her tools were warm support and meticulous attention to detail. Her insights showed me where to go, how to get there, and how to know when I had finally arrived.

To Rhoda Friedrichs, Professor of European and Medieval History at Douglas College, my special thanks for suggesting not only scholarly references but plot ideas; to Minna Rozen, Professor of Jewish History, University of Haifa, for answering my questions about Jewish law and customs; and to Lee Saxell, Professor of Midwifery at the University of British Columbia, for explaining how babies come into the world.

To all the many wonderful writing teachers I have had the pleasure of studying with over the years: William Deverell, Joy Fielding, James N. Frey, Jonathon Furst, Elizabeth Lyons, Bob Mayer, Barbara McHugh, Kim Moritsugu, Anne Rayvals, Peter Robinson, and John Stape.

To my writers' group: Carla Lewis, Sandy Constable, and Sharon Rowse.

To my friends: Katherine Ashenburg, Lynne Fay, Shelley Mason, Jim Prier, Gayle Quigley, Elana Zysblat, Gayle Raphanel, and Guy Immega for their help and support.

To my much beloved daughter and insightful reader, Martha Hundert.

To my stepdaughter and talented editor, Kerstin Peterson.

And to my great friend and gentle critic, Beryl Young.

To the art department at Random House/ Doubleday for sending my baby out into the world with such a beautiful face, and to Bhavna Chauhan for championing my book and offering editorial support.

And finally, to Ken, my husband and best friend, who has always known how to keep the pot boiling, the stakes high, and the disbelief willingly suspended.

FURTHER READING

Andrieux, Maurice. *Daily life in Venice at the Time of Casanova*. New York: Praeger, 1972.

Ashenburg, Katherine. *The Dirt on Clean*. Toronto: Knopf Canada, 2007.

Brown, Patricia Fortini. *Private Lives in Renaissance Venice*. New Haven: Yale University Press, 2004.

Butler, E. A. *Silkworms*. Aberdeen: University Press Aberdeen, 1929.

Calimani, Riccardo. *The Ghetto of Venice*. Milano: Arnoldo Mondadori Editore, 2005.

Chojnacki, Stanley. *Women and Men in Renaissance Venice*. Baltimore: Johns Hopkins University Press, 2000.

Cohen, Elizabeth S. and Thomas V. *Daily Life in Renaissance Italy*. Westport, Connecticut: Greenwood Press, 2001.

Cohen, Mark R. (translated and edited by). *The Autobiography of a Seventeenth-Century Venetian Rabbi*. Princeton: Princeton University Press, 1989.

Davis, Robert C. (ed.), and Benjamin Ravid. *The Jews of Early Modern Venice*. Baltimore: Johns Hopkins University Press, 2001.

Defoe, Daniel. *Journal of the Plague*. New York: Indy Press, 2002.

Klein, Michelle. *A Time to Be Born: Customs and Folklore of Jewish Birth*. New York: Jewish Publications Society of America, 2000.

Laven, Mary. *The Virgins of Venice: Enclosed Lives and Broken Vows in the Renaissance Convent*. London: Penguin Books Ltd., 2003.

Lawner, Lynne. *The Lives of Courtesans in Venice and Rome*. New York: Rizzoli International Publishing, 1991.

Mee, Charles L. *Daily Life in the Renaissance*. New York: American Heritage Publishing Co., 1975.

Plumb, J. H. *The Italian Renaissance*. New York: First Mariner Books, 1961.

Pullan, Brian. *Rich and Poor in Renaissance Venice*. Cambridge: Harvard University Press, 1975.

Roden, Claudia. *The Book of Jewish Food: An Odyssey from Samarkand to New York*. New York: Knopf, 1996.

Rosenthal, Margaret. *The Honest Courtesan*. Chicago: University of Chicago Press, 1992.

Roth, Cecil. *History of the Jews in Venice*. Schocken Books, 1976.

Ruggiero, Guido. *The Boundaries of Eros*. Oxford: Oxford University Press, 1989.

Tenenti, Alberto. *Piracy and the Decline of Venice 1580 – 1615*. New York: Longmans, 1967.

Tuchman, Barbara. *A Distant Mirror: The Calamitous 14th Century*. New York: Ballantine Press, 1987.

Wills, Garry. *Venice: Lion City*. New York: Washington Square Press, 1971.

Zeigler, Philip. *The Black Death*. New York: Harper Perennial, 1971.